A TICKET TO MURDER

ABOUT THE AUTHOR

A Ticket to Murder is the fifth novel of Phil Hall, and the fourth in his Surrey Hills series to feature his daring duo of dysfunctional detectives. A future story is in development.

He has previously contributed film reviews to a University magazine and a chapter to an anthology. He attended K.E.G.S. in Chelmsford and studied Economics at UEA, Norwich before embarking on a career in marketing – the perfect grounding for writing. Phil lives in Surrey with his wife and daughter.

His first book was a domestic thriller called Dream House; you can find more details on the website www.philhallauthor.com or dive straight in and buy it from Amazon.

A TICKET TO MURDER

**Someone's missed a beat
in the Surrey Hills**

by
Phil Hall

DISCLAIMER

All characters and events in this publication, other than those clearly in the public domain, are fictitious and any resemblance to real persons, living or dead is purely coincidental.

All rights reserved. No part of this publication may be reproduced, stored in a retrieval system, or transmitted in any form or by any means, without the prior written permission of the publisher.

Published details: Amazon

Published June 2025.

Copyright © PE Hall 2025
Print Edition

For
Margaret and Eddie

A
TICKET
TO MURDER

ONE

Ron McTierney and Scott Bee emerged from Wembley Park tube station, two small ants in a huge army of people heading towards the famous stadium. As they inched along Wembley Way the towering arch came into view long before the main building. The iconic white steel structure, curving elegantly over the stadium was illuminated against the night sky casting a soft glow. It was late July, and the sun hadn't yet disappeared, but it couldn't compete with the brilliant LED light show that the stadium was flaunting to herald the first of the long-awaited Oasis concerts to hit London. The lighting added a sense of grandeur and energy, like a beacon calling people to the site.

A thousand yards away Scott and Ron, striding towards the light had succumbed to the aroma of fried onions and stopped at a dubious looking burger van.

"Get extra onions on mine will you, and a slice of cheese."

Scott nodded his understanding as he reached the front of the queue. He pressed his debit card against the small money machine, took a burger from a young Asian lad and passed it across to Ron, then shuffled to the side to the rickety table stacked with condiments. It wasn't quite the height of English cuisine but on a night like this, it hit the spot. The two friends munched through their burgers, smiled warmly at each other and continued their slow amble to the stadium. The nearer they got, the more they could feel the anticipation in the air, the crowd's excitement palpable. It had been 16 years since Oasis had played live in London, and this was the hottest ticket in town. After the euphoria around their recent concerts in Manchester, the expectation was sky high.

The boys edged towards their Mecca as the numbers around them grew.

"It's not quite Bruce Springsteen, but I'm looking forward to this," said Scott throwing the greasy burger wrapper into a bin.

"That's a bold admission from the man who never looks forward to anything."

Scott frowned, "Bruce was magnificent. He gives everything at every performance. The last time he played here, he was on stage for just short of four hours. That's more than you do most working days."

"Great. But back to tonight, we're in entrance E, that's over there, come on. I hope they play 'Cigarettes and Alcohol', I think '(What's the Story) Morning Glory?' is their best album."

"That track is on their first album, 'Definitely Maybe', I think you'll find."

Ron narrowed his eyes at Scott's pedantry but let the comment pass. Eventually the friends found their seats.

"I don't know how you managed to get these tickets, they're superb, we're only a couple of rows from the royal box,' said Scott looking around admiringly.

"Don't mention it. I thought it was about time I got you out of the house and listening to some decent music for a change. You can't spend your life listening to Springsteen all day, every day."

"These must have cost you a fortune. I remember the outcry at the time about the ticket price going up as the queues got longer. How long did you spend hanging on the internet?"

"Not long. Now don't worry, you're worth it. You're a good friend."

"But I feel I owe you, come on tell me how much you spent?"

"Scott, will you drop it. You're becoming a bore. Just sit back and enjoy the music. It's a present, don't ruin it."

Scott opened his mouth to protest, but Ron wasn't having it. "You're not a politician, so you can accept a gift without breaking the law or feeling guilty."

Scott nodded, "Okay, thank you."

"But you can buy the beer tonight," said Ron leaning back into his seat.

Scott Bee doesn't do spontaneity, he's out of his comfort zone, and he's babbling away to cover his anxiety. This is a switch for the friends because ordinarily Ron McTierney does the talking. But tonight, they are off duty. Scott Bee, the daytime detective inspector had dressed down in a lightweight fawn jacket on top of brown corduroy trousers, Ron, his detective sergeant was wearing jeans and his ubiquitous black leather jacket.

The lights dipped, a fog machine kicked in creating a haze on the stage, a roar of expectation floated around the stadium and built into a crescendo. The first bars of 'Cigarettes and Alcohol' broke through the hubbub; a familiar silhouette strutted across the stage to the microphone and the crowd erupted.

As the first song ended, Liam Gallagher slouched back to the microphone and grunted to the audience. "Good of you dickheads to turn up."

The rest of his diatribe was lost amongst the cheering of the crowd. A tall man in a black coat pushed his way along the row in which Scott and Ron were sitting, accompanied by the usual moaning as people were forced to stand up to let him pass. As he reached Scott, he grabbed his right wrist with one hand and shoved an envelope into his hand, no words were spoken, and the man moved on quickly before reaching the end of the row and heading for the exit.

"What's he doing? They're just getting started," said Ron.

But Scott didn't answer. Ron turned to him expecting a reply, but Scott was staring at the envelope in his hand.

"What's that?"

"I don't know that guy just shoved it in my hand."

"Maybe it's an invite to the after-show party."

Scott raised his eyebrows, turned the envelope over in his hands, but there was nothing written there. He picked at the seal, then tore it off and pulled out a single sheet of paper, folded in half. He opened it and read the four printed words.

LOOK UNDER YOUR SEAT

Scott and Ron exchanged nervous glances.

"Go on then."

Scott leaned forward and stretched under the seat; he moved his right hand around. "I think there's something here." He tugged at a package. "It's stuck."

"Give it some welly."

Scott got up from his seat and crouched on the concrete, he squeezed his arms under the chair and wrenched at the package, which came away in his hands. He passed it up to Ron and returned to his seat. "This is starting to get a bit suspicious."

Ron looked alarmed, turned it over in his hands, there were no markings on the khaki package. He put it to his ear. "It's not ticking. Have a quick look and we can get back to the concert."

Scott broke the seal and looked inside. He gasped and pushed the package back down on his lap, and grabbed Ron's shoulder, "Where did you get these tickets from?"

"I told you, off the internet."

"Did you actually buy them, or is this some scam of yours?"

"What do you mean?"

"Take a look – there's a stack of £50 notes inside the package, taped to the bottom of the seat, you mysteriously bought on the internet."

"Cash! Wow! How much?"

"Sssh. Keep your voice down, we don't want a panic."

"Huh. No one is listening to us, while the band's on stage. How much?"

"I don't know, I'd guess £20,000 pounds."

Ron's eyes bulged. "It's mine by the way."

Scott rolled his eyes. "There's something else in here." Scott pushed his fingers deep into the packet and pulled out a thin white envelope. He showed it to Ron.

"Maybe it's the name of the person who left the money."

"Don't joke," said Scott as he opened the envelope, "it's a ticket for a train journey to Exeter for tomorrow."

TWO

THE TWO FRIENDS spent the return journey back to Scott's house in Outwood, debating what to do with this discovery. Detective Inspector Scott Bee was tall, pale with wiry, short, black hair, he took a sip of carbonated water from a small bottle. He was a traditional detective; meticulous, observant and wedded to proper procedure, but despite that handicap he got his man more often than not. Beside him was Detective Sergeant Ron McTierney, he was not as tall as Bee, with short blonde hair and a round face that always lit up with an easy smile and a glint of mischievousness in his eyes. His upbeat attitude radiated joy, making everyone around him feel at ease. It was a wonder he had ever made it in the police force.

"We're police officers, we have a duty to investigate."

"It's probably some nutcase, who's watched too many spy movies. Besides tomorrow's Saturday, I've got a promising date with Natalia. I don't want to miss it."

"You know we have to do this."

McTierney didn't answer, he knew Bee was right, but he didn't want to give up without a fight. He stared out of the window of the London Victoria to Redhill train searching the darkness for an escape. "If you feel that strongly, then why don't you go on your own?"

A TICKET TO MURDER

"You know I can't do that. It's a two-man job; one to sit in the seat and one to keep an eye on the other passengers to see who's taking an interest."

McTierney pursed his lips, why did Bee have to be so meticulous. "Okay, okay. But if Natalia won't re-schedule, you owe me big time."

"She will. What female can resist your charms?"

McTierney waved away the false praise. "Come on what's the plan?"

"I'll buy a ticket for the same train but sit on the opposite side of the carriage and watch anyone who makes contact with you. There must be a second part to this. Someone has gone to an enormous amount of trouble to set this up. It could be something big."

"Is that your plan, buy a ticket and see what happens?"

"It's a start. After that we'll improvise. I'll take the money just in case. Whoever set this up will only be expecting one person on the train, so with two of us we'll have the advantage."

McTierney nodded but didn't appear to share Bee's enthusiasm.

"We'll travel as two separate passengers, so no communicating, no chatter, nothing until the third party has broken cover."

"Okay."

"Keep your phone on and we can trade text messages, that won't be too abnormal but keep your phone on silent."

"What time's the train?"

"It's an afternoon train; it leaves Paddington at 3:05 p.m. and arrives in Exeter two hours later."

"Hmm. It'll ruin the whole day. You know whenever

people sing about train journeys, it's always the last train. The Monkees had that song, 'The Last Train to Clarksville' and ELO sang about a 'Last Train to London'. Clearly our man isn't a poet."

"No, he's probably a cold-blooded killer."

"Has your man recorded anything about a train?"

"Of course. 'Downbound Train' is on the 'Born In The USA' album, but that's a lament for a lost love."

"Can we leave Natalia out of this?"

THE FOLLOWING MORNING, Bee and McTierney shared a car to Redhill station and then Bee left McTierney to his own devices, although they caught the same train into London, they travelled in different carriages. Bee opted to alight at East Croydon and completed his journey by an overground train, leaving McTierney to travel into London Victoria and follow the London Underground across the capital.

As Bee walked into Paddington station he was struck by the grandeur of its architecture, a mix of historic and modern design. The vast iron and glass roof supported by graceful arches allowed natural light to flood the spacious concourse creating a sense of openness. Although Bee imagined that it didn't feel quite so open on a weekday rush hour. He crossed the station and headed for the overhead timetables; their train was scheduled to depart from Platform 12 and had no delay. Bee noted the planned stops, Reading, Taunton, Tiverton and Exeter St Davids. That would allow their mystery man to get on or off at any station. But four stops was manageable, it could have been a lot worse. He looked at the next train on the board; Cardiff featured seven stops.

He stepped away and looked for a food kiosk, because he didn't want to risk having to visit the buffet car during the journey. The choice was wide but uninspiring, he collected a tuna baguette and his regular bottle of sparkling water and made his way towards the platform. As he walked he felt the station come alive; a Duke of Edinburgh trekking party were huddled around a teacher staring at a piece of paper trying to decide which train to catch, and a couple of tourists were asking a porter for directions, a young student galloped across the concourse with a coffee in his hand. Altogether the platform buzzed with energy; 20 minutes and the train would depart, and yet there was no sign of McTierney.

The London to Exeter route is operated by Great Western Railways and features an InterCity Express, Bee was pleased to see that the train at Platform 12 looked brand new. He handed his ticket to the guard at the end of the platform.

"First Class sir. That's the penultimate carriage. Enjoy your trip."

Bee nodded and began his walk along the platform. He stepped into coach one and checked the seat numbers, he would have to walk to the far end of the train. Bee and McTierney had seats in the last section before the luggage rack at the end of the carriage. McTierney had a seat facing the luggage rack, while Bee was on the opposite side of the compartment facing all the way down the train and giving him an excellent view of anyone approaching them. The contrast was stark, McTierney would have no outlook at all. Inwardly Bee nodded his approval at whoever had set up this situation, McTierney's seat was at an immediate disadvantage.

Bee took his seat early and began evaluating the other passengers as they boarded the train and looked for their seats. He assumed the contact they were searching for would know the layout of the carriage and would be able to walk directly to their seat without delay. For a moment he considered whether the mystery man might deliberately put on an act to deflect suspicion, but why? At this stage the plan was falling into place for whoever had stuck the package to the bottom of the seat at Wembley. There was no need for complications.

The first person to enter the carriage was a business man; he wore a dark blue suit but no tie. Bee wondered why he might be travelling on a Saturday. But he looked confident, strode down the carriage, appearing to know where his seat was, but stopped in the area before Bee and then took a seat facing away from the action. Bee dismissed him.

Following quickly behind the man was a young couple, hands entwined, eyes only for each other. Bee considered that neither could be more than early twenties. Neither was your typical contract killer or hitman. The man had a rucksack on his back and was leading his damsel down the coach, they stopped and checked their tickets half way down.

Surely, these can't be in first class thought Bee, and then admonished himself for his snobbery, but breathed a sigh of relief as they continued into the next compartment.

Next to appear was an elderly lady, neatly dressed, she stowed a large case in the luggage rack behind Bee and stood looking for her seat. *This would not be good* thought Bee; he didn't want any bystanders to be in the middle of anything that might happen. She took a seat opposite Bee, smiled at him and took out an Agatha Christie novel from her bag.

Bee checked his watch, five minutes until the train was due to depart. No sign of the mystery man and no sign of McTierney either. If his DS didn't make it in time, the entire plan would be in jeopardy. His thought process was broken by baby's cry. A young mother shushed her child as she cradled her baby in one arm and carefully manoeuvred along the aisle. The mother looked a little flustered as she balanced a bag on one shoulder with her infant on the opposite hip and searched for a seat number.

Bee gulped and winced. *Please keep walking or better still turn around you shouldn't be in first class.* His prayer was answered as the young woman slipped through the adjoining door to the next carriage. Bee breathed a sigh of relief and leant back against his seat. *I've become a terrible snob; I don't want anyone else to sit in first class. No. It's their safety I'm focused on.*

Bee hadn't forgiven himself when he saw a beautiful blonde girl walking casually down the train, unsure of where her seat might be. Bee's heart missed a beat. Please keep walking, if you sit opposite McTierney, the whole plan will go up in smoke. She stopped a few paces before Bee and looked up to read the seats numbers illuminated above the seats. She looked around, noticed Bee staring at her and approached him. "Excuse me sir, I'm searching for seat 2, could you help me please?"

Disaster. That's the seat opposite McTierney and she had the cutest French accent that Bee had ever heard.

"Bien sur mademoiselle. C'est ici"

"Ah, you speak French, that is so good."

"No, not really," said Bee retreating back to English and to his corner with the disapproving look of the elderly lady.

Bugger! Bugger! Bugger! I might as well get off now!

Bee sat cursing the situation and debated with himself whether he should switch places with McTierney and take seat 3, but before he had reached a decision he spotted McTierney walking down the carriage. As he arrived at the final compartment he quickly recognised the situation and slipped Bee a knowing grin as he took his seat opposite Miss France and introduced himself.

THREE

THE DARK HOLLY green train slid silently out of the station, steadily gathering speed as it hurried through the west London suburbs and started the 193-mile journey to Exeter. Bee was surprised by the amount of graffiti along the trackside. *How do people get access to these places. Why do people do it?* Although he had to concede that some of the images on display were deserving of a wider audience.

He dragged his mind back to the situation in front of him as the train sped through Iver station. Although the die had been cast, Bee wasn't convinced that their contact was on the train. In theory he had two hours to make an appearance, so there was no rush. Bee hadn't seen anyone yet who fitted the image he had in mind, but he continued to examine each passenger he could see. As his eyes moved to his left he noticed that his colleague in seat 3 had adopted a different approach to their adventure.

McTierney was engrossed in conversation with the blonde mademoiselle and Bee could see that McTierney was enjoying the moment. Miss France had a much softer voice than McTierney and Bee couldn't make out many of her words. But McTierney spoke loud enough to give him a good idea of how the conversation was progressing.

"What's my job?"

Oh Lord please don't tell her that you're a detective working on an undercover case!

"I don't think I can tell you, if I did I'd have to shoot you!"

Don't do that, you're a police officer.

"Don't worry, I wouldn't do that, I can think of much more fun things to do than that." The girl giggled and Bee felt nauseous.

"Do you work for the government then? I bet you're a spy."

"I couldn't tell you if I was. You'll just have to imagine whatever you want."

Bee wanted to block out the imagery but found himself drawn to the conversation.

"My name?"

Don't tell her your name you idiot!

McTierney paused as if he'd somehow picked up on Bee's thought. He glanced across the aisle, turned back to the girl and said, "It's Bee, Scott Bee, but my friends call me Bumble."

Miss France sniggered, and Bee felt a wave of anger rise up in him. *The little sod has taken my name!*

Bee slumped back in his seat engulfed in a fog of disappointment, while the old lady opposite him looked up from her book with a frown. Bee offered a half-smile by way of an apology, but the woman took the opportunity to speak.

"You look unhappy, if you don't mind me saying."

"It's nothing really."

"Since we're talking would you mind if I asked you for some advice?"

Bee was caught by surprise, but gathered himself and

shrugged his shoulders, "Of course, I'm not sure that I know much, but go ahead."

"It's my family; my only son has invited me over to his house for the weekend. But it's really an ambush, he and his manipulative wife are going to pamper me tonight and then hit me with emotional blackmail tomorrow morning."

Bee tried to keep his expression neutral. His mouth parted as he contemplated replying, but the old lady hadn't finished.

"My only grandson attends a private school in Reading, and it's suddenly become quite expensive, as you may know the government has changed the law. Tracey, my daughter-in-law has got herself pregnant yet again and is going to have to give up her job. Although my son has an excellent job, they are still going to feel the squeeze. I suspect they want the bank of granny to fund the education of her grandchildren."

Bee nodded his understanding, not sure whether he was required to speak yet, but it seemed not.

"The trouble is I don't particularly like my grandson; he's an ill-mannered nasty little bully. Although I have the money, I'd much rather spend it on little trips. I know if I say yes to this, there will be another request next year. What should I do?"

Bee couldn't recall the last time he'd been asked for his opinion; it was something that didn't happen to him. He didn't have complicated family politics in his life, he had no experience of what the lady was asking him, but he wanted to help her. "Families can be difficult," he hedged.

The old lady looked unimpressed, so Bee decided to be bold.

"My advice would be to tell them the truth. Tell your

son, you don't like his wife or your grandson and that you're going to give your money to the cat's home. But prepare yourself for a lonely life."

The lady looked shocked at the response.

"If you can't face being alone, and I can tell you from experience it's not easy. Seize the moral high ground and offer the money before they ask. It'll make the decision feel much better, even if you're not really making the decision."

The lady appeared even more shocked at this response.

"Once you had your son, you signed up for this. Maybe you didn't know the details, but the contract was made. All your life, you worry, you care, and you pay, because the alternative of losing them is unthinkable."

The old lady's shock morphed into a smile of understanding. The train's audio system announcing that they would soon be stopping at Reading. The lady returned her novel to her bag and got up from her seat. "You're a wise man, someday you'll make someone very happy."

With the lady gone, Bee resumed his vigil, evaluating every new passenger who joined the train. Two young lads walked all the way through the carriage and disappeared from Bee's register. Ditto a mother and daughter, but a single middle-aged woman, took a seat in the next area having stopped and looked around in the area where Bee and McTierney were seated. Bee pondered the idea of a female contact. There was no reason why it couldn't be a woman, although somehow he had always assumed that the mystery person would be a man.

As the train departed, a member of the train catering crew appeared at the far end of the carriageway pushing a well-stocked trolley. He stopped at each set of seats and offered a selection of drinks and snacks to the passengers.

Eventually the conductor arrived at the final area and asked McTierney and his new friend if they would like anything from his trolley. McTierney grabbed the opportunity to offer his companion a drink; she hesitated but McTierney persuaded her to take a small bottle of wine, reassuring her that it wouldn't be English. McTierney then asked for a beer for himself, the waiter looked surprised. "Wouldn't sir rather have a Coke?"

McTierney scowled at the suggestion, "No thanks. I'll have a beer."

"I don't think the tins of beer are that fresh sir, I think they've been stored close to a heater. The Coke would be better."

"No. Not keen on the stuff, I've have a beer and take my chances."

"But sir."

"No come on, I'll have that one on the top of the trolley. I'm sure it'll be fine."

Before the conductor could resist, McTierney reached across and grabbed the can from the trolley.

"Let me leave this one with you in case you need something refreshing later on your journey."

The conductor pushed the can of Coke across the table towards McTierney.

"No, don't worry. You keep it," said McTierney placing it back on the trolley.

Across the aisle Bee couldn't believe what he was seeing. *Just take the bloody can you idiot.*

"I'll take that can of Coke please," said Bee.

The conductor spun round and glared at his new customer.

"I'll get you a fresh one sir,"

"No that's okay I'll take the one you have there."

"But it's been handled now."

"No problem I'm sure the contents are fine."

"Can't be too careful sir, I'll get you a fresh one."

"That one is fine."

"It's no trouble sir."

Bee could see perspiration starting to appear on the conductor's forehead.

"Please I'd like that can, there's no need to find another."

"It's no bother sir. The bottom part of my trolley is a chilled cabinet, a cold one will taste so much better." The guard bent down, opened a door and rummaged around inside for a new can of Coke. For a few seconds he couldn't find one. He pulled out a 7 Up, a Sprite, but then at last he plucked a deep red coloured can from the bowels of his trolley. Bee could sense the relief on the man's face.

"Here you go sir. Told you it was no bother. There's no charge for soft drink and snacks in first class sir. Would you like a snack to go with it?"

Bee kept his eyes glued to the man while he pondered. The man offered a weak smile, but it quickly cracked, Bee half expected him to turn and run.

"What have you got to offer?", he asked slowly.

"You know, the usual, crisps, chocolate bars and a few peanuts. There's a wider selection in the buffet car at the other end of the train if you're hungry." The man was starting to recover his composure; Bee had one more card to play.

"I'll take a Snickers bar, if you have one?"

"Certainly sir. The man stretched across his trolley and picked up a bar and passed it to Bee. As Bee took it from his hand, he stared him directly in the face. "And another can of Coke please, I have a weakness for the taste, and you did say it was free."

The man shuddered, Bee could feel the anxiety flood over him, "Certainly sir," he mumbled and hurriedly bent down again to resume his search in the bowels of the trolley. Bee could hear the frantic rattling of tin cans as the conductor searched for another Coke tin. Eventually he found what he was looking for, resurfaced and offered the can to Bee. Bee smiled as he took it, but the smile wasn't reciprocated. The man couldn't wait to escape the carriage, but Bee needed only a few seconds to log his facial features.

Age 45 to 50. Five feet eight tall, West Country accent, brown eyes, brown hair recently cut, no facial hair but a large mole above his top lip. He would be easy to find when the train arrived in Exeter, especially as he had a name badge declaring him to be Jon.

As the guard lined up his trolley to push it through to the next carriage, McTierney called out to him "Tell you what, I've changed my mind I will have that Coke. I never like to turn away a freebie."

FOUR

EXETER ST DAVIDS railway station was the final stop for the GWR train. It's a provincial railway station sitting quietly in the centre of the city. Originally built in 1844 to support the ambitions of Isambard Kingson Brunel it has undergone several renovations. Despite holding the position as the busiest station in Devon, it offered limited services to the London traveller. A modest brick building with faded signage and a single clock above the entrance. Weathered benches lined the main platform with the occasional weed pushing through cracks in the concrete. The station with its simple charm and unhurried pace felt like a place where time moved more slowly.

Bee exited the train ahead of McTierney and stepped away from the express to allow other passengers to leave. He looked up and down the length of the train hoping to see the conductor who had delivered the Coke can, but he didn't appear. His concentration was broken by the voice of his partner, McTierney who was still chatting to his French companion as they got off the train. McTierney caught his eye and subtly nodded towards the exit.

Exeter is a historic city, dating back to Roman times, known for its blend of ancient charm and modern vibrancy. At its heart stands the magnificent Exeter Cathedral, with its

Gothic towers overlooking narrow cobbled streets lined with independent shops, cafes and pubs. The River Exe snakes through the city, offering quayside walks, whilst remnants of Roman walls and medieval buildings hint at Exeter's rich past. Exeter Castle, a Norman landmark overlooks the leafy Northernhay and Rougemont Gardens.

For the casual tourist the county town of Devon had much to offer. But not for two detectives from Surrey. McTierney watched wistfully as a taxi whisked Miss France off to her destination. He joined Bee standing in front of a row of shops and the two men began walking towards the centre of the town. They didn't speak until they had crossed Bonhay Road and began climbing St David's Hill.

"I bet you thought I hadn't clocked that the Coke can was the key."

"You hadn't."

"Course I had."

"That guard was desperate to hand it to you and all you could do was demand a beer."

McTierney smiled.

"Need I remind you; you are working."

"I was undercover."

"Oh yes, using my name. Thanks for that."

"No one's going to confuse you for me."

"I think we can both say amen to that. Anyway, stop arguing, what's special about the can?"

McTierney pulled the can from his jacket pocket and rolled it around in his hands. He frowned and repeated the process, then turned it upside down. "That's strange – I can't see anything unusual."

Bee tutted, "Pass it over." He repeated the actions

McTierney had just completed but came up with the same conclusion. "There's no message. You haven't lost it have you?"

"No!" Shouted McTierney grabbing the can back and turning it over again.

The two detectives looked at each other.

"Shit!" said Bee, "I was convinced it was the can. Did anyone else make contact with you?"

"No. Although I'd like to make contact with Sophie."

"Miss France?"

McTierney grinned like a schoolboy.

"Down boy."

"Come on, let's go get a drink, while we think about what to do."

"Wait that's it. It's in the can. You need to drink the contents."

"I'm not drinking it. You drink it."

"I've already had two cans today; that's enough for anyone."

McTierney shook his head. "The things I do for the police."

He pulled open the tin and took a long swig. "Aargh."

"Poisoned?"

"No, but there's something in the can." McTierney yanked the can away from his mouth and poured the contents on the pavement. A silver key dropped onto the ground and bounced towards a drain. Bee lunged forward and managed to catch it. He wiped it dry on his trousers and spun it around in his hands. It was attached to a small plastic tag which carried the number 22.

"Left luggage compartment in the station perhaps," he offered.

"Let's go see, and I'm fine, thanks for asking."

The pair turned to head back to the station carefully sidestepping a group of students from the university who were heading out for a night on the town.

"Early start," said McTierney.

"So says the master. By the way did you know JK Rowling attended Exeter University? Apparently there are several Harry Potter related sites around the city."

McTierney threw his head back in disgust, "How do you know this stuff?"

He led the way back into the station, stepped around a vagrant lying on the station floor and walked over to the ticket desk. Now the London train had cleared the station, the hubbub had died away and the place was quiet again. The young man behind the counter pointed to his left and the two detectives gathered around the short row of left luggage lockers. There were 24 in total arranged in three rows of eight. Number 22 was at the far end on the top, as far away from prying eyes as it could be.

"At least there is a 22," said McTierney as he pushed the key into the lock. It clicked and sprang open. He reached in and pulled out another khaki package, which looked remarkably similar to the Wembley one, although perhaps a little larger. McTierney closed the locker, turned his back towards the station and slipped his finger under the seal breaking it in an instant. He slowly tipped the package up placing his free hand under the opening to catch the contents. A black pistol dropped into his hand. He and Bee exchanged astonished looks. McTierney opened the chamber, and his eyes fell on a full magazine of six bullets.

"Is there anything else inside?"

McTierney passed the gun to Bee and felt inside the packet, he pulled out a single sheet of paper. He unfolded it and held it open for both to read.

LG MUST DIE

"Didn't see that coming," said Bee. "It looks like you've been hired to make a killing."

"Me? Or us?"

"Sorry. You know what I mean. Us. Let's see if we can track down the conductor who gave you the can of Coke. This is getting serious. I made a note of his name when we were on the train."

Bee led the way back to the ticket desk, flashed his police identity card at the young man and asked to speak to the station manager. Three minutes later, he and McTierney were sitting in a cramped, rectangular room tucked away behind the last platform. A worn wooden desk cluttered with paperwork and an old black landline telephone separated them from a middle-aged plump man. The walls were adorned with faded timetables, a calendar and several photographs charting the development of the station.

"Good of you to see us at short notice," said Bee. "We're working on an unusual case which began in London but has brought us to Exeter."

The station manager nodded gently as if he faced this situation every day of the week.

"We'd like to talk to one of the catering crew from the Intercity Express that arrived here at 5:15 p.m. I'd say he's in his late forties, about five feet eight tall with brown hair and brown eyes. His name is Jon."

"Ah yes. That'll be Jon Eastham. But I don't think you'll be speaking to him today. He was on the Penzance train. It left five minutes ago."

The customary look of disappointment fell across Bee's face.

FIVE

THE EUROPCAR OFFICE in Exeter is situated in Marsh Green Road a 15-minute walk from St Davids station. Bee and McTierney ran it in eight minutes and arrived three minutes before it closed. The office was a simple no frills building situated close to waste ground, which backed onto the railway line. There were a few rental cars parked outside and more on open land at the rear. Inside, the space was small but functional, with a linoleum floor and a few plastic chairs along one wall. A grey counter stretched across the room, behind which hung a clutter of car keys on hooks each with hand-written tags. Sunlight filtered through a dusty blind on the shop front casting a warm glow over the faded travel posters on the wall. The air smelled faintly of coffee, while a single employee sat behind the desk tapping on a computer. He looked up in surprise as the two policemen burst into the office.

"We're just about to close."

"We're the police, we need a car," puffed Bee.

McTierney flopped onto the counter, "We need something fast; I'd like a Chevrolet because in all the rock songs ever sung it's always the Chevrolet that has the most fun!"

Bee swung round, eyes bulging. "What? No!" He turned back to the assistant. "Please ignore my colleague, he gets emotional around cars. We'll take whatever you've got to hand."

Ten minutes later and with three copies of the paperwork in Bee's pocket, the pair walked around to the back of the car lot searching for a blue Volvo C60.

"I can't believe you took a Volvo. I'm too young to drive a Volvo."

"Don't worry you're not driving. I hired it as a single driver."

McTierney hid his disappointment well and took control of the car's satellite navigation system and music. "The sat nav says 101 miles, 1 hour 55 minutes, that'll be eight-fifteen by the time we get there. You've got to beat that."

"I don't."

"Come on everybody tries to beat the sat nav, that's the point of having one. It's a challenge."

"The point of the sat nav is to help you get to your destination. What road is it recommending?"

"Looks like the A30 most of the way and it's dual carriageway, early evening no traffic. Put your foot down, I'm in the mood for a long beer."

Bee took his time to extract them from Exeter city centre, but once on the A30 with McTierney's prediction proving to be correct, he made good time. It was just after 8 p.m. when he reached the outskirts of Penzance and pulled off the ring road to follow the signs towards the town's railway station. The town was surrounded by hills and the lights of the place seemed to shimmer in a bowl below them. They drove past large villas, which had been turned into guest houses all labelled with exotic names; Seashell Retreat, squeezed in between Sandpiper's Nest and Seabreeze Cottage. Each had a

'No Vacancies' board.

McTierney ventured that "Most of these guest houses are full, and those that aren't, have to pretend to be, to save face."

Bee rolled his eyes, "You're such a cynic. This is high season; you'd expect them to be full." The station is the end of the line for Great Western Railways and made the provincial station in Exeter look like a major terminus. Bee pulled into one of the parking spaces outside the station.

"Let's hope Jon Eastham hasn't rushed home."

"Actually, I think you've beaten the train. It's one of those that stops at every milk churn down the line. We had a lot of them in Norfolk when I was living up there."

When the two detectives alighted from the car they felt a sudden chill; the sun hadn't quite dipped, but it was obscured by the tall buildings which surrounded the station. Bee shivered, "Beginning to wish I'd brought more clothes."

"Yeah it's suddenly cold down here."

"Ten miles further and you'd be standing on Lands End staring out at the Atlantic Ocean."

"Let's get this over and done so we can get back to civilisation."

"I think the best we can do tonight is Exeter."

"That'll do."

The two detectives headed for the station entrance. Penzance station was a modest, single-story building with chipped paintwork and ivy creeping along the brickwork. A simple wooden sign displayed the station's name in the now familiar cream and maroon livery of the Great Western Railway's boards. Inside, a narrow ticket counter sat opposite the entrance, at the end stood a Costa Coffee franchise outlet and beside that a vending machine hummed softly in the corner. The station was deserted. Bee walked over to the ticket desk and spoke to the woman behind the glass. Within a minute he was back alongside McTierney.

"Doreen says that the station master left an hour ago. Our train should arrive in the next five minutes and then there's one later train to come."

McTierney frowned.

"In case our man switched trains and is coming home on the last train."

Bee's fear proved unfounded and after the 15 passengers had alighted from the train and made their way through the exit gate, Bee spotted the elusive catering man Jon Eastham walking alongside the train. McTierney had stood out of sight, in case his presence spooked Eastham, but as the conductor got close to the exit McTierney stepped into the light. Eastham recognised him but by then it was too late. As the light flashed across his face, Bee seized the moment.

"Mr Eastham, we're the police. We'd like a quick word with you. But you're not in any trouble, we just want to ask you a few questions."

Whether Eastham was reassured by Bee's words or whether he was too tired to run, he didn't resist and followed the detectives into the main building. With the Costa Coffee franchise closed the only available room was the waiting room and together the three men nearly filled the place.

Bee sat opposite Eastham and led the interview, keeping the details to a minimum. As the junior officer here, McTierney is technically on note-taking duties, but that is a task that doesn't come easily to this DS; it all seems redundant to him since he possesses a near perfect photographic memory. But of course, Inspector Bee won't see it like that and nor will it count if McTierney is asked to make an appearance should this adventure ever end in a court case. But for one reason or another McTierney leaves his notebook in his pocket and hopes that Bee has scribbled down enough to get them out of that particular black hole should it appear at some point in the future. Bee kicks off the interview.

"So, tell us how you came to deliver a coded message in a tin of Coke?"

"I didn't know it was a code. I thought it was a joke, a wheeze. This guy approached me at Paddington station, offered me a grand to hand the Coke tin to the person sitting in seat 3, coach B. He said it would make his day. It seemed like easy money. I don't make much money on the trains, so a grand for one little tin, it was too good to turn down."

"You didn't think it sounded a little strange?"

"Well, yes it was a little strange, no doubt about it, but as I said, he offered me a grand. At that point, who cares about strange?"

Bee pursed his lips. "What can you tell me about the man that made you this offer?"

"Not a lot really. He was standing in the shadows by the far platform, I couldn't see his face, plus he was wearing a big hat, one of those with a wide brim." Eastham waved his hands around his head to give Bee the general idea.

"Yes okay. What about his voice?"

Eastham thought for a moment. "Deep. A bit deeper than yours. And he spoke a bit like you. If I had to guess I'd say he came from London, not from down here."

"What about his height?"

Eastham looked from Bee to McTierney and back again. "He was tall. I'd say he was more your height than your partner's."

"Okay. Thanks. Anything else?"

"Can I keep the money?"

"Sure, why not."

Eastham's face exploded into a big grin. "Thanks mate. The missus will be chuffed."

Further investigation established that Eastham had worked on the railways for thirty years since leaving school, was well-known on the network and recently had to pay a hefty medical bill for his wife which left him a little short of money and a prime target for someone.

Bee smiled and turned to McTierney. "Anything you want to ask?"

McTierney stepped towards the man "Yes, if money was no object which hotel would you choose in Exeter?"

Eastham thought for a moment, "I've never been there, but I've heard a few passengers say good things about the Rougemont Hotel on Queen Street. It's close to the Central station."

As Bee and McTierney prepared to leave, Eastham called out to them, "I just remembered something. When he handed over the packet of money, I noticed the man had a tattoo on the back of his hand, or rather where you'd expect a watch to be. It looked like a fish."

As the two detectives made their way back to the car, Bee turned to McTierney, "Why did you ask him that question about hotels and money being no object?"

"Because that's the situation we find ourselves in; looking for a hotel in Exeter with £20k in our pockets."

"You know we can't spend that money. It's evidence."

"Not all of it needs to be evidence."

SIX

BREAKFAST AT THE Holiday Inn was more than likely a much plainer affair than it would have been at the Rougemont Hotel, but it also cost around half the amount. Detective Scott Bee took a light breakfast of fresh pears, and a bowl of muesli washed down with an apple juice and a cappuccino, while Ron McTierney took full advantage of the buffet option. He began with a bowl of Frosties and followed this with a Full English which was as full as his plate would allow; three pork sausages and four rashers of bacon, rounded off by two slices of toast and accompanied by an orange juice and a pot of tea.

"Are you sure you've got enough on your plate?"

"Who knows when we're going to eat again. It's Sunday, we'll probably spend all day on a train with a buffet car offering stale sandwiches."

Bee shook his head in disbelief, "Come on, eat up, we've got a train to catch, and this one will be 'sans femmes'."

"It'll be what?"

"Without women."

"What a horrible idea. But at least you didn't say without beer!"

"It's nine-thirty on Sunday morning; you don't need beer at this hour."

McTierney shrugged and the pair, still dressed in yesterday's clothes, walked from the hotel to the station where they had arrived yesterday afternoon. But this time they had no pre-booked tickets; a quick review of the respective prices put the two detectives in second class sitting on cloth back seats. Their train departed at 9:30 a.m. with most of the seats around them empty. Bee had picked up The Sunday Times from the station newsagent but hadn't finished the first article when McTierney broke the silence.

"Why do you think whoever is behind this dragged us all the way to Devon to hand us the next piece of the jigsaw puzzle?"

"Yes, I'd been wondering that."

"All of this could have been done so easily in London. Paddington station has left luggage lockers, as does Victoria, and even Redhill for that matter. I could have had my Saturday with Natalia."

Bee eyed him suspiciously.

"Okay, maybe not Redhill, but we didn't need to come all the way down here."

"Perhaps the perpetrator has a connection to Exeter, or maybe it's a test of our commitment."

McTierney grunted, clearly dis-satisfied with the answer. Bee folded the news section of his paper and placed it on the seat beside him. "What I do know is that we need to get back quick, or our new Chief Superintendent Springfield will be spitting blood."

"Ah, the evil queen of numbers. Hopefully Itzkowitz has been holding the fort on the detective desk. She was on the rota for yesterday, and I haven't heard anything from her."

"By the evil queen I presume you mean our new chief

superintendent."

"The same. She's always on my case. I don't know what I can do to please her."

"I think she's a new broom sweeping clean, looking to make her mark. Try to keep your head down and don't let her hear you call her the evil queen."

"Fair point."

"As for Itzkowitz, I've not heard anything either. I think she's smart, she'll be okay. You probably know her better than me. Do you think she's going to stay in the UK, or will she head back to New York one day?"

McTierney screwed up his nose while he thought about the answer, "Don't know. Probably depends on whether she finds someone to settle down with. I believe she's tricked some poor chap into dating her. Some guy called Jake, but I haven't met him yet, she's quite guarded about her personal life."

"I wouldn't criticise her for that. We spend so much time in front of the public, it's hard to retain any privacy."

"Unless you have a house in the middle of nowhere."

Bee dipped his nose and looked over his glasses at McTierney, "Is that a word of complaint about your current living quarters? You are free to move out if you want. It has been over three years now."

"No, no I like it. It's just sometimes it would be nice to be nearer to civilisation."

Bee shrugged, "While we're talking about keeping the boss happy, something you could do to please me, would be to give me your preference on a new colour for the kitchen. It's long overdue a fresh coat of paint. I was thinking something warm like a sunshine yellow or an apricot colour."

McTierney blew out his cheeks. "I don't much care."

"How about I paint a few strips on the wall, and we see how we feel?"

"How about you stop talking like we're a couple. It's disturbing. I hope you don't expect me to do any painting."

Bee raised his hand in submission, "Okay. You win. Here have the paper, I'm going to see if I can get a coffee. You want something?"

Bee wandered through the carriages, rocking from side to side against the seats. When he arrived at the buffet car two assistants behind the counter were discussing proposed staffing changes on the railways. Each was upset about the proposal to reduce staffing numbers on the trains, but neither noticed Bee waiting to be served.

"We need our union to make the rail companies see sense."

"Can't provide a decent service to customers if they keep taking away the people who make it work."

Bee wondered if there was a second buffet car further down the train, but he'd already walked through five carriages. Then the train rocked, and he lurched forward grabbing the counter. Both protagonists turned to face him.

"Are you alright there sir?"

"Could I get a couple of large coffees please?"

Bee returned to their carriage and moved to pass over McTierney's coffee cup, but as McTierney reached for it, Bee pulled it back. "You only get this if you tell me the truth about the Oasis concert tickets."

"Er, I did," croaked McTierney.

"No, you didn't. I remember when the tickets went on sale you were obsessed with getting one and threw a tantrum when you were on shift when they became available."

McTierney retreated into his seat and didn't respond.

Bee fixed him with a stare, "If you'd suddenly acquired a pair of tickets you wouldn't have been able to keep quiet about it. So come on, what did you do to get them?"

McTierney reached for the coffee, "You don't want to know."

Bee kept hold of the cup, "Yes I do."

"Really, you don't."

"Yes I do!"

"Okay."

Bee released the cup and took his seat. McTierney took a sip, drew himself up in the seat and turned to face Bee.

"You remember last week I had to go up to Croydon to help them out on the major case that's due to come to court in the next couple of weeks?"

"Aha."

"They've been desperate to nail this guy for years and I got the feeling that their case is a bit weak."

"Who is it?"

McTierney screwed up his face. "Some Russian, Dimitri Taranovsky. I thought he might be a jewel thief, but it turns out he isn't."

Bee leant his head back and racked his brain for a moment, "This is the guy known as Tchaikovsky. A nasty piece of work, a Russian who kills people with piano wire. Apparently he started his career with the killing of his piano teacher when he was 12, after she told him off for missing his scales or something."

"Yes that's the name, I thought you'd like that, consider it classy?"

"Classy? The guy's a killer. There's nothing classy about that."

"Anyway, the searches were all focused on trying to find some extra evidence to put this guy away. I was asked to help the local team search a few of Tchaikovsky's properties; his office, his club, and his house."

Bee nodded, his memory was returning, "This is the guy who in recent years has become a major gangland leader in South London."

"Yep, that's him. The Croydon boys seemed to think he was the biggest."

"But the police have struggled to get him convicted for anything. From what I've read he seems to have had a charmed life. Always getting away at the last minute."

McTierney shrugged his shoulders, "Maybe not this time, as the word in Croydon was that there is a witness, a young girl who has come forward saying that she saw him kill a man in March. That was why he was taken into custody and why we were searching all his properties for evidence that might help the case."

Bee moved uneasily in his seat. "That would be tremendous. South London will be a lot safer with Taranovsky behind bars. But what's this got to do with the tickets?"

McTierney took another sip of his coffee and glanced out of the train window. "I found the tickets when I was rummaging around his desk in the study at his place in Croydon."

Bee looked askance at McTierney, "Oh no, I don't want to hear this."

"I figured they would only go to waste, because Taranovsky was in custody, so I slipped them into my pocket and carried on."

"That was idiotic. Beyond belief. Now we're both guilty of theft. We can file that under 'bloody stupid'!"

"I didn't think anybody would ever find out."

"Someone always finds out! If this comes out, Chief Superintendent Springfield will crucify both of us!"

"So, we don't tell anyone."

Bee hung his head in his hands and felt his career flashing past him. Slowly he lifted his head and looked at his partner with a mixture of disbelief and fury. "Don't tell anyone, huh! Don't tell anyone, we've stumbled across £20,000, plus a locker with a gun and bullets and we don't tell anyone about it. That's your plan."

"I admit it needs a bit of work, but yes, we can sort it."

Bee shook his head and slumped back into his seat; his hands flopped down beside him. He opened his mouth to speak but couldn't find the words. Eventually he spoke. "I don't know if I can do this. If this comes out we're both finished."

"You have to. You have to help me, otherwise I'm sunk."

Bee turned and stared out of the window. McTierney let him sit for a minute, then nudged his shoulder. Bee turned his face towards him. "You haven't heard the bad bit yet."

Bee's jaw dropped, but he was incapable of speech.

"Taranovsky's lawyer got him released on Thursday evening, so he will know someone took the tickets."

SEVEN

IT WAS 8:45 a.m. on Monday morning in the new Reigate police station. Recently appointed Chief Superintendent Lisa Springfield was on the prowl searching for her detective team. Her twenty-five years of experience gave her an authoritative stride; she was dressed in a sharp, tailored uniform. She benefited from a commanding posture, walking tall and alert with eyes that were both observant and thoughtful. Her jet-black hair was neatly tied back in a no-nonsense approach that reflected in her attitude to the role. She had only been in the job for a few months having transferred down from Glasgow to replace the retiring Chief Superintendent Beck. She enjoyed the clean southern air, but little else about the role pleased her. Most of her charges lacked urgency, they all seemed content to drink tea and fill out paperwork all day, and that, as far as Springfield was concerned, would not get her promoted to the next level. She had endured a difficult weekend entertaining her younger sister and her ghastly children, whom she had wanted to yell at but had been unable to do so. But now, in her own domain, somebody was going to pay.

The original Reigate police station was a casualty of the reinforced autoclaved aerated concrete scandal, known in the trade as RAAC. It, along with numerous other public buildings, many of them schools built in the 1960's had been evacuated and now stood empty waiting for a plan to rebuild it, as officials feared that the lightweight alternative concrete could collapse if and when exposed to excess water, and there had been a lot of water in Reigate of late. Most people in the know believed that the police would never return to their former station, the potential land value for the space was far too great for the council to let this golden opportunity slip by. The council recognised the need for a police force, it was just an inconvenience to provide them with a large building in the town centre from which to do their policing. For the time being, they had been forced to relocate to St David's House in Wray Park Road, and co-habit with the Fire Service. It meant that the 77 CCTV cameras used by the police to monitor the roads and general public of Reigate were left unmonitored in their old building. A testing time for all involved. But Lisa Springfield didn't suffer any of that inconvenience. On her first morning she had identified the largest office in the new building, and she hadn't looked back since.

Springfield set off around the building on the first of her three daily patrols. Sharing a station with the local fire brigade was not part of the plan when she had first heard that she was in the running for the top job in Reigate, but she was wise enough not to make a fuss when the offer came through. Whenever she entered a new area, the casual conversations ground to a halt; the officers had quickly learnt that Lisa Springfield didn't tour the office to make polite conversation, she did so to ensure everyone was working. Up on the first floor the air was cool with the faint scent of coffee; this was the new home of the CID team, but this morning there was only Carol Bishop present. Springfield stopped, surveyed the scene, tutted and walked slowly across the floor to Bishop's desk. She decided against trading pleasantries with a junior officer and offered her an abrupt nod instead before turning back towards the stairs. She took a step, changed her mind, and turned back to DC Bishop, who hadn't looked up from her laptop. Springfield spoke fast, partly to convey the idea that she was busy and partly because she was busy. She liked to be involved in every aspect of policing at the station and that took a lot more hours than she was paid for. "When the inspector finally arrives, send him to my office. Immediately."

"Yes Ma'am." Bishop, warmed by what she believed to be a compliment dived into her work with a greater intensity.

★ ★ ★

MEANWHILE SIX MILES away in an isolated farmhouse in the small village of Outwood, and after a protracted journey home from the West Country involving a three-hour delay outside Swindon station, Reigate's two leading detectives were taking a late start. At least one of them was doing so, Bee had risen early and been out to re-stock their fridge, while McTierney had enjoyed an additional hour in bed. As the kitchen clock ticked past nine o'clock they met by the kitchen table.

"While you were lounging around in bed, some of us have been up doing things."

"Oh yeah, put the kettle on while you're over there."

Scott rolled his eyes, but obliged, nonetheless.

Ron shook the last remnants out of a cereal box and reached for the milk bottle that Scott had placed on the table.

"So, what have you done?"

"I called into Sainsbury's for some fresh milk," said Bee, pointing at the bottle in McTierney's hand. "Then I took the opportunity to buy some sample paint pots and then I dropped off some old clothes to the recycling point."

"Yippee. The world has been saved!"

"It all helps. But I nearly didn't go through with it."

"Sudden pang of guilt that no one would want anything that you once considered fashionable?"

"No. But while I was at the supermarket, sitting in my car, the Oxfam man turned up to collect the clothes that people had donated. He was having a bit of a rummage around and rejecting some of the items that he encountered. Those that made the grade were transferred to the back of his van. He was taking ages, and I had to fight the temptation to abandon my visit and return tomorrow."

Ron stared back across the kitchen table. "You don't really think people get judged by the quality of whatever they decide to recycle do you?"

Scott allowed a long pause to develop.

"Oh shit. You do."

"No," said Scott, avoiding Ron's face. "I don't need to. I got out of the car and made my way over to the man and his van. I was unsure whether to put the bags into the container so that he could remove them seconds later or whether it would be presumptuous to chuck them straight into his van. But he saved my blushes. 'Thanks, mate', he said. Taking them from me and pushing them into his vehicle alongside an appalling coffee table and some unsightly trousers."

Ron shook his head. "That's made your day, hasn't it!"

Scott eyed him dismissively, "Come on, let's get to work.

I've just had a text from Carol warning me that the chief is on the warpath."

★ ★ ★

SPRINGFIELD SPOTTED BEE and McTierney arriving together and determined to test her new detective team; would Bishop pass on the message quickly and would Bee react instantly? She would give him three minutes. By nine-thirty-seven the trial period had expired, and Springfield retraced her steps to the detective area on the first floor of the improvised station. Bee was standing by the coffee machine collecting three coffees when Springfield appeared at the end of the hall.

"Bishop, did you give my message to Inspector Bee when he arrived six minutes ago?"

Carol Bishop swung around in her chair, caught in the headlights like a scared rabbit. Not sure what to say, she stuttered, paused and fell silent.

"She did, yes Ma'am," said Bee. "I needed a drink to whet my whistle before coming to see you. I'm rather wedded to my routines."

"Good of you to show some backbone Bee. I like that."

Bee offered a weak smile and walked across to the open plan area where the four-person detective team was based while they were sharing premises with the fire service. He placed the plastic cups on the desk. McTierney grabbed the first, Springfield took the second and Bee moved the third closer to Bishop. Springfield took a sip from her cup, grimaced at the taste. "There was an emergency call into this department on Saturday afternoon, what was the outcome?"

Bee, McTierney and Bishop all exchanged vacant looks.

"Does anybody know?"

The three vacant expressions turned to concern and then apprehension as Springfield's mouth began to twitch. Finally, Bee took control of their response. "Fran Itzkowitz was here on Saturday covering the desk. If there was an emergency call, I'm sure she would have covered it. She's a good officer."

Springfield drilled her eyes into Bee and then McTierney "Where were you two on Saturday afternoon?"

"Err, at home."

"What are you the odd couple?"

Bee tittered, "Yes Ma'am."

"Itzkowitz didn't close out the day log and she's nowhere to be seen. Are you expecting her to be in here today?"

"Yes Ma'am."

"Find her and then tell me what happened on Saturday afternoon and then ask Itzkowitz to complete her paperwork. I like an efficient station with all the paperwork done."

"We all do," said McTierney from behind the chief. Springfield spun round and eyed McTierney suspiciously. "Glad to hear it, McTierney."

She stepped away from the group, "Inform me the moment you locate Itzkowitz. I want to see a completed call log before the end of the day." With that Springfield left the three detectives to discuss the absent Fran Itzkowitz.

EIGHT

BEE REVISITED THE coffee machine at the end of their floor and returned with a fresh cup.

"I wouldn't have bothered if I was you. This stuff tastes horrid. How I miss Juliet now we've been forced to move into this ghastly monstrosity of a building," said McTierney.

"Yes, I agree," offered Bishop, "It's cold, crumbling and has a weird sense of neglect and dread. You know I just can't get used to this building, I wish we were still in the old station. We've been here for six months, but it feels like a lifetime."

"Actually, it's been ten months," said Bee. "We moved in on 23rd of September last year."

McTierney shook his head at Bee, but he didn't notice and carried on.

"I think we can all agree that the coffee is worse," said Bee grimacing at his own plastic cup. "But first things first, what do we know about this inquiry that came in on Saturday and do we know where Itzkowitz is?"

It was the same answer to both questions. Bee tried an easier option, "Bishop can you call Itzkowitz and see where she is? McTierney can you retrieve the daily log, and we can see what came in on Saturday?"

"Sure. It's appalling these officers thinking that they can

walk in at any time of the day. We have standards!" He raised his hands in mock defence before anyone could say anything.

Ten minutes later, three quarters of the Reigate CID team were gathered around the central table in the solitary meeting room on the first floor. In days gone by the room had been an elegant drawing room with a view south to the lawns of the neighbouring houses. But times change; now the room had a new life as the standard ops room for the CID team, but the transformation wasn't yet complete. The meeting room was plain and unremarkable with neutral-coloured walls and a large generic plastic topped rectangular table in the centre. Several standard office chairs were neatly arranged around it, a couple exhibited torn fabric. Overhead, a pair of fluorescent tube lights cast a harsh flat glow. The only remnant from the old case room in the Reigate Road station was the whiteboard that Bee liked to use to map out their cases. The door had been closed all weekend and the air felt stale and offered little inspiration or energy.

Bee opened the call log to Saturday's page and read the last entry. "A call came in at 3pm. Looks like Itzkowitz answered the call to go to the Holmethorpe Industrial Estate on Saturday afternoon and has not been seen since. The caller asked for a detective to come over and check out a potential robbery on Ormside Way. But there's no address listed and no phone number either, which suggests the number was withheld."

"Either that, or Itzkowitz couldn't be bothered to enter it. She must have known it, to know where to go."

Bee acknowledged the truth in McTierney's words, pushed his glasses up his nose and then turned his attention to Bishop, "Any joy in locating our American colleague?"

"She's not picking up on her mobile, it goes to voicemail, and I've left a message. Sorry, but I don't have any other number. To be honest, I don't even know where she lives. I think it's near Priory Park. I've heard her talk about walking in the park but never known exactly where she lives."

Bee turned his attention to McTierney.

"Don't ask me, I've never been to her place."

"Hmm. I just thought that since you'd employed her you might know more about her."

McTierney screwed up his face, "What can I tell you? American from The Bronx. Crossed the Atlantic and started in the Guildford force. Moved here two years ago when we needed a new DS. Eats weird shit, talks funny, but a decent officer. Don't think she'd do anything stupid."

"Unlike your good self."

"Unlike me," laughed McTierney.

"Okay. Can you dig out her home address and drop by to check all is well."

★ ★ ★

THE HR MANAGER furnished McTierney with Itzkowitz's home address which turned out to be in Glovers Road, Reigate. She was renting an early-Edwardian semi-detached house which matched hundreds in the local area, all packed together on the southern side of the town. McTierney wandered up to the front door, pressed the bell, banged on the door, and lifted the letter box to shout through it. All to no avail. He moved to the kitchen window and peered through but there was no sign of life. Unperturbed, he opened the side gate and walked around the property to find the back door. He lifted the lid from her green waste food bin and looked down on a mess of food debris. Yes, this is the right place, he thought. He banged on the back door, but once again there was no response. He returned to the police station with no news.

While McTierney was in the heart of Reigate, Bee headed up to the Holmethorpe Industrial Estate on the outskirts of Redhill to see if he could trace the original call from Saturday afternoon. He parked up at one end of Ormside Way and started his walk. Bee was comparatively unfamiliar with the area. Years earlier it had been a cosmopolitan commercial area of fascinating contrasts; of the drab and the delightful; of boarded up premises and thriving small businesses; of decay and regeneration – a private sex shop at one end of the estate and a car repair shop at the other. But most of that had gone now.

He wandered between empty warehouses and factory buildings, once bustling with activity, which now stood abandoned, their windows shattered or boarded up. Graffiti scarred the walls, and the once bright signs of industrial optimism had faded and peeled away, giving the place an air of decay.

He marched across cracked tarmac and past rusted fences where overgrown weeds had slowly overtaken the edges of the pathways; it was a desolate sight. But every hundred yards there was an oasis of activity as a new business start-up had emerged and was aiming for the sky in a race with the weeds as industry reflected nature. Bee identified five potential premises where he thought Itzkowitz could reasonably have been called to investigate. He approached each in turn but none of them had any knowledge either of making a call to the police or of seeing a police officer walking around the estate on Saturday afternoon. More disturbing for Bee was that there was no trace of Itzkowitz's car. He returned empty-handed to the station hoping that McTierney had produced a better result.

The three colleagues revisited the same bare white table that they had left not two hours earlier and discussed their options.

"Should we be worried?" asked Bishop.

The ten second pause answered her question, although Bee attempted to deny it. "No, Fran Itzkowitz is a smart officer, she wouldn't be considered to be an 'at risk' person. She's mentally and physically stable. She knows the area, I'm sure there's a logical explanation for what's happened, we're just not privy to all the facts at the moment."

"Yes, absolutely," added McTierney. "She's probably booked a hair appointment and forgotten to tell anyone."

Bishop offered a weak smile, "Maybe she slipped away for a weekend treat with her new man."

"We ought to check that. Does anyone know his name?"

NINE

BEE AND MCTIERNEY left Bishop at the station to gather as much background information as she could on Fran Itzkowitz and set off to Wembley stadium. Bee hoped to use the surveillance cameras to identify the mystery man who had given him the envelope on Friday night.

In stark contrast to the arduous slog that had characterised their journey on the Friday evening, slipping around the M25 to the national football stadium on a Monday lunchtime was a doddle; even parking at the retail centre proved easy. But the biggest difference was in the aura around the stadium; with the arch no longer illuminated the arena had lost some of its majesty.

"We have to tip our hats to Bobby," said McTierney.

Bee frowned.

"England's best footballer never to play for Manchester United," McTierney continued.

"Is that how you remember him? He captains us to our greatest ever victory and all you can think about is club football."

"Club football is much more important. As pleased as I am that we won the World Cup, and I hope we do again, it's the club games that get the pulse racing."

"Really? You'd choose tribal games over uniting the

nation in a common cause."

"Every week."

"The national team transcends personal differences, whenever there's a major tournament the community comes together. It's a collective experience strengthening national identity. Peace and goodwill abounds."

"Yes I know all that, but it doesn't have the same intensity as the club games. Whenever there's a break in the league competition for a series of international matches it's so dull."

"Philistine."

The debate had brought the pair to the Bobby Moore statue; they walked around it twice, McTierney tapped the base and stood back to take in the full view.

"I can't believe you can rubbish the national game and then come here and idolise our cup winning captain. It makes no sense. What would you do if we were visiting Old Trafford?", asked Bee.

"I'd be there for hours, but as yet I've never been."

"Of course not, every Manchester United fan lives in Surrey. Look, rather than getting excited about your fantasy Manchester United team that's never going to occur, why don't you give some thought to what these messages mean? They're clearly linked, and the creator is expecting you to do something."

"You mean us."

"Yes, I'm thinking about it too. I can't escape it."

"No. I mean we need to do something. The message was under your seat."

"Oh yes, the seat that came with the stolen ticket." Bee stared at his partner. "But whatever. It strikes me that there must be another link in the chain, and we need to work it out. Come on, let's see if we can find someone to let us look at the security cameras."

McTierney led the way into the main entrance at the stadium but hadn't got far when a burly security guard approached him. "Sorry, I can't let you in – it's a security thing."

McTierney enjoyed these encounters, and flashed his warrant card, "Yes you can – this is a police thing and a murder to boot, so open the gate."

The guard was taken aback, apologised, asked them to wait and disappeared inside.

"A murder?" asked Bee.

"It would've been had he tried to play Jack the Lad with me."

It wasn't long before the two detectives were sitting in a plush office with James Murtey, head of security for Wembley Stadium. Bee explained the situation to Murtey who appeared sympathetic if a little sceptical. Murtey explained that although Wembley stadium used over a thousand surveillance cameras, none of them would have been in operation before the event started. That was standard procedure; partly because there were few if any people to watch and partly because although video disk space costs money, it costs a great deal more to pay people to monitor the screens. But Murtey took the edge from their disappointment by allowing Bee and McTierney full access to review the recordings from the night of the concert.

Murtey delivered the pair to a middle-aged man called John who was situated in the video control room. The cramped room had barely enough space for a desk. It was cluttered with a bank of multiple monitors from the stadium;

numerous cables coiled across the floor and stacks of external hard drives haphazardly placed around the room. The walls, bare except for some pinned notes and technical diagrams, seemed to close in on the three men. The air was thick and stuffy with a faint smell of body odour, mixed with stale coffee lingering from the half-empty cup on a shelf that had probably been there since Friday. There was a mustiness about the place, as if the windowless room hadn't been ventilated in a while, compounded by the whiff of burnt electronics from overworked devices. The space was functional, not meant for comfort with just a single chair, while the solitary dim fluorescent tube added to the claustrophobic atmosphere.

"Don't get many visitors up here," said John in the understatement of the year. Both Bee and McTierney scanned the room urgently looking for an escape route.

"I'll go get some lunch for us," said McTierney, but Bee pulled rank on him, "No. You get started, I'll get lunch. I've just remembered something else I want to check out."

McTierney scowled but settled down to his task. His new friend John appeared delighted at the prospect of some company and McTierney capitalised on his enthusiasm, allowing him to drive the video screens as he searched their database for cameras focused on section 122 where he and Bee had been on Friday night. McTierney stood looking over John's shoulder as he quickly found the relevant three cameras. Each replay showed the live time in the corner of the screen and McTierney watched as John ran the tape through at double speed. Each of the cameras focused on their seats picked up the assembly of the crowd, McTierney noted the arrival of himself and Bee but none of the cameras identified anyone stopping by their seats and affixing a package to the bottom of seat 378.

"Have you got any recordings from earlier in the day?"

John shook his head, "No these are the first recordings of the day."

"Okay, let's see if we can trace the man who bumped into my colleague."

That challenge proved more achievable for the Wembley security system and soon McTierney was watching footage of a tall man walking down from a higher area and then into their row and making his way along the whole row, before stopping to put an envelope in Bee's hand. The man had a cap on his head and was wearing a dark coat. John paused the video on the moment the envelope was passed over.

"Can you zoom in on the image?"

"A bit, but we'll lose some of the clarity."

John did as requested, but it didn't help much. McTierney thought that the mystery man had done this kind of thing before and was well aware of the risks of video surveillance. "Doesn't help much. Okay let's see if we can follow him after he leaves us."

The man walked straight up the steps away from the pitch without looking left or right and disappeared from view.

"Have you got any cameras surveying the concourses where all the food vendors are situated, John?"

"We do."

A couple of minutes later and McTierney was staring at a new image; this camera feed showed a row of food outlets; in contrast to the previous images there were no people in these. Then thirty seconds after he had disappeared from stadium camera 227, their mystery man popped up on stadium camera 124. As he left the area, he glanced to his left and seeing the empty stalls he strode across to buy a burger and fries.

"Pay by card, pay by card," pleaded McTierney, but the man handed over a £20 note and then waved away the change.

"Is that a tattoo on his hand? Can you zoom in again?"

John obliged and there on the screen on the back of the mystery man's wrist as he stretched out to take his burger was a black hammer. It wouldn't be visible at first glance because it was positioned across the man's wrist but as he stretched his shirt sleeve receded and exposed the marking.

"Perfect. Can you get me a still of that close up?"

When Bee returned weighed down with burgers, fries and cups of Coke, he found McTierney standing outside the security room deep in conversation with his new friend.

"Busy?"

"All done and dusted. We're just reminiscing about previous visits here. John's dad was here for the final in 1966, can you believe it?

"Yes. I can."

"And he saw Manchester United win the European Cup in 1968."

"Another United fan living down south. What a surprise. Now what did you discover?"

McTierney recounted their success with the video camera and passed over a black and white still of the mystery man's right hand. Bee nodded his approval and said, "Bit disappointing not to get a name or a face but an interesting tattoo, that might be enough for the database."

Then he shared his own achievement from the last hour. He'd been to the ticket office and collected the email details of every person buying a ticket in their area, and the adjacent sections of the ground. The list ran to nine pages. McTierney offered a cursory glance at the sheet.

"Bishop's going to hate you, when you give that to her to sort through."

Bee offered a weak smile, "Got to be done; we need to identify the man with the envelope."

TEN

Bee didn't sleep well on Monday night; he couldn't escape the idea that he and McTierney had stumbled into a mafia-esque crime syndicate which wouldn't end well. He left a note on the kitchen table for McTierney telling him that he would drive by Itzkowitz's house on his way into the station. The note finished with a request for McTierney to get his backside into the office before 9 a.m.

Bee manoeuvred his old Mercedes car around the quaint residential streets of south-central Reigate. This part of the town offered a mix of charming traditional homes with the occasional modern development squeezed into the landscape. The older homes offered brick facades many with pastel painted fronts, bay windows and small front gardens. The early hour meant that the street was full of parked cars all along one side, Bee was grateful that Itzkowitz's short driveway was clear as he squeezed his car on to it.

But, as he had expected, there was no sign of Itzkowitz herself in Glovers Road. Bee caught one of her neighbours heading off to work and stopped her to discuss the missing police woman. The neighbour shook her head, offered her concern, hoped the story would end well, then checked her watch and scuttled off to the train station. Bee spotted a couple of black refuse bins scattered along the road. He walked up to them, lifted their lids, both were empty. It seemed like 'bin-day' was Monday in this part of town. He wandered around the back of Itzkowitz's house, her bin was parked along the alley way. He lifted the lid, it was three quarters full of black bags, so it was clear that Itzkowitz hadn't been at the property since Saturday. As he drove through the slowly awakening town and up to the new police premises on Wray Park Road, he made a decision. Itzkowitz had been missing for at least 24 hours. It was time to make this official and put her name on the list of missing persons.

McTierney surpassed himself and joined Bee and Bishop in their new operations room 20 minutes before the deadline Bee had given him. Bishop brought him up to speed with the unsurprising news that Itzkowitz's mobile had been turned off and no one was picking up on her home phone. She concluded, "I'm getting worried about Fran, this is so unlike her."

"I think we all are," added Bee, and McTierney concurred.

Bee took the lead, "We'll make this an official inquiry now, so we can get everyone working on this. That should make a big difference. I arrived early, and I've been reading through her recent reports and case notes. There's nothing in any of it to suggest she might be following a lead that would take her out of the area."

Bee allocated a few tasks amongst the team; McTierney was to return to her house and take statements from all the neighbours, enter the house and then try to track down the mystery boyfriend. Bishop was asked to obtain a photo that could be used for the public and then try to contact family in the US. Bee gave himself the unenviable task of sharing the news with Chief Superintendent Springfield and issuing a statement to the press.

"We need to find her phone and trace her credit cards, see if they've been used recently. Anyone know who she banks with?"

Nobody did, but Bishop suggested talking to HR and getting the bank details via the payroll. Bee nodded, agreed a 12-noon progress meeting back at the station and watched his team head off in search of their missing colleague, before shouting after them, "Any developments, call me immediately."

★ ★ ★

BEE'S PHONE HADN'T rung all morning, and he could see from his desk in the corner of the first floor that Bishop wasn't having a lot of success. He wondered how he was going to offload the extra work he'd picked up from his visit to Wembley the previous day. But for now, that would have to wait. All too soon McTierney returned to the fold. Bee could tell by his slow gait that he hadn't unearthed any interesting leads. He motioned to Bishop and the threesome congregated back in the ops room. Bee took a deep breath and was about to speak when Chief Superintendent Springfield entered the room.

"If you're discussing our missing officer, I want to be part of it. And if you're not discussing her disappearance, I want to know why?"

"We were just about to hold a review, please do join us, Ma'am," said Bee pointing to an empty seat.

"Tell me, what do we know?"

Bee pushed his glasses up his nose and gave a quick summary of the situation up to that morning and then handed the baton to McTierney.

"I have statements from all the neighbours; no one has seen her since Saturday morning. In all likelihood she would have checked into here at 2 p.m. for her shift. The call log suggests she took a call at 3 p.m. and headed off to Holmethorpe Estate in Redhill. I can't find anyone who has seen her since." He looked around the room for confirmation, both Bee and Bishop nodded their agreement. "Whilst I was at her property this morning, I secured entry."

Springfield raised an eyebrow. "How?"

"Nothing dramatic, I watched a YouTube video a few years ago and bought a skeleton key from a dubious source and together they've helped me on several occasions."

"I don't think I should be hearing this, McTierney."

"It's okay Ma'am, he used the keys on my house a couple of years ago."

"And that makes it all right, inspector?"

"Maybe not, but perhaps on this occasion, in view of the circumstances."

"Hmm. We'll talk about that another time, keep going for now."

"There's not much to say, except that her house looks normal. I had a quick look round, checked all the rooms. No sign of Itzkowitz. There's no suggestion of her packing to go anywhere and I picked up her passport, so we know she hasn't left the country."

Springfield grunted and then took control, "I'll tell you what we're going to do. Yes this is serious, a missing officer always has the potential to be significant, but I don't want to go public yet. If we do, and Itzkowitz turns up we'll look ridiculous. So, I'll give you three officers to conduct door to door inquires to go wherever you want over the town."

Bee looked aghast, "If we don't go public we are missing out on the help of thousands of people."

"I'm well aware of the limitations inspector, so I'll make you a deal. You find her car, her phone and her bank cards and then we'll go public. For now, we'll call it an amber alert. You can inform all our patrols and issue them with a photograph and details of her car. But we keep this strictly within the Reigate team. If anyone leaks it, I'll be down on them like a ton of bricks."

Bee slumped back in his chair and his colleagues looked stunned.

"We'll review again at 4 p.m. Wednesday, I'm out of the office tomorrow."

Springfield rose from her chair and left the room.

The team sat in silence for five minutes, "Did I hear that right?" said Bishop, "She's giving up on Itzkowitz."

"You did. We all did. But I'd rather think of it as she's just protecting her reputation, in case Itzkowitz turns up."

"That stinks," said McTierney, "I'd like to think if it was me out there, that there'd be a bit more than three officers knocking on doors asking polite questions."

Bee clapped his hands together, "Don't forget that in addition to the three officers, there's us three dedicated to this full time. Let's agree what we're going to do."

"I still have to make a start on the bank details," said Bishop.

"Fine. You do that and see if you can get any details on this supposed boyfriend. I think McTierney, and I should go back to Holmethorpe Estate. It's the last place we believe she's been."

McTierney nodded, "It's a shame we couldn't move all the camera surveillance equipment when we had to evacuate the old building when the concrete started crumbling. We could do with looking through the video footage and seeing where her car has been."

"Good thought."

"Tell you what, though. I'll pop back later tonight and use my skeleton key before the evil queen takes it from me."

"Yes, I like it."

"Ah, damn. It'll have to be tomorrow; it's quiz night at The Bell."

Bee lowered his gaze at McTierney. "Okay, I'll go after the quiz."

ELEVEN

"DIDN'T YOU CHECK this industrial estate yesterday?"

"Yes, but only the buildings that were operational. I'm starting to think that there's something sinister about Itzkowitz's disappearance so I think we should check all the unused properties."

McTierney offered a wan smile, "Yes, I hate to say it, but Itzkowitz was brought up in The Bronx, she knows how to handle herself. She's not going to get lost in a place like this."

"And she's too experienced to jet off for the weekend without telling someone."

"Where does that leave us?"

"I don't want to go down that avenue yet."

"Come on, we have to. The boss isn't going to bother about this for another two days. We owe it to Itzkowitz to consider all the options."

Bee turned his head to face McTierney. "Okay, yes, you're right. But if it's a kidnap it's not right. It doesn't stack up."

"Agreed. Why kidnap a police officer? For starters it's high risk, and then where's the note?"

"I don't know Itzkowitz well, but she doesn't strike me as the average kidnap victim. Her family is in the States, and I don't get the sense that they're rich."

"This might be a ton of work for someone, but perhaps we should start to consider if there's anyone in the US who might have a grudge against Itzkowitz, who's suddenly been released from jail and popped over the pond to settle a score."

"If only we had the person who interviewed her available to us." Bee held his gaze on McTierney.

"Okay, I interviewed her, but I didn't have much time to mess around with detail, I needed someone to join the team, while you were otherwise occupied."

"The word around the station is that once you discovered her initials were FBI, she'd got the job, purely on the basis that you could say 'action FBI'."

"Don't know where you got that idea from," smiled McTierney.

"No?" said Bee. "Just for the record, I understand that the joke is wearing a bit thin for her."

"If we find her alive, I promise never to say it again."

BEE AND MCTIERNEY drove through Redhill and stopped at the southern end of Ormside Way. This was the area where most of the active units were based, and the area had a purposeful atmosphere. It was only when you travelled north on the road that more units became vacant, and the mood changed.

"Supposedly this is where she came on Saturday. Let's park here and walk."

Automotive repair garages dominated the scenery; the buildings were typically low and wide with large open garage doors revealing a hive of activity inside, with various cars raised up on hoists; tools were scattered around workbenches as mechanics in grease-stained overalls hammered away on repairs, the ubiquitous radio blasting out to the street. A distinctive smell of motor oil, rubber and petrol fumes mingled in the air.

"I spoke to these first two garages, and both work Saturday mornings, but finish at lunchtime, so they couldn't offer any help."

"Although, if you knew that and wanted to lure someone to a proper address it would make a perfect cover."

"Yes it would. Let's check what time the place cleared on Saturday."

The Autocare manager confirmed McTierney's suspicion that the building had been vacated just before 2 p.m. on the Saturday and that the forecourt had been left vacant so could theoretically have been used by anyone after that time. Unfortunately, they didn't have a surveillance camera in operation, but the manager was keen to reject the idea that their premises could have been used for illegal purposes.

Bee and McTierney took advantage of the manager's sudden guilty conscience to wander around the unit. There was nothing obvious to suggest anything untoward had taken place.

"Of course, there's been a full crew in here for the last couple of days, steadily trashing any evidence that we might find."

"And we're close to the roundabout and the other parts of the industrial estate. Let's try our theory at the next repair garage further up the road. That's a bit more out of the way. Would be a bit easier to construct something."

"I'll tell you something else about this place, it's not easy to pick up the numbers on these units. If you didn't know where you were going, and judging by the station log, Itzkowitz didn't know, you could easily get lost and confused up here."

250 yards further along the road there was a bend to the left and another automotive repair outlet appeared with the same characteristics as the previous one, including the hours of operation. Bee and McTierney made another walking search of the property with similar results. They walked back to the edge of the road and looked across it at a desolate building that had once been a hot-tub dealership. The former glass and wood façade was weathered and stained with tall weeds pushing up through the cracked concrete forecourt.

"What's that caught in the grass on the left?" asked McTierney.

Bee squinted, took off his glasses, polished them and squinted again. "Don't know. Let's have a look."

They crossed the road and McTierney bent down to retrieve a dark brown chocolate wrapper from the grass. He held it up for Bee to see.

"Who do we know who eats American chocolate bars made by Hershey?"

"I can only think of one person. Stuff it in an evidence bag and we'll take it back to Dr Kelly and see if he can find some fingerprints on it."

McTierney obliged, "The weather's been half-decent since Saturday, we might get lucky and find something."

Bee smiled for the first time in three days. "Let's have a snoop around here and see what we can find. For a start it looks like there's been a car parked in here in the recent past. You can see the grass and the weeds have been flattened back a bit. Have a wander around the back and I'll give Dr Kelly a call and get him out here sharpish."

"Isn't he going to wonder what's going on if there's no body?"

"Maybe, but I value his perspective."

McTierney shrugged his shoulders, "He'll be lost without a dead body. I heard he once took a corpse to a party as his plus one!"

Bee eyeballed his colleague over his glasses and McTierney took his cue to leave. He pushed his way past a rusted gate and disappeared to the rear of the building. Aside from a few broken window panes and some discarded oil drums there wasn't much to see. He pushed against a rear door but to no avail. He leant against the window pane, rubbed away some of the grime and peered in the rear of the unit. The sun burst into the back of the warehouse and illuminated a concrete floor. A couple of packing cases stood in the middle of the floor but otherwise the place was deserted. Off to the left there was an office, the door had been left open, but McTierney couldn't see inside. He stood on an outside water tank and tapped out the remaining glass around the broken pane, reached in, twisted the handle and opened the window. He clambered through, dusted himself down and walked around the building. The only area he couldn't see was the office, but this didn't hold any surprises. He made a full circuit of the unit, stopped by the front door and kicked around some of the post that had been collecting on the floor. It looked like no one had been there for months.

Meanwhile, at the front of the building Bee had dashed back to collect his car and was now busy cordoning off the front area with some police tape from the boot of his car. He pulled on a pair of purple nitrile gloves, and disposable shoe coverings and started to examine the tyre marks. Before he had got far, Dr Kelly and a forensic officer arrived from the station. Bee stepped back to brief the pair, then left the officer to begin the detailed search.

Dr Kelly was an overweight, yet fastidious pathologist who had worked with the Reigate team for four years. His West Indian roots compelled him to recognise himself as a cricketer first and man of science second, yet through his time in the county he had developed a great respect for Bee's methods.

"I appreciate the call inspector, but without a body, I'm not sure how I can help you?" He put on the lugubrious voice he reserved for serious occasions, post mortems or batting collapses by the West Indies.

"I'm hoping to avoid finding a body, but I wanted your thoughts on what might have occurred here. You know I hate to jump the gun and make assumptions, but I fear time is against us, so I'm breaking with tradition and taking a leaf out of McTierney's book."

"Steady. That's a slippery slope."

Bee smiled, reflecting on the frequent clashes between his DS and the pathologist, "There's some evidence to suggest Itzkowitz was here on Saturday, can you cast your eye over what's here, let me know if you agree and then speculate on how the situation unfolded."

"Speculate? I'm a man of science; I like my facts. But I like our American colleague, she and I trade notes on where to find the best burgers, and I'll do whatever I can to help find her."

★ ★ ★

MEANWHILE, BACK IN the station Carol Bishop was ploughing on with her desk research. Bishop was a conscientious officer. She worked hard and followed orders but rarely put her head above the parapet. Her previous seven years in the drugs team at Reigate station had taught her to keep her nose clean, but also that there was nothing to be gained from putting yourself at risk. Now that she had transferred to Bee's detective team, she had found her old habits difficult to break, but today her concern for her friend's safety was overriding everything else. She worked like a dervish, hassling public companies and threatening any objector with fearful consequences whenever she encountered a jobsworth who felt reluctant to provide the police with information.

Bishop began with Itzkowitz's bank details and spending pattern. The payroll team had provided the bank details and a couple of phone calls added the extra dimension; the bank card had been used on Friday evening, July 25th and not since. There was no unusual activity on the account and the bank agreed reluctantly to put a stop on the account and to alert Bishop if any attempt was made to use the card. Bishop ticked that one off her list and discovered a similar pattern with Itzkowitz's phone records. Through Friday night and Saturday morning she tracked Itzkowitz's movements by the various phone masts where the signal was bouncing around in the Reigate and Redhill area. She didn't detect anything untoward from the spider graph that the pattern created, but it all stopped at 3:45 p.m. on Saturday afternoon. At that point the phone had been turned off and hadn't been detected since.

Finally, Carol Bishop ploughed into the social media accounts of her colleague. Itzkowitz was a compulsive user of Facebook and X and posted on one or the other on a daily basis and sometimes on both, but neither platform had been visited by Itzkowitz since Friday night. Yet another indication that she had disappeared on Saturday afternoon. Bishop went back through Itzkowitz's recent records and logged the date, time and topic of each posting she had made. She couldn't determine if there was a pattern, she assumed that there wasn't but left the records on Bee's desk for him to review. She added to it a list of the regular contributors with whom Itzkowitz interacted. Top of the pile was an image and the name of Jake Rivers, who Bishop believed to be Itzkowitz's new boyfriend.

TWELVE

TUESDAY EVENING IS quiz night at The Bell in Outwood, and Ron McTierney rarely needs an excuse to visit the pub, so, with his penchant for quizzes and the prospect of some decent real ale it should be no surprise that he had created a regular quiz team amongst his friends. Also, no surprise that his regular appearances in the pub had allowed him to commandeer a particular table, known to everyone who worked in the pub as 'Ron's table'. But what might be a surprise is that on this particular Tuesday evening his regular team of four was down by a player. A last-minute cry-off by Dean Grant from the Caterham station looked like it might leave Ron's team in the lurch. He took his pint of Fuller's London Pride and walked to the back of the pub to make a desperate call.

The Bell is a classic rural pub, set in a picturesque English village with a large green, a cricket pitch, a village hall and church. The rustic, centuries-old building was supported by oak beams and offered an open fireplace. The furniture was wooden with the occasional cushioned bench spread above a flagstone floor and the icing on the cake for McTierney was the absence of a jukebox. Although Scott didn't know it, it was close proximity to the pub as much as the low rent and convenience that kept Ron living with his friend.

Scott headed to the front of the pub; he glanced at the encased stone bell that dominated the front wall and pushed open the heavy wooden door. The three wise monkeys which adorned it caught his eye. I wonder which Ron will be tonight, he thought, undoubtedly not the one who speaks no evil. He glanced around and spotted the quizzers all collected to the left-hand side of the pub. He nodded at Ron and walked over to the table and took a seat, Ron pushed a pint in his direction.

Scott reached over and picked up a triangular prism shaped card from the middle of the table, he turned it in his hand and read, "Quiz team Aguilera." He frowned but took a sip from his pint and nodded his thanks towards Ron.

"Thanks for coming over at short notice. I was worried that you'd be engrossed in some paperwork."

"I was, but I thought a friend in need and all that. I'm happy to step up from the subs' bench."

A blonde woman next to him sniggered. Scott looked at her, then offered his hand, "I'm Scott, as you'll probably know. I guess you're Natalia."

The woman looked surprised, "No, I'm Josie, who's Natalia?"

Ron glared at Scott but composed himself by the time Josie turned to him and asked, "Who's Natalia?"

"She's nobody, a girl who sometimes works behind the bar."

Ron was spared any further questioning by Darren picking up the mic and starting the quiz. He explained that there would be eight rounds including one music round and one picture round. This was greeted with a ripple of chatter across the seven tables that were competing. Ron took control of the answer sheet only referring to his teammates when an answer eluded him. The music round passed Scott by – there being no questions that featured Bruce Springsteen. It was much the same with the photo round, each picture being a celebrity. He broke his duck when he was able to remember that the bell after which the pub was named, and which stood in the wall beside the front door, was cast in 1635.

"How do you know that?" asked Ron.

"I noticed it when I walked past it tonight."

At the halfway stage, Darren announced a 20-minute break and invited the teams to refill their brains by visiting the bar. Scott scowled at the concept, but Ron needed no invitation to go to the bar. Josie, who hadn't contributed a single answer to the team, brought her 45-minute sulk to a close by announcing that she was leaving and Scott found himself being questioned by the fourth member of the team, a young man who introduced himself as Bob.

The second half commenced with Darren reading out the scores and positions of the teams; Quiz Team Aguilera was placed third with 32 points, five behind the leaders. Ron leaned in across the table, "The Duffers often win, I think they're all teachers, but I'm expecting good things from us in the second half – there'll be a geography round to come, so we'll play our joker on that one."

Before the geography test, Darren produced a round of missing authors in which the teams had to identify the author of a list of classic books. Ron threw the pen down in disgust, but Scott picked it up and filled in nine of the ten answers, before sliding the sheet back. Ron glanced at the list and spotted Raymond Chandler's name adjacent to the title 'The Big Sleep'. Ron's eyes lit up, "He's your favourite sleuth if I remember correctly."

Scott nodded contentedly and then pulled the sheet back to add another answer.

"I'm glad I invited you now," smiled Ron.

But his face lost its happy smile when the next round was announced as 'quotes'. Again, Bee filled in the most answers; correctly identifying JF Kennedy as saying "Don't ask what your country can do for you. Ask what you can do for your country." Then against "The way to get started is to quit talking and begin doing," he wrote 'Walt Disney, not Ron McTierney'. He followed this with remembering the speaker of "Be yourself, everyone else is already taken," as Oscar Wilde and "I am your father" as Darth Vader, although he doubted that Vader was the only person to say it.

Eventually, the long-awaited geography round arrived under the guise of Places. Ron announced that Quiz Team Aguilera would be playing their joker and picked up the pen expecting to get full value from his geography degree and began scribbling away as Darren asked for the capital cities of Bulgaria, Latvia, Costa Rica and Greenland. He paused to consider the spelling of Ouagadougo when Burkina Faso was mentioned but continued to write. When he'd completed the page he pushed it back across the table and sat back in his chair. Scott pulled the page towards him and Bob and ran his finger down the sheet. He cupped his hand around his mouth and said, "I believe the European Parliament building is in Strasbourg not Brussels."

Ron shook his head.

"It's the European Council, which is in Brussels."

"No, it isn't," said Ron, ending the debate.

Even when the teams changed papers to mark each other's answers and Ron saw that the Duffers team had Brussels as the answer to the last question, he dismissed it as tosh. But after Darren read out the correct answer as Brussels, Ron's shoulders slumped, and he pushed the pen across the table in defeat.

Scott rubbed his shoulder, "You still got nine correct and with the joker that's 18 points."

"We're not going to catch that lot. Coming second is coming nowhere."

Ron's prediction proved correct and once again Quiz Team Aguilera fell short. Even the second prize of a bottle of wine did little to improve Ron's mood. Scott chose his moment carefully and suggested that now was the time to slip back into Reigate and try Ron's magic skeleton key on the old police premises. Together they walked back to Scott's house and jumped into his old Mercedes and drove the five miles into Reigate.

"Apologies for my faux pas at the quiz with Josie. I just assumed she was Natalia."

"Hmm."

"It's to be expected, if I've not been briefed and I'm a late second choice."

"Second? Don't kid yourself, you were fourth choice. And even with your brains, we didn't win!"

"Apologies again, I'm not on form tonight."

"Say that again, there's corpses on old Kelly's table on better form than you."

"That's a bit tasteless, considering we're searching for our colleague."

"Yes, sorry, just a bit disappointed by the quiz. Let's make amends by getting the camera feeds from the old station."

"Ah disappointment, my favourite subject, if only there'd been a round on that in the quiz."

Ron raised his eyebrows, but it wasn't enough to stop Scott delivering.

"Disappointment gives us a benchmark to measure enjoyment."

"Does it?"

"Come on, even you must have experienced a bad pint of beer sometime."

"No, don't think I have."

"You're just saying that to irritate me, I know. But let's turn the argument on its head, what's the best pint you've ever drunk?"

Ron smiled, "A much better topic, but that's a tough choice, there's so many good ones. The London Pride in The Bell would be a contender."

"Okay, let's cut through your waffle; cars, I know you hate any Ford, and you adored your old Jag, so you have two extremes. This gives you a degree of perspective from good to bad, from enjoyment to disappointment."

"How do you know this crap?"

"I read."

"Pity you didn't read any books with pictures in, you might have been some help on the photo round tonight."

Scott ignored the jibe. "Plus, disappointment helps build resilience; helps you cope with adversity, and it shows you what's important and what you really value."

"Maybe you should think about that next time you're alone with Carol Bishop. Tell her you care for her."

At last Ron had found the right response to take the wind out of Scott's sails. He fell silent for a couple of minutes. "I do care, but I don't want to let her down. I don't think I'll be around for long; this world is too hostile, too horrible and I doubt I'll die of old age."

"Careful, your glass is overflowing again."

★ ★ ★

REIGATE NESTLES IN the heart of Surrey and is one of those attractive market towns mixing rural history with accessibility to London, a compelling combination which keeps the property prices high. At night the busy town transforms into a tranquil but vibrant spot. The 13th century Reigate Castle grounds and Priory Park, with their ancient walls and tree-lined paths take on a quiet, serene beauty, perfect for a peaceful evening stroll. Nighttime also reduces the traffic to a near-zero level, which enabled Bee to slip quickly into the old police station situated along the main A25 road. A barrier blocked the main area of the car park, but he was able to pull off the road and stop the car.

"Right, don't be too long. Just borrow the tapes which should be in the surveillance control room on the first floor. Use the torch on your phone to save putting any lights on."

"Yes. I do know. Turn the car around for a quick exit. I'll see you in five minutes. While you're waiting, there's something you can do for me."

Bee looked up in surprise.

"The quiz got me thinking. I think I should have a motto. Something in Latin, which is where you come in. You know, 'always gets his man', 'hard but fair', that kind of stuff."

Bee's jaw fell open. When McTierney disappeared, he

moved the car as McTierney had suggested, then looked up at the sky, a fingernail moon illuminated the station. Bee was mesmerised by the sharp image and allowed his mind to wander back to the subject of Carol Bishop. Part of him felt relieved that it wasn't her who had gone missing, then he admonished himself for the thought, it was bad enough with Itzkowitz missing. His phone pinged and he looked down to see a text from Bishop. He spun around in his seat believing for a moment that she must have been aware of his thoughts, but there was no one around him. He read the text, it was work related. All his texts were work related. It took his mind away and he didn't notice the security guard approaching his car until the guard's dog barked and Bee flinched in his seat.

"What's going on here, then?"

"Oh, nothing. I used to work here, and I dropped by for old time's sake." Inwardly Bee cringed at the feeble nature of his lie.

"Is that right?"

Bee fumbled for his police badge and passed it apologetically across to the security man.

"Inspector Scott Bee, hey, I've heard of you. You're the copper who nicked that bent one aren't you?"

"Yes, er, that's me."

"Good job. Now what are you doing here? My alarm tells me that someone's just opened the back door here. If it's not you, it must be your mate."

"Really? That's news to me, I'm here alone."

The security guard flashed his torch into Bee's car and across to the passenger seat. "That jacket's yours is it?"

Bee looked at McTierney's black leather jacket, thought to himself that he'd never be seen dead wearing it, turned back to the guard and smiled, "Yes, I brought it in case I fancied a walk. The temperature starts to drop at this time of night."

"If you're going to walk, sir, don't leave your car here. You'd be surprised how many people want to break into these premises. I get a call almost every night."

"No, of course not. I won't. Really? People want to break into a police station, I can't think of anything worse."

As Bee was digging himself deeper into his pit of lies, McTierney came racing around the back of the station and the guard's Alsatian began to bark. The guard fought to hold him back. McTierney jumped into the passenger seat, "Success." Then he looked across at the guard. "Who's your friend?"

Bee decided to come clean and explained the real reason why they were at the station, although he omitted the part involving their missing colleague. The security guard stood shaking his head, "I knew something was up. Trouble is the boss will have seen the alarm; I'll have to make a report."

McTierney stepped out of the car and walked around to the guard. "How about we make a deal? You think of some way of explaining the alarm to your boss, I'm sure you can do that, and I'll give you one of my special cards." McTierney reached into his wallet and pulled out a police business card with his name on it. "I'll sign the back and anytime you are in trouble with the police, just show this card or call me and it'll make all your problems go away. Think of it as a 'get out of jail free' card."

"Can you do that?"

"Not normally, but a bit like you, when faced with a challenge, I can be creative."

The guard smiled and saluted as McTierney climbed back into the car.

"Did you really do what I think you did?"

"Desperate times and all that."

Bee shook his head.

"Come on. Can you imagine what would have happened if he'd called in the uniformed boys? The evil queen would have gone ballistic, and, if it made the papers, I don't dare think about the consequences. She hates me already."

"Dare I ask how many 'get out of jail free' cards you've issued?"

"That's only the second one down here and there's a few back in Norfolk. But I am trying to give up the habit."

Bee blew out his cheeks in disgust. "I don't want to know anymore. But I do want to know what you discovered in there."

McTierney reached inside his shirt and pulled out a couple of video disks. "Here you go, the disks covering Holmethorpe Estate for last Saturday."

"Good man. While you were in there mucking about, Bishop sent me a text, she's tracked down Itzkowitz's boyfriend. He lives in White Bushes, near the hospital. Fancy making a late-night call?"

THIRTEEN

THE ADDRESS BEE and McTierney were seeking was in Greenwood Drive, White Bushes, just south of the main accident hospital in the area, East Surrey Hospital. It's a quiet suburban area with a mix of housing types, most of which were built in the late 20th century. In the daytime there's an open common area close to the hospital, which is often full of young children, but at 11 o'clock on a Tuesday night the clientele has changed, and a couple of youths watched Bee's Mercedes drive past. The house they wanted was at the rear of the estate backing on to the open land which stretched all the way down to Salfords, the next village. Bee's car rumbled over a series of jagged potholes as they approached their target.

When the pair walked towards the white wooden door, McTierney turned to his partner, "Good cop, bad cop?"

"Let's get a conversation going first."

McTierney nodded, "At least there's a light on." He pressed the bell and hammered on the door. A young man, perhaps in his early thirties came to the door. He had long hair, a goatee beard and was wearing a purple waistcoat over a pale-yellow shirt on top of faded jeans with rips in the knees. He looked the two detectives up and down but didn't speak, instead he took a drag on his rolled-up cigarette.

Bee took the lead, "Good evening, would you be Jake Rivers?"

"Is it about my bike?" His face lit up. "Don't tell me you've found it after all this time. I've even put a new lock on the back gate."

"No, not the bike," said Bee, "we're two detectives from the Reigate station; I'm DI Bee and this is DS McTierney." The pair flashed their warrant cards. "Sorry to bother you late at night. We're investigating the disappearance of Fran Itzkowitz, and we believe you know her. I wonder if we could come in and have a little off the record chat. I should stress that you are not under arrest, or even under suspicion, but we're concerned about our colleague and a chat here rather than taking you down to the station, would be much quicker for everyone concerned."

"No worries man. I'm just kicking back, listening to some tunes. Not been back long from my shift at the hospital. You've got an hour or so before I'll be hitting the sack."

Rivers turned and walked into the lounge. The room offered a broad selection of seating; a worn grey three-person sofa occupied one wall, under the front window was a single brown armchair and a red bean bag completed the range, a large TV screen was fixed to the main wall.

"Make yourselves at home," said Rivers waving an arm at the sofa, "Do you want a drink? I was in the middle of fixing myself a beer. It helps me unwind." Bee looked around the room; there was clutter everywhere, even on the sofa there was a jumper, and a newspaper spread across the seats. An ironing board stood open against the wall. Somewhere deep inside him Bee felt his stomach flip, the place was so untidy, a total contrast to the way he tried to live. Even McTierney wasn't this bad.

Rivers continued walking through to an open plan kitchen which adjoined the lounge. McTierney's eyes lit up at the suggestion of a beer, but Bee stopped him and called out their requests for two coffees. Bee tidied up the paper and the sweater and the two detectives took a seat on the main sofa, Bee nudged McTierney and pointed to a guitar case in the corner of the room.

With drinks sitting in front of everyone, Bee opened the questions, "Could you explain to us how you know Fran Itzkowitz."

"Yeah, sure. She came to see a show where I was playing in a pub in Dorking. She seemed to like the music and hung around after the concert finished, we got talking and that was that."

"You're a musician? When you opened the door I thought you said you'd just finished a shift at the hospital."

"I do both. A porter at the hospital during the week and at weekends I'm the James Taylor of Redhill."

Bee smiled. "I wonder how the real Mr Taylor feels about that?"

Rivers shrugged, "Don't suppose he cares much."

"Back to Miss Itzkowitz, how long have you two known each other?"

Rivers leaned back in his chair and blew out his cheeks, "A month or so, the gig would have been on a Friday night, so that's the 20th, something like that."

"Of last month?"

"Yes that's right. It was at the pub in the centre of the town."

Bee stopped to record that in his notebook. "Can you describe your relationship with Miss Itzkowitz?"

"Do you mean are we sleeping together? Yes we are."

"When did you last see her?"

"Last Wednesday, we had a drink at her local, spent the night together and then I came back here on Thursday morning. I had a late shift that day."

"You've not seen her since."

"No. I did think she might come over on Sunday, but she never showed up."

"You didn't think of trying to contact her?"

"No."

"Any reason why not?"

"Not especially. If she didn't want to show, that's cool by me."

"Is it common for the pair of you to not speak for a few days?"

Rivers wobbled his head as if weighing up his answer, "Yeah, not uncommon, we, both work funny hours and all that."

Bee nodded and exchanged glances with McTierney. "Itzkowitz hasn't been seen since Saturday afternoon. Where were you Saturday afternoon?"

"As I said I was here from about eleven onwards, before I went into work for a shift at six in the evening."

"Can anyone verify that?"

"Not the afternoon bit, but there's plenty who saw me at the hospital, and anyway you have to clock in and out."

The conversation paused while Bee jotted down another note.

"When you and Miss Itzkowitz parted on Thursday

morning, was it on good terms?"

Rivers started to shift in his chair, "Yes. What are you trying to get at here? If she's gone missing, it's news to me."

"We're just exploring some options, as I said at the start, you're not under caution. Do you know anyone who would wish to harm her? Has she crossed swords with anyone lately?"

Rivers shrugged his shoulders, "Not especially, she doesn't talk about her police work."

"Okay. Do you have a car?"

"No, I've got a small van, the one out the front. I need it for moving my music equipment around."

Bee nodded his acceptance, "Okay, I think that will do for now. Let me give you a card and if anything comes to mind about where Miss Itzkowitz might have gone, please give me a call."

Rivers took the card, "Sure." But the rest of his sentence was broken by the door bell ringing. All three turned their heads to the door but nobody moved.

Bee gestured towards him, "Perhaps you should answer that."

Rivers got up and walked to the door. He opened it, and a young brunette strode into the room, she kissed him on the cheek, "Hello babe." Then she noticed Bee and McTierney, and paused, "Oh, I didn't realise we had company." She walked past everyone and continued up the stairs.

Rivers looked uncomfortable but didn't acknowledge the girl's entrance. McTierney took up the gauntlet, "Who's she?"

"Sylvia. Sylvia Jones," mumbled Rivers.

"And does Miss Itzkowitz know about Miss Jones?"

"Er no, but you know how it is, we never said we'd be exclusive."

Rivers looked from Bee to McTierney and back to Bee hoping for some support. Bee stared at him in astonishment.

"No," said McTierney. "He doesn't know how it is but let me tell you something. We're going to find Fran and, when we do, you're going to do the decent thing and come clean with her." He allowed the point to register, but Rivers didn't reply. "Because if you don't I'll be back to haunt you. The next time there's a murder in the district, it'll be yours. Not as the victim, but I'll frame you for it."

Rivers looked shocked at the suggestion, "You can't do that."

It was Bee's time to speak. "You'd think not, wouldn't you, but I know him, and the rules don't apply to him. Good evening, sir."

The two detectives sat in Bee's car contemplating what had just happened.

"Thoughts?"

"He's a scumbag," offered McTierney.

"You think it's the boyfriend?"

"It's always the husband or the boyfriend, why would this be any different?"

"No evidence, no body for that matter. Isn't it a bit early to be arresting someone for murder?"

"No, I can feel it in my bones."

"I would say that Rivers never once asked what had happened to her. It was like he already knew. He didn't show any emotion. At least not until you threatened him."

"See. It's him, he's guilty."

"Perhaps. I might acknowledge that we have a suspect, even a prime suspect, but as yet we don't have a crime."

FOURTEEN

BEE TOOK THE long route back home via the temporary station in Wray Park Road to allow him and McTierney to drop off some information for Carol Bishop, which would allow her to make a start on their latest discoveries and, in turn, would allow the pair to head north to Croydon first thing in the morning. The station had only a skeleton crew at midnight, and the pair were able to walk into the station and up to the CID area without needing to explain themselves to anyone. Each stopped at their own desks to write a covering note. McTierney left the two disks he had taken from the original police station, while Bee left the list of attendees who had been in their block at the Wembley concert, and then on top he wrote a note explaining their suspicions surrounding Jake Rivers and asked Bishop to prioritise delving into his background.

★ ★ ★

"WHERE'S THE DYNAMIC duo this morning?"

Chief Superintendent Springfield had used one of her superpowers and crept up on Carol Bishop without making a sound.

Bishop jumped in her chair and spun round looking

guilty. "Oh, er, I'm not sure. I wasn't expecting them to be here this morning, although there's still time for them to appear." Bishop glanced at her watch, noticed that it was a little after nine and qualified her response, "Well, maybe."

Springfield focused her gaze on Bishop, and it pinned her to the chair. "Are you busy?" she asked, ignoring the obvious fact in front of her. "I'd like to talk about this incident." As was her way, Springfield went straight to the point. "What line of enquiry is Bee following?"

Bishop swallowed hard, "I'm not sure that I'm fully up to date, but I know he's been to the industrial estate where we believe she went on Saturday afternoon and yesterday I tracked down Fran's boyfriend and he and McTierney called in on him last night."

Springfield digested the information then spotted one of the notes that Bee had left on the desk. Bishop spotted it at the same moment, but didn't dare react. Springfield reached out, picked up the sheet and read it. "So, Bee thinks the boyfriend might be a suspect in a missing person's case."

"I don't think Inspector Bee would consider him a suspect just yet."

Springfield allowed her eyes to wander around the room and then returned to Bishop. "You're very loyal to your inspector. I find him hard to read. Tell me about him."

Bishop blushed but composed herself. "I think he's a good officer. He's thorough, fair and trustworthy, but he's not comfortable dealing with people."

"Hmm. How so?"

"Well, he will only infrequently offer praise or gratitude but when he does it's lavish and over the top, as if he's trying to make amends for the lapsed time."

Springfield nodded as if she was making a mental note.

"I don't think he knows it, but he's liked immensely, and people trust his judgement." Bishop was warming to her task. "If he said 'go investigate the local cinema' then people would return with the A to Z on the Everyman. It's not charm because there is none, it's not because he's easy to work with, because he isn't, but he seems to know the right thing to do. Or perhaps, he seems to be able to sniff out the right course of action. I trust him impeccably."

"I hope you're right on this Itzkowitz case, because it doesn't feel right to me. If you see Bee before I do, remind him that we have a 4 o'clock review, here."

Springfield turned and left Bishop in peace, who felt sweat pouring from her armpits. She reached across her desk and picked up a few sheets of computer print, the list of attendees from Wembley stadium, she let out a deep sigh of relief. She was grateful that Springfield hadn't picked up this sheet, because Bishop didn't know what it represented or why Bee had asked her to review it.

Bishop began with the boyfriend, and it didn't take her long to compile the back story of Jake Rivers; – his conviction in the summer of 2018 for theft in the holiday resort of Great Yarmouth set the standard. With a little digging she quickly painted a portrait of his life, as she did she wondered how much of it was known to Itzkowitz. Jake Rivers was born in Beckton, East London in April 1989, making him 36 years old. He'd left school at 16 and drifted in and out of jobs and in and out of houses. He'd spent time all over London; worked as a delivery person, a waiter, a barman and a hospital porter. More recently he moved to East Anglia and worked in the Norfolk and Norwich University Hospital. It was while he was here that he'd found himself on the wrong side of the law after he'd been caught picking pockets on the Yarmouth seafront. This had resulted in a three-month custodial sentence, of which Rivers had served two months. He dropped off the radar after that and popped up again 18 months ago when he began to work at the hospital in Redhill. His social media feed emphasised his music career, although Bishop doubted the word career was appropriate. Nonetheless she was attracted to the idea of a musician and decided to call the pub in Dorking, The Surrey Yeoman, where the couple had met. Bishop wasn't expecting much from the call, given the weeks that had passed since Rivers gig, but the barman remembered him well and recounted a colourful tale which ended with the comment that Rivers was now barred from the place, and that 'it was only some cop who jumped up and started flashing her badge at everyone who saved his arse from a beating.'

She pushed her chair back and went in search of a coffee and wondered what her friend had seen in this man.

Upon her return, Bishop switched her focus to Itzkowitz's car and the pair of digital discs that McTierney had retrieved from the old station. She knew Itzkowitz drove a pale blue VW Beetle with a 17-registration plate and a I heart New York sticker on the rear bumper. McTierney had taken the feed from the camera which covered the main junction in Redhill where two major roads intersected, the A23 and the A25. Bishop watched the traffic flow and in the middle was the vehicle she wanted. Itzkowitz manoeuvred across the junction, slipped past a couple of slower vehicles and headed north up the A23. A second camera picked her up further along the London Road as she turned right into Frenches

Road, which would lead into the industrial estate, but there were no further images. What they needed was a camera from the industrial estate, she made a note. Maybe one of the businesses had a security camera in place, that might capture the car passing by.

Bishop picked up her two remaining tasks: checking the list of attendees at Wembley and searching the police database for any past offender with a distinctive feature of a black hammer tattoo. Although she felt a loyalty to focus on the requests made by Bee, she knew the black hammer job would be easier to complete and potentially would take them further forward in the case. Her dilemma was solved by the appearance of Officer Rockford, one of the extra officers assigned to the case, by Springfield. He was tall and slim, but Bishop thought he was a touch lanky. He walked with an upright posture. Dark hair and eyes to match. Bishop briefed him on the Wembley list and suggested that as a typed list was unusable, he should call the stadium, arrange for one of the administrators to download an electronic list and then begin contacting each one individually.

Criminal records information is held on two main systems: the Police National Computer and the Police National Database. The National Computer records convictions, reprimands, warnings and arrests, while the National Database holds police intelligence reports. It's here that they store biometric information, and on occasions they will use it in conjunction with 'live' facial recognition which compares images from video footage to a database of suspects. This is what Bishop was seeking. The system allowed Bishop to search by a variety of facial features and distinctive markings. She typed in 'tattoos' and set the computer searching through over two billion records.

While the computer was searching, Bishop switched to the phone records of Itzkowitz; she knew that her colleague was a social monster and always on her phone. No surprise, then that all the calls Itzkowitz had made in the few days leading up to the Saturday were to named individuals, but one name appeared more than most, it was Rivers. "We keep coming back to this guy," said Bishop to her laptop screen. She switched to the calls received log but there wasn't the expected reciprocal number of calls received from Rivers. *A one-way relationship*, thought Bishop, as she logged a question for McTierney to follow up on. The database concluded its search and provided Bishop with a list of over 10,000 tattoos. She pursed her lips in frustration and narrowed the search to tattoos featuring black hammers. This didn't take the database long at all, it found zero. She continued to tweak the wording of her search and after half an hour concluded that the police had encountered 25 men and six women with hammer tattoos, but none with an image that would compare with the picture McTierney had given her from the security camera at Wembley.

Her desk phone rang; it was a detective from Itzkowitz's former precinct in New York; he was responding to a request she had sent yesterday asking about Itzkowitz's time in the NYPD. Bishop had Itzkowitz's CV in front of her, – the one McTierney had used when he'd decided to offer her the job nearly four years ago. The American detective agreed to put the essential details in an email and send it over but wanted to give her two key items first hand. Bishop began scribbling away and by the time the call had ended she felt she hardly knew her colleague. She looked down at the notes she'd recorded and the CV she had been given by HR, – apart from the name there was little to connect them.

Her notes listed that Itzkowitz had killed three men and seriously wounded another in the course of her duty. But worst of all, one of them was an unarmed kid. There was doubt surrounding the circumstances, but the backlash had been intense at the time, and Itzkowitz had been advised to leave the city for her own safety after a gang had issued a kill order on her. Now the gang leader had been released from prison for a minor offence and was known to be making threats against the police again.

Bishop blew out her cheeks and pushed her chair back, Itzkowitz's long story about coming to England to broaden her horizons was starting to unravel. It was evident that McTierney hadn't made any background checks.

FIFTEEN

BEE SUFFERED ANOTHER in his series of bad nights' sleeps; he'd woken as the sun rose with his mind full of disciplinary reviews, concert tickets and embarrassing confessions. He drank some water to clear his head, but any sleep disappeared when he rolled over to look at the clock. As he lay awake, he couldn't escape his fear that something terrible had happened to Itzkowitz and although he'd felt strangely encouraged by his remark of the previous evening that there was still no crime, inwardly he recognised that this was only a matter of time. At 6 a.m. he resolved that they should return to the beginning and go back to the house where McTierney had picked up the Oasis concert tickets, a week ago, when this crazy adventure began. By seven-thirty he'd woken McTierney and shared the plan.

"What? No. Why? There's no connection between the concert and Itzkowitz's disappearance. We should be focused on pursuing that dodgy boyfriend of hers."

"It's where things started unravelling."

"No, it isn't."

McTierney's rant was interrupted by a bleep on his phone as a text message arrived. He raised his hand to Bee to stop the debate. "This might be Natalia, can you give me a moment."

Bee retreated from the kitchen and stepped outside of the house to enjoy a fresh summer morning. The air was still cool from the night but was gently warming as the sun rose in the sky and began painting his house front with a soft golden hue. The birds had been up for hours, and their songs provided the soundtrack to the day. Bee felt his mood being lifted and resolved that, if McTierney wouldn't join him in heading north, he would go on his own. But this concern was soon shown to be unfounded.

McTierney joined him at the front of the house and was unusually subdued. He kept his eyes to the floor as he said, "Yes, I think you're right, maybe we should take a look at the Taranovsky connection."

Bee swung round in surprise. "Really, what did Natalia say to convince you?"

"It wasn't Natalia. It was a text from an unknown number which says, 'You've not done you're bit. Get on it.'"

Bee's eyes were on stalks. "Show me."

McTierney handed over his mobile and Bee read the note. "This raises a whole new set of questions."

"Really," said McTierney disconsolately.

Bee's mind was racing. "Someone thinks you've made a deal with them to do a job and given what we've discovered on our travels over the latest few days, I'd say your generous friend with the Oasis tickets thinks he's paid you £20,000 to kill someone with the initials LG and is getting upset with your lack of progress."

"You think so? Well, I never."

Bee ignored the jibe; he was engrossed in the text. He turned the screen to McTierney, "Look there's a typo in this, that might be significant."

"What?"

"Our correspondent has typed 'you're bit', when it should be 'your bit'. That might help us identify him."

McTierney rolled his eyes, "Are you saying we rule out all the ex-public-school students across the country, because this suggests some dumb-arse comprehensive student? Unless, of course, this is a smart comprehensive student who's smarter than you public-school toffs and playing the double bluff."

Bee blanched, "Is there a chip on your shoulder? Something you want to say?"

"No. It feels like it's you with the prejudice."

Bee looked hurt. "Not at all. I'm just saying it's unusual and worthy of consideration. But we still don't know if, or how, this is connected to Itzkowitz. If the initials were 'FBI', we'd be getting somewhere, but they're not."

McTierney grunted, "I know this smacks of self-interest, but I do think you're forgetting the important point here, the one about some lunatic having my personal phone number."

"Yes. But on the positive side, we have a potential direct line of communication to the perpetrator."

"That's no comfort."

"Of course, it could all be a coincidence or a mistyped number with the message meant for someone else."

McTierney looked at him in disbelief. Bee smiled, "But we don't believe in coincidence."

In the face of the new information, the detectives agreed to head north to Croydon, but as McTierney reminded Bee, Taranovsky had been released on bail and could easily be at home, they decided to start by a visit to one of Bee's old pals, Detective Inspector Ian Jackson, who had worked with Bee in Hendon and had recently joined the South London team.

McTierney insisted on driving, arguing that it would save them 20 minutes with him at the wheel. As McTierney's car joined the A23 at Merstham, a few miles from Bee's house in Outwood, he sighed as the road quickly filled with a steady stream of cars, vans, and buses all inching their way north. The pace alternated between crawling, complete standstill, and brief spurts of movement as they passed through numerous sets of traffic lights and roundabouts. The rush hour commute into Croydon was a stretched-out caterpillar of red-lights for 25 miles.

Bee had phoned ahead to set up a meeting with Ian Jackson, who was waiting for them when they arrived, twenty minutes late for their appointment.

"Typical of you country policemen to be late. Wouldn't get away with that in the Met," he joked.

Bee offered a weak smile in response, but Jackson hadn't finished. "What was it? Sheep rustlers out in the green fields of Reigate?"

"London traffic," said Bee, looking for sympathy that wasn't apparent. Jackson rolled his eyes and turned to face McTierney, "Hi, I'm DI Ian Jackson. I spent a few years with this man when we were learning the ropes in Hendon."

McTierney shook his hand the three men moved away from the entrance to the station.

"I presume you still need coffee to function, so let's drop down to the canteen and get that sorted, then I've booked a room for our discussion."

With drinks in hand, Jackson led them into meeting room three up on the first floor. It was a windowless, beige box with blank walls and a slightly scuffed carpet in a muted grey colour. A plain rectangular table stood in the centre with half a dozen plastic chairs scattered around. A pair of fluorescent strip lights cast a harsh unflattering glow creating a room that was both too bright, yet lifeless at the same time. McTierney turned his nose up at the environment; "We might be country bumpkins, but we don't work in squalor."

Jackson looked offended, "Who upset the princess?"

Bee, forever keen to avoid conflict, spread his arms between the two. "Excuse my colleague, things are getting tense in our station, our colleague DS Itzkowitz has disappeared."

Jackson looked surprised, "A missing detective? I hadn't heard."

"No. It's all off the record and strictly hush-hush at the moment." Bee leaned in towards his ex-colleague, "so you can't say a word."

Jackson maintained his look of alarm.

"We only discovered this on Monday, and the chief was dubious about the veracity, so she opted to keep the lid on our enquiries until we're sure about what's happening."

"And are you?"

Bee looked across the table at McTierney, and back to Jackson. "No. It's fair to say we've been running around like idiots for the last couple of days; we're picking up lots of pieces but it's not clear how they all fit together."

"It can be like that at times. But I don't see where I fit into this investigation."

Bee took a sip of coffee, then a deep breath and began. "One of our loose ends relates to the Taranovsky case." Jackson's ears pricked up. "I wonder if you could give us some background."

Jackson smiled, "This case has a life of its own, but, as you probably know it's not mine. Detective Chief Inspector

Ryan Cooke has taken personal charge of the case."

McTierney nodded, "I met him when I was up here on loan last week. Big, fierce looking chap with a black moustache."

Jackson smirked, "Yes, that's him. Doesn't like to hear anyone disagree with him."

"Like most Met detectives," added Bee. "How did he take Taranovsky getting out on bail a week or so ahead of his big trial? He must have been livid. How was it possible? Taranovsky must have the best solicitor in the UK on his team."

Jackson grinned, "Does he ever. Some double-barrelled ponce who's full of himself. But we had the last laugh. Taranovsky's back in custody."

"How come?"

"Word has it that the Assistant Commissioner for Met Operations, Matt Dickens, got involved and demanded a new judge look at the appeal and he reversed the initial decision. So Taranovsky is stomping around his cell 20 feet below us as we speak."

"No way!" shouted McTierney.

"That's more than a little unusual," said Bee.

Jackson smirked, "Off the record, as it seems most of this conversation is going to be, there are rumours bouncing around that Taranovsky has a judge on his payroll. No evidence as far as I know, but it would explain a few things."

The trio continued a conversation debating the challenges faced by detectives in upholding the law and the role played by judges in the process. It was a debate that required more coffee. But eventually, Bee brought their discussion back to his reason for visiting. He explained how he and

McTierney had been to the Oasis concert on the previous Friday and how this had led them to Exeter and then they found themselves in possession of a gun and £20,000 with an order to kill someone with the initials LG. He concluded with the recent text message demanding that Ron get on with the job.

Jackson listened intently, tried to probe how McTierney had acquired the concert tickets, but Bee waved him away. But he did have a key idea to throw into the mix. "As much as it might be fun to believe that the 'LG' in question is Liam Gallagher from Oasis, I can give you a more likely alternative, considering whose property you took the tickets from."

Bee and McTierney looked across the table in anticipation, while Jackson enjoyed his moment. "I'm willing to bet that 'LG' stands for Lily Gandapur. The young girl who is the star witness for the prosecution. She's the one who claims she saw Taranovsky kill a security guard in her office."

SIXTEEN

JACKSON AGREED TO drive his old friend to the home of Dmitri Taranovsky in the upmarket Croydon suburb of Kenley, but as he did he shared his reservations. "I don't mean to question your skills, but what do you hope to find? We've had our own forensic team all over this place; there won't be a single inch we haven't checked."

"I don't doubt that Ian, but there are two factors that make this different. Number one; Taranovsky would have known you were coming so he wouldn't have left anything incriminating that he didn't want you to find. But then he was released, probably thinking all the searching was done before his trial, then out of the blue, he's picked up again and enjoying the 1-star service of Croydon police station. That wasn't part of his plan, so perhaps he got sloppy. We need to be thorough and see if he made a mistake."

Jackson nodded his acceptance of the logic.

"Secondly, we have a new approach. All your forensic boys were searching for clues relating to the crime connected with that murder, but that doesn't apply to us. I'm convinced Taranovsky is involved somehow with the disappearance of our DS. I don't know how and I don't know why, but it's too much of a coincidence that all this is happening at the same time. So, we will be looking for anything that helps us make the connection. That's something that wouldn't have been on the radar of your teams."

Again, Jackson approved of Bee's rationale. The thoughtful mood was shattered by McTierney who threw a question at Bee from the back seat of Jackson's sleek blue BMW 5 series.

"Do you know the best thing about this case, while we're working undercover?"

"No, tell me."

"No paperwork! I haven't filed a report all week." McTierney began to laugh.

"Not that you're known for the quality of your report writing at the best of times."

Jackson interrupted the banter, "Okay, here's the game. I know you want to be thorough, but we need to keep this short. I wouldn't want to explain to anyone the circumstances behind this visit."

"I think we can all agree with that," said Bee. "Can you give us 15 minutes?"

"Fair enough. I'll hang around at the front of the building and stop any unwanted visitors, but don't be late."

Bee nodded his agreement.

"Oh, and you'll probably meet the delightful Irina, Taranovsky's girlfriend. She's a diamond."

Bee turned his face to meet Jackson. "She's always dressed up to the nines and will have spent an hour or two on her make-up. Won't be a hair out of place."

"She must be experiencing a change at the moment," said Bee.

Jackson laughed as he nosed his BMW through a set of electric gates and stopped his car on the gravel drive of a huge six-bedroom property on Tandridge Road in Kenley. The three men walked to the front door and Jackson pushed the doorbell which played the Cannon section from Tchaikovsky's 1812 Overture. Bee smiled. "Taranovsky likes his nickname," explained Jackson.

"I thought that last week, but this is a smart house," said McTierney, admiring the architecture, "You don't get one of these from driving trains, no matter how many times the union goes out on strike."

The elegant wooden door was opened by the aforementioned Irina, a young woman in her mid-twenties with a fair complexion and a natural rosy glow to her skin. She wore rings on every finger except the significant one, complemented by extravagant fingernails. Her striking blue eyes were framed by dark long lashes and high cheekbones, but her alluring appearance changed the second she recognised DI Jackson.

"What do you want? Haven't you caused enough problems?"

"Good morning Irina, I have a couple of colleagues who need a quick look around. We won't be here long."

Irina looked unimpressed. "You men are always yapping; you've got no rizz. Where's your warrant? You should have something I think."

Jackson offered her his sweetest smile, "These gentlemen are in a bit of a hurry Irina, so if you could overlook the lack of a warrant, we'll be in and out in 15 minutes."

Irina glared at him but suddenly agreed to his request, "Okay. You give me two minutes to finish the laundry, and I let you visit. But no more than 15 minutes. I keep my watch on you."

Jackson nodded in agreement and Irina disappeared inside momentarily before returning to the door. She opened it fully and Jackson beckoned Bee and McTierney to enter the house. "Thanks Irina, we won't be long, and anyway soon all of this will be over. Dmitri's trial is almost upon us and once he's behind bars, we won't bother you anymore. Because you won't be living here."

Irina turned her ire on Jackson and Bee and McTierney used the opportunity to slip by. They stepped inside into an impressive double-storey lofted entrance hallway with natural stone marble flooring.

"Which rooms did you search last time?"

"I was on the ground floor," replied McTierney.

"Okay, take upstairs this time. See what you can find that might relate to Itzkowitz, but we'll have to be quick, I get the feeling that Jackson is out on a limb for us here."

McTierney nodded and scampered off upstairs, leaving Bee to head off to the garage. Ordinarily a house search would require a methodical approach with a team of several officers systematically working from room to room. They would examine every space, every drawer, every cupboard, photographing many items of interest and bagging and logging others. But Bee didn't have that luxury. He started with the garage thinking that Taranovsky had only a short time back in his house and would probably have driven at least one of his cars. It was a hunch, but after five minutes of opening and closing boxes and looking around shelves, Bee abandoned the idea and transferred his attention to the kitchen.

The kitchen was spotless, open and spacious. Bee stood in the doorway and thought it was probably larger than his entire ground floor. An expansive island sat in the centre with a glossy quartz countertop. Bee focused on the numerous small drawers, pulling each one open, rummaging inside and pushing the drawer closed. This was no good, they just didn't have the time to make a thorough search. He reached the end of the row and spun around in frustration. He had five minutes left. Okay, the study.

Like all the other rooms in the mansion, Taranovsky's study was excessively large. It had a floor to ceiling bookcase along one wall, the shelves were lined with books on every conceivable subject, and a few photo frames broke up the monotony. Bee glanced at the first few book covers; Taranovsky had a such a wide-ranging collection; there was Shakespeare, Chaucer, Dickens, Tolstoy, Nesbo, Jackie Collins and Anthony Horowitz. Bee ignored them and looked across at the opposite wall; a full-size Salvador Dali hung in the middle, 'The Hallucinogenic Toreador'. Bee wondered for a moment if it was the original but rejected the idea. In between a desktop computer sat at one end of a large mahogany desk, – no point in looking at that, thought Bee, the forensic team would have been all over it and anyway it's far too obvious. Bee looked out of the study window, Jackson seemed to have calmed Irina, and the pair were sharing a cigarette by Jackson's car.

Bee returned to his forte, the line of books. He had dismissed them as just for show, no one had reading tastes that wide, but perhaps that was the clever bit. And there it was, not a book, but a photograph of Taranovsky and two friends, the one on the right was tall and had his arm stretched around Taranovsky's shoulder. His hand dropped down on the front of Taranovsky's chest and on the back of it was a tattoo of a black hammer. Bee picked up the photo and went to find McTierney.

They rejoined Jackson outside, who checked his watch and smiled at Bee, "Good job." Then he turned back to Irina and indicated that she could return to the house. As she disappeared Bee tapped his shoulder. "Quick question for you."

"Sure."

"Did you say Taranovsky was back in custody?"

"I did."

"And he was in custody, this morning?"

"He was. Where is this going? What have you found?"

Bee grinned but continued, "So he couldn't have access to a mobile phone this morning around eightish?"

"No. He shouldn't have."

"Hence it's reasonable to assume he couldn't have sent a text this morning to McTierney telling him to get on with killing LG."

Jackson wavered slightly, "Reasonable assumption, but not altogether impossible. You know how these things work sometimes."

"Okay, so we have a third person to consider."

"A third person? I didn't even know you'd found a second."

Bee took the photo frame from under his jacket and passed it to Jackson. The three men stood around it. Bee pointed to the man with his arm around Taranovsky. "This man on the right looks like he has a black hammer tattoo and could be the man at Wembley stadium giving out train tickets. Don't suppose you know who he is?"

Jackson pursed his lips for a moment. "I think I could get

you a name, but I'd have to ask the chief."

"That would be good, then I think we can file this under 'a useful morning'."

Jackson nodded. "Now it's your turn to do me a favour."

"Oh yes?" said Bee looking surprised.

Jackson led him away from the house to make sure they couldn't be overheard. As Jackson spoke, the colour drained from Bee's face, and he took a step back from the conversation. Jackson reached out and grabbed his shoulders. It was clear the conversation was becoming intense. Bee lowered his head for a moment, then stood up straight; it appeared he had come to terms with whatever Jackson had asked. The pair shook hands and walked back to re-join McTierney.

SEVENTEEN

"WHAT WAS THE favour that Jackson wanted?"

Bee and McTierney were back in McTierney's car and heading away from Croydon police station.

Bee tilted his head towards McTierney and said quietly "He asked if we could help him with the protection of their witness in the Taranovsky case, this Lily Gandapur."

"And you said, 'no way'."

Bee didn't answer.

"Oh, come on, how can we?"

Bee remained silent.

"We have to prioritise finding Itzkowitz."

"We do."

"And we don't have the resources. The chief will do her nut. She's not Miss Cuddly at the best of times and if you go and land this on her plate, she'll explode."

Bee looked out of the window at some of the large houses which bordered the A23 south of Purley and mumbled "I wasn't thinking of telling her."

McTierney hit the brakes and Bee lurched forward in his seat. "What did you say?"

Bee turned back to face McTierney. "You heard. I'm thinking of concealing her at the house and not involving

Springfield or any of the Reigate team, other than us and Bishop."

"Are you crazy?"

"Look. You landed this crap on our table. I'm trying to find a way through it."

"By making it ten times worse!" Shouted McTierney.

"Have you got any better ideas?"

The two men fell silent, retreated into their shells for a couple of miles before McTierney spoke. "How the hell are we going to protect her?"

"We don't, we hide her in plain sight."

McTierney opened his mouth to protest but didn't know where to start and he closed it again, allowing Bee to expand on his plan.

"Jackson told me that he's convinced that Taranovsky has friends in the Met who are out to kill this Gandapur girl and, in doing so, save him."

McTierney's shoulders tensed, he tightened his grip on the wheel, and he took a sharp intake of breath. Turning to Bee, he said. "That's not good, but it's not strictly our problem."

Bee ignored the interruption, "Over the last month there's been two close shaves and he's certain there will be another. They've been trying to move her around, but he feels that there's a mole in the team who's leaking information to one of Taranovsky's gang and it's only a matter of time until they get lucky. Worse still, he thinks that the closer they get to the trial date, the more desperate the gang will become, and it could end up in a gun fight or even a pitched battle."

"So much better to bring all that shit down to our patch.

We haven't had a good gun battle for a few weeks."

Bee offered him a weak smile, "Just hear me out."

"Go on then."

"Aside from helping a good friend, and possibly avoiding the death of a key witness, and perhaps a nasty gun battle, we would be helping to bring a repugnant criminal to justice."

"Oh shit, you're going to bring decency and honour to the debate. Next you'll be saying it's the right thing to do."

"But it is the right thing to do, and you've not heard the best argument yet."

"Go on, slay me."

"The photo on the bookcase with the tattoo tells us that Taranovsky is connected to your concert tickets fiasco, and I'm convinced that Itzkowitz's disappearance is also connected."

"So now you're saying, it's my fault, and that's why we need to look after this waif and protect her from a group of crazed killers bent on terminating her."

Bee's face hardened as he turned to look directly at his colleague "Let's not forget why we're in this mess. I still don't know if we're doing the right thing. It wouldn't be so bad if Beck was still in charge at the station, but Springfield's only been in situ a matter of months, and I don't know how she'd react to all this subterfuge." He paused. "Not well would be my guess."

McTierney shook his head but said nothing.

"I'll call Jackson, and we'll arrange it for tonight."

EIGHTEEN

BEE PUT HIS mobile phone back in his jacket pocket, turned to McTierney and smiled. "The deed is done. I'll drive up tonight and meet Jackson. He's going to make it look like she's escaped and is on the run. Not totally unbelievable given the aggravation she's being facing of late."

"Won't Jackson get the bollocking of his life from his boss?"

"Probably, but he feels it'll be worth it if we keep Gandapur alive until the trial."

"A week in the doghouse and then glory."

"Hopefully."

"Let's hope Springfield doesn't make your stay in the doghouse any longer."

The colour drained from Bee's face.

"Only joking. I'm sure she'll be delighted with the outcome. But more importantly, what did you think of Irina?"

Bee was taken aback by the question, "Nothing really. I suppose I feel a bit sorry for her caught up in all of this. She seems a bit young to be involved with a major criminal."

McTierney rolled his eyes, "That's not quite the angle I was thinking of. More along the lines of Russian gangsters, or even gangsters from any country shouldn't have pretty girlfriends. It's not right. There's no justice in the world."

"Oh yes. I guess it was the blonde hair that did it for you."

"Yes, the hair, but also the smile, the figure, those fingernails, everything really. But regardless, my point is still valid."

"It is, but as every seasoned detective in the country will tell you, there's precious little justice in this world. But it's our job to make sure there is at least some."

McTierney smiled and turned the car radio up as the DJ played a Bon Jovi track. Bee grimaced and turned it back down and started another conversation.

"While we're in the mood for looking around houses, let's go back and have a thorough search of Itzkowitz's place. Bishop sent me a text telling me that Springfield will be sending a team in this afternoon to go through it with a fine-tooth comb, but I'd like us to have a look around before they trample over everything."

"Fair enough boss."

★ ★ ★

BY COMPARISON TO the mansion they had been exploring in Croydon, the three-bed semi of Fran Itzkowitz felt like a shoebox, but Bee insisted on them maintaining a thorough approach.

"Stick some gloves on and take the upstairs, while I look around downstairs."

"Sure. But what are you hoping to find?"

"I don't know. Look for anything unusual that could explain her disappearance. As you keep pointing out there is no evidence to link her to the Taranovsky case, or any other case for that matter, but she's missing for a reason."

The two men parted company at the bottom of the stairs and Bee began his search in the kitchen. He noticed the calendar hanging on the wall; Itzkowitz used it solely for social engagements. There was nothing marked for the day, but she had written 'Jake' into Saturday night for the day she'd disappeared, so clearly she had been expecting to see Jake that day, even though he had downplayed their relationship. A row below she had 'Sainsbury delivery at 8 p.m.' written in for Thursday evening, so clearly she intended to be at home tomorrow. Bee dropped the calendar into an evidence bag and continued to search.

Ten minutes later he heard McTierney clomping down the wooden staircase. He came into the kitchen and put two items on the table. "Exhibit A, Itzkowitz's laptop and exhibit B, her diary."

Bee sucked air over his teeth and looked uncomfortable, "We can pass the laptop over to the IT team at the station, they'll make quicker progress than we will. I presume someone has already been checking her work computer."

McTierney shrugged his shoulders.

Bee nodded, "I'll ask Bishop."

McTierney held up the diary, "This might be more interesting."

Bee offered an awkward smile, "Yes. Maybe, but I'm uneasy at the idea of reading a colleague's personal diary."

"Agreed, but this is a different situation. We're not schoolboys flicking through the diary of a girl we fancy in the sixth form; this is a case of a missing person."

Bee viewed him suspiciously over his glasses, "Clearly we went to different schools."

"We did. But come on, we're doing this for the good of

the case. Suppose she mentions some guy we don't yet know."

Bee broke eye contact with McTierney and glanced around the kitchen. He rubbed the back of his neck, while McTierney stood waiting. "Okay. You're right. I guess we should."

McTierney smiled and flicked open the diary and turned to Saturday's page. "Nothing for the day she went missing." He turned another page, "Or the day before." He flicked back another few pages and Bee resumed looking through the kitchen drawers.

"Wait, this might be interesting."

Bee stopped and turned back to his colleague.

McTierney continued, "I must tell someone; I can't go on any longer feeling this way. He fills my every thought. I make up reasons to be in his presence."

Bee stopped what he was doing and leant towards McTierney.

"He's the kindest, most thoughtful man I've ever met. I must find a way to tell him how I feel. I would do anything to have him to myself."

Bee was agog as McTierney continued to read. "He never seems to notice me, but I will make him love me. I know I can do it and then we'll both be so happy."

"Who is she writing about?"

McTierney held up his hand to silence Bee as he read. "He's just so wonderful and sexy, the hunky Inspector Scott Bee." McTierney burst into laughter, "Jeez, you're so gullible!"

Bee clenched his fist and spittle formed at the side of his mouth. "Will you stop clowning around and do something useful? I'm putting my career on the line here to help you and all you can do is sod about! Go through the damn diary properly."

McTierney looked shocked at the outburst, dropped his eyes to the floor and mumbled an apology. "Sorry, just trying to lighten a difficult time." He let out a heavy sigh. Then he spoke more softly, "I read the diary upstairs. It mentions Jake Rivers a bit and there was some other bloke called James earlier in the year, who we ought to check out. His details are in here. I'll go and see him tonight."

Bee acknowledged the statement with a nod and the two detectives continued to look around the house but couldn't find anything to explain why Itzkowitz might have disappeared. McTierney left Bee in the kitchen and wandered into the lounge. He picked up a photo of her in her NYPD uniform smiling at the camera and with a huge bagel in her hand overflowing with lettuce and sauces. He pulled a face at the food but then began to smile. He flopped down onto the sofa.

"Lord, I know I don't believe in you, and you probably don't believe in me, that's okay, but let me make a deal with you. If you help me to find Fran Itzkowitz I swear I'll never moan about her smelly food ever again." He paused, "And I'll even take her out to lunch every Friday and let her buy some of that disgusting red cabbage stuff she seems to think is healthy."

"Not making promises you can't keep are you?" Bee was standing in the doorway. McTierney swung round and looked flustered. "No. No, not at all."

Bee wandered over and sat next to his colleague on the worn, blue sofa. "I miss her too you know."

The two men sat in silence looking in different directions, until McTierney broke out of his reverie. "Hey, do you remember that time a couple of years ago, just after she'd moved across from Guildford and she was in Sainsbury's buying a few bottles of non-alcoholic lager?"

"Oh yes, she was going through the self-service check out when the machine beeped at her and a young assistant came over to check her age, and she couldn't understand why they were checking her age on non-alcoholic lager. Then you explained to her that even non-alcoholic lager still has some alcohol in it, and she became agitated and wanted to write to the government to complain."

"Ha. Yes. But as I said at the time, the key question is why was she buying non-alcoholic beer?"

Bee rolled his eyes, and the pair fell back into their own thoughts about their missing colleague. An idea flickered across Bee's mind, a soft frown creased his forehead, but he let it float away, and his eyes returned to the floor. The quietness of the house seemed to engulf the pair. McTierney was lost in his thoughts.

At last Bee spoke. "I remember Itzkowitz dragging the three of us; you, me and Bishop, over to some Greek party in Guildford. I think it was the birthday of one of her old colleagues. The one with a Greek husband, I don't remember her name."

McTierney looked up but didn't speak.

"I've never known someone so keen on food as this guy. Not only was he eating everything in sight, but he seemed to get as much pleasure from encouraging others to eat, and he wouldn't take no for an answer. If he doesn't have a restaurant, he surely should. I remember eating pies of all types, heaven knows how many calories I consumed that evening. But it was fun and Itzkowitz made it all happen."

McTierney offered a half-smile, "It was always food with her." He paused then added "And who can forget that loud raucous laugh?"

"Ha, yes, you can always tell when Itzkowitz is in the building. And we won't forget it, because we'll hear it again. As soon as we find her."

The mood was broken by a sharp rap on the front door. Dr Kelly and his forensic team had arrived as requested by DCS Springfield. Bee and McTierney exchanged looks and agreed to leave the experts to do their thing. As the pair got to McTierney's car, Bee tapped his partner's sleeve. "When we have this review with the chief, let's be careful what we tell her. There's more than one element here I don't think we should reveal."

"She's not going to like that."

"I know, it's counter-intuitive to restrict resources when we're on a missing person's search. But I can't think of any way of explaining the concert tickets, the money, the trip to Exeter or the gun without getting ourselves into hot water. It feels like the world is closing in on us. We're going to have to tread carefully."

"That's not going to leave a lot to talk about."

NINETEEN

SPRINGFIELD GATHERED EVERYONE in the ops room for the 4 o'clock review. She had arrived early and was inspecting the CID area as the rest of the team appeared. She took position at the head of the table and scrutinised each person as they filed in, causing them to scurry to find an empty seat, seemingly to put everyone even more on edge. Finally, she started to speak.

"You've had 50 hours on this disappearance, let's hear what you've uncovered."

The team exchanged anxious looks, unsure of where to start. Bee leant forward to explain their position. "The team has been working solidly on the case, I can update you on some items, but I'm not up to speed on what's been happening in the office, it's a moving feast."

Springfield acknowledged his admission, "I understand inspector. Now can I suggest you put some of the details up on the white board. As I recall that's the traditional approach to these cases, and it will help all of us focus on the main points."

Bee did as he was asked, stood and walked to the white board. He looked at the blank open space. He didn't like blank pages; he preferred writing pads which had lines. He performed better with boundaries and rules, even though he might sometimes cross the boundaries, he liked structure and formality, a complete carte blanche filled him with horror, especially when he was feeling uncomfortable with the story he had to write.

Bee picked up the blue felt pen and felt Springfield's eyes burning into the back of his head. Then inspiration struck, he began a star chart and put Itzkowitz's name in a box in the centre of the white board. He drew an arrow to the right, wrote 'Jake Rivers', and turned to explain that he was the boyfriend of their missing colleague. That he and McTierney had interviewed him informally and been left with some concerns. Bee concluded, "He remains a suspect."

Bishop raised her hand and looked between Bee and Springfield, Bee smiled at her, "Do you have something more on Rivers?"

"Yes I do. Lots."

There was a buzz of excitement around the room as everyone focused on Bishop's next sentence. "I trawled through Fran's phone records today and there are a lot of calls between the two, mostly from her. It looks like they last spoke on Friday, twice in fact."

"That's interesting, because he told us he hadn't heard from Itzkowitz since Wednesday night, Thursday morning."

"So that's a complete lie."

"It is. When we saw him he seemed to have another girl with him, and gave the impression that Itzkowitz didn't know about it."

Bishop shook her head and pressed on. "But the text messages from Rivers are the most revealing. It looks like he'd been asking Itzkowitz for money; it's not clear how much."

"Not going to be £50 is it?" said McTierney.

"No, I guess not," agreed Bishop. "It seems Itzkowitz refused his request because the texts from two weeks ago take a nasty turn. He tells her he's going to make her pay for refusing him."

If Bishop didn't have their full attention before, she did now.

"Then he goes on with lots of unpleasantries. Not quite a threat to kill her, but close."

"We need to speak Rivers urgently," it was Springfield. "Bring him in."

"I'm on it boss. I'll get down to the hospital where he works, once we finish here," said McTierney.

"Good." Springfield turned back to Bee, "What else have you got inspector?"

Bee shuffled his feet uncomfortably. "We've focused a lot of our time on the idea of a kidnap. McTierney and I trawled through the area she was called to on Saturday and there's some light forensic evidence to suggest she was there."

"Tell me more."

Bee found the bridge of his glasses with his forefinger and pushed them gently back into place. He hoped it would lend an academic touch to what he was about to say. "We can trace Itzkowitz's car to the general area of the Holmethorpe Industrial Estate. Although we would benefit from having the traffic surveillance cameras relocated from the old station to here." He paused, offered a quick glance in the direction of Springfield who scribbled something in front of her, then Bee pressed on. "At the site we found a US chocolate wrapper, Itzkowitz is known to favour, plus car tyre tracks. I believe Dr Kelly is trying to validate our suspicions."

"Hmm. I'll be amazed if he does. You're not giving him

much to go on."

"No." admitted Bee. "There's been very little evidence at this point."

Springfield opened her mouth to speak but Bee continued before she could jump in.

"I believe the lack of clues is itself a clue." He paused for effect. "It tells me that this is the work of a professional; not necessarily an assassin or a trained kidnapper, perhaps someone skilled in abductions or serious crime in some form. He could have experience of security work, be a former member of the military or even the police."

He noticed Bishop twist in her chair, and she caught his eye. "Although I think Bishop has uncovered some useful information here." He looked across the desk with imploring eyes and Bishop came to his rescue, recounting the details that she'd uncovered over the last couple of days.

When she'd finished Springfield made a point of complimenting her on her work and concluded by telling Bee, "It's a pity you've not been as productive as some of your team. What, exactly, have you two been doing?"

Bee looked at the ceiling, not wanting to catch the eye of McTierney. McTierney looked at the floor not wanting to catch the eye of Bee, and certainly not the eye of Lisa Springfield. Bee bit his lip, hoping that no one would jump to his defence and mention all the work he had been doing. To divert attention, he returned to the white board and added a new column to reflect the new lead; Babylon, the name of the New York gang member, as provided by Itzkowitz's American former boss. He turned back to face the table.

"I believe the house-to-house enquiries and our own

search of Itzkowitz's house suggest that she left home voluntarily. It's later that the problems arise. However, without a body, I think we have to consider that this is probably a kidnapping. I would go further and say that the American threat is much more likely to end in a straightforward killing, rather than an abduction. So, while I wouldn't discount him from the investigation, my feeling is that he's not in play at the moment. However, Rivers remains a prime suspect."

Springfield relaxed a little at the analysis and Bee took the opportunity to add a few extra dimensions. "If I may, I'd like to share some questions which I've been struggling with and some concerns I have with the case."

"Go ahead."

"Assuming this is a kidnapping, where's the ransom note?" He let the question hang in the air, but nobody answered. "There's been no contact at all. That's unusual and it worries me. I hate to say it, but it makes me think that Itzkowitz isn't coming back unless we find her."

Bishop gasped at the statement, but nobody challenged the logic.

"Then we have Itzkowitz's car. Or the lack of it. If she's been abducted then what happened to the car? We're fairly sure it was in the industrial estate on Saturday, but it's not there now. It suggests that maybe there were two people involved in the kidnapping. It would certainly make it easier to achieve, not just the abduction on the Saturday, but it takes manpower to sustain a kidnapping. It's not impossible for a lone wolf, but a team of two or three certainly makes it easier and yet both of our prime suspects are individuals. So, who would be their accomplices?"

Bee left another pause, and this was also greeted with a silence, so he continued. "We have to recognise that no one debuts as a kidnapper. It's not where a criminal starts. They work up to it. They start with something petty, get away with it, then get a bit more adventurous. But even then kidnapping is not for the casual, opportunist crook. It takes planning, organisation and experience. There's every chance our boy, and it's nailed on to be a man, is in our database somewhere. I was hoping that Kelly would find a print of some sort at the likely abduction scene but that's not happened. With all that we know about Rivers, I'm struggling to believe that he fits the profile."

Bee searched the audience for a response, but aside from a nod of the head from McTierney none came, so he persisted. "Let me change tack slightly. I've been trying to put myself in the shoes of the kidnapper, trying to think how he would have thought. I have a couple of questions that I can't answer, but they feel significant. Firstly, why here? I mean why Reigate station, why Itzkowitz? And then why Saturday afternoon?"

Springfield decided it was time to chip in. "The answer to those last few questions is easy if you believe that either Rivers or this American, Babylon is the culprit. They have personal grievances with Itzkowitz which might explain a potential kidnap, although I take your point about manpower."

Bee smiled at Springfield, "Yes, that's the obvious response, but it raises the next question. How would our caller know who was going to answer the call? How would he know it would be Itzkowitz who would be responding and going into an ambush on the industrial estate? Unless the caller had inside information and knew the rota. It's a one in three chance of getting Itzkowitz, not great odds and considering how well the abduction appears to have been completed I would say our criminal doesn't play the odds."

Springfield recoiled at the dismissal of her point as obvious but had no answer to Bee's rationale. But he had one more point to make. He took a deep breath. "Unless, of course, the kidnapper wasn't targeting Itzkowitz at all. Instead, he was targeting the police, us, and if he was maybe he hasn't finished."

Bee's comment was almost a throwaway line, but it sent a shiver around the room as his colleagues exchanged nervous glances and twisted in their seats. Springfield cleared her throat and took back control of the meeting.

"Let's focus on what has happened and not speculate on what might happen. Do we really think this is a kidnapping? Because if we do, there are specialist agencies in London who we could call upon to help us. Sophisticated teams with experience and inside information, usually ex-police or ex-military, but smart operators. I attended a conference on kidnapping a couple of years ago and you'd be surprised at the number of foreign nationals who are targeted in London."

Bishop perked up at the challenge but didn't dare offer a number.

"Virtually 50% if I remember correctly."

Bee looked unconvinced. "I know I mentioned kidnapping as an option, but one issue for me is I don't believe Itzkowitz, or her family, are wealthy." He looked across the room at McTierney, who nodded his agreement. "So why go to the trouble of kidnapping a police officer if there's no jackpot at the end?"

"Yes. Why indeed?" Said Springfield, she paused considering the point. "We'll hold off from contacting this outside team for now but keep it in mind. But let me say clearly that we will not rest until we find Itzkowitz. The life of a potential hostage comes before every other consideration. I understand that some of our own people are upset and nervous and I want to provide some reassurance that we are doing everything we can to find Itzkowitz. This is our number one priority. I am ready to expand the numbers working on the case and put more manpower out on the street. If we can't protect our own police officers, how on earth can we protect the public?" She looked around the table for support, but nobody said anything. "I'm surprised, I thought you would all be pleased that I'm prepared to up the ante on this case. What's wrong?"

Bee's stomach lurched; this was a route he didn't feel comfortable taking. Yes he wanted to find Itzkowitz, but he didn't want to expose the little adventure that he and McTierney had been on since Friday night's concert. He looked across the table at his colleague, but McTierney had his eyes glued to the floor. "Oh, I don't know," he said. His fingers trembled around the pen he'd been holding, so he abandoned it and sat down on his hands to keep them still. "I think there are too many unanswered questions at the moment. We don't really know that this is a kidnapping yet."

Springfield glared across the table, so Bee tried a different tack. "We could set a lot of hares running and then discover that it's something completely different."

"Like what?"

Bee sensed that his boss was getting ready to explode. He shrunk in his seat. "I don't know, but I'd recommend caution."

Springfield slammed her fist on the table and Bee jumped. "I want to show this bastard who's taken Itzkowitz that he's not winning. That no one can do this to us. To the police. Are you telling me you're not with me?"

Bee looked across the table at his friend; his loyalty to McTierney was at breaking point; ordinarily he would be fully committed to the job, but he didn't feel he could abandon his friend. Honesty had been the cornerstone of his career, but now he felt he was drowning in lies.

"No, no not at all. I'm 100% committed to finding Itzkowitz." Bee faltered, "I'm just not sure this is the moment to go big and public."

Springfield took a deep breath, "Very well inspector, we'll hold that decision for a couple of days. But before we break, let's revisit the action points. Bee, McTierney you pick up Rivers." The two men nodded their agreement. "I'll get a team into the old station and pick up all the traffic camera feeds so we can get them relocated to here and for that matter we'll pick up all the security cameras from the garages on the industrial estate."

She turned her attention to Carol Bishop. "Bishop, you follow up on the US gang member; get a proper name, a photo, all the information you can, use our facial ID systems to track him. Find out if he's entered the country and if so where. Then Bee, you find him and eliminate him from our inquiries."

Springfield returned to Bishop, "Then dig into Itzkowitz's recent past in Guildford. Find out if there's anybody there who might have a grudge against her."

Bishop scribbled a note on her pad, but Springfield

hadn't finished. "What do we know about Itzkowitz's parents?" Three blanks faces stared back at her. "Fine, Bishop, can you get me some contact details, we may need to talk to them at some point."

Once again the room fell silent. Springfield looked around at her colleagues, "Despite the reservations of our inspector I'm going to upgrade the security at this station. I'll be putting in a request for a digital CCTV camera on the only accessible entrance taking photographs of everyone on entry and exit. Together with a biometric entrance security system that requires both a fingerprint and a six-digit code that changes every week."

There was a stunned silence around the room, but nobody dared challenge the idea.

Springfield closed the meeting, "That should be enough to be going on with for now. I want an update this time tomorrow," she looked directly at Bee as she spoke. "And then another face-to-face review on Friday afternoon in this room. I assume we will all make that."

TWENTY

"INSPECTOR BEE, COULD I see you for a moment?"

Bee spun round in surprise, "Yes sure." He expected Lisa Springfield to speak to him there, but instead she started to walk away from the CID area. He hesitated unsure if he should follow, Springfield realised he wasn't walking with her, stopped and turned back to face him. "Now!" She barked.

Bee wore a puzzled expression but dutifully followed Springfield across the floor, down the stairs and out to the front of the building. She had the first office in the old Gothic building, meaning that they had a five-minute walk through the converted old country house with its solid wooden doors, carpeted walkways and occasional coffee machines squashed into every alcove.

Although Bee and Springfield had worked together in the new premises for close on four weeks by now, this was the first time he had been called into her office. She pushed the big white door which creaked as it opened. Inside, the former reception room hadn't given up all of its rural charm; two large arch windows let in ample natural light, a fireplace stood in the centre of one wall, while the mantel was adorned by an antique clock and a pair of Egyptian vases. This was crowned by a high ceiling which gave the office a touch of elegance. But functionality and practicality were taking over in the rest of the room, with a compact seating area, modern bookcases and filing cabinets completing the picture. In pride of place on the front of her large oak desk stood a large photograph of Lisa Springfield standing with her arm hooked around another woman. Bee tried to look away but found himself drawn back to the image. Springfield caught his eye, "My partner Maddie. She's a fabulous woman. I'm not quite as open about my private life as my predecessor was, I believe he invited the team to social gatherings at his home. Fear not, I won't be doing that, but if you do get to meet her, I'm sure you'll like her."

"The pleasure would be all mine."

Springfield smiled. "Inspector Bee. Always says the right thing. Always does the right thing."

Bee looked embarrassed and shifted his weight from one foot to another, "I try," he mumbled.

Springfield left him standing while she looked at him and then invited him to take a seat. "So, what was that charade this afternoon?"

Bee's mouth went dry, but he didn't dare swallow. Despite the late hour, Springfield's eyes shone and searched, spotlights swirling around his head looking for a weakness. "Charade? I don't know what you mean?"

Springfield stared at him, "Come now inspector, we both know you were putting on a performance upstairs."

Bee flinched but didn't respond.

Springfield leaned back in her chair, "Okay, I'll go first. I didn't take this job to spend my productive years smelling the roses in Reigate. Nice place that it is, I have ambitions beyond this little town. But it's a competitive business. I get the sense that you don't bother with all that political chicanery and that's fine. But while I'm in charge here, we play by my rules."

She looked directly at Bee to ensure he was following. Bee didn't say anything, but he maintained eye contact.

"So, I'm looking to impress. Impress those above and I have two strategies in place to succeed. Would you care to hear them?"

"I would," lied Bee.

"Firstly, I keep a tight, yet clean ship. We all work hard, and we work together. We solve crime, we keep people safe, we get noticed."

Bee smiled in acknowledgement.

"Secondly, I will root out any bad or corrupt police officers. We owe it to the general public to give them a police service; they can be proud of. We've been given a position of trust and responsibility, and we have a duty to live up to those expectations. There is no excuse for letting those standards drop and I will not entertain poor standards."

Bee recoiled at the intensity of the statement.

"I don't think you have anything to fear on the basis of corruption; people tell me you are as honest as the day is long. But I'm not yet convinced by your wingman."

Bee allowed himself a quick smile, "He's a better detective than people give him credit for."

"That's as maybe, but I hear he has some unorthodox methods."

Bee squirmed in his seat and wished for the conversation to be over. "I really couldn't say, he's always behaved impeccably whenever I'm around." Bee pushed his right hand into his trouser pocket and pinched his thigh to keep himself concentrating on the conversation.

Springfield eyed him suspiciously. "Your loyalty does you credit, even if your choice of friends leaves a bit to be desired. Have you ever considered that McTierney has collected you? You're not an obvious friend to him, but rather someone who can be useful, either now or in the future. But I'll leave you to ponder the merits of DS McTierney and return to my reason for bringing you here. I have the feeling that you are working against me, following your own agenda or thinking that you can't trust me. I'm here to say that you can." Springfield allowed a pause to develop, but Bee had played the same game in the interrogation room and didn't respond.

"You'll find me fair. I'll give you a topical example. After the little show you put on up there with your team, we could have had this chat in front of them. I could have bawled you out in front of them and made you look small. But I'm not like that. I let you come down here and I'll let you determine how much of this conversation you replay when you're reunited with them."

"That's very reasonable of you Ma'am. It's much appreciated. I'll tell you this, that I try hard not to pass on bad news to my team, but I will share any positive reviews."

Springfield smiled at the idea, "Highly commendable inspector, and in the spirit of openness allow me to say this. Don't make an enemy of me, because I'll crush you like a fly." Bee looked up at the threat and didn't doubt it for a second. "I've told you about my mission, don't think for a moment that I'll allow any regional detective, no matter how smart he might believe he is, to derail that ambition. It's my way or the exit door. Understand?"

"Yes Ma'am."

"Very good. So, here's one last chance to come clean about whatever is going on upstairs. Tell me everything or I'll find out in any event and then there'll be hell to pay."

Bee blew out a shaky breath. He wasn't used to a boss who was on top of her game. Whereas old man Beck had been on the long ride to retirement, Springfield was still climbing the ladder of ambition. He would need to sharpen up his game. "Thank you for your honesty Ma'am, but there's nothing else to say."

Bee moved to leave his seat but quickly realised that he hadn't yet been dismissed. Springfield watched as he lowered himself back into the chair. "Don't bring the house down on your career out of some misguided loyalty to a friend."

"I wouldn't, Ma'am."

TWENTY-ONE

BEE WALKED AWAY from Springfield's office with hunched shoulders and his hands thrust into his pockets. There was a heaviness to him, which wasn't normal. He wasn't comfortable keeping the truth from the chief superintendent, he felt sure this would blow up in his face. As he walked along the main corridor he suddenly thought Springfield was behind him and he spun around to check, but it was just his conscience. He turned back and sighed and found himself face to face with McTierney.

"What do you make of the evil queen's performance today?"

Bee grimaced, "She's okay. Just trying to do her job."

McTierney took a step back. "Wow. As someone who always sees the best in people, which is a very annoying trait by the way, when you say someone is 'okay', that translates to she's a 'total bitch'."

It was Bee's turn to look shocked, but he didn't correct his colleague.

"It was certainly a bit uncomfortable earlier. You did a good job keeping the evil queen at bay."

"Did I? She's on my case now. We need to get this LG business solved and fast, or I'll be filing it under 'career disaster'. The boss is all over it." Bee glanced back over his shoulder as he spoke, nervous that he might be overheard. His mobile beeped and he jumped in fright.

"Is that the queen, calling you back?"

Bee fumbled with his phone but opened the message. As he read it the colour drained from his face.

"Bad news?"

"Yes and no."

McTierney waited for an explanation. Bee motioned to him to step into an empty interview room and closed the door behind them. "It's Jackson. He's suggesting we make the switch with Gandapur tonight. He wants me to meet him at 9 o'clock."

"That's good isn't it?"

"On most days yes, it would be good news. But coming on the same day that I've misled the boss and been told to focus 100% on the Itzkowitz case, it's not good timing."

"But you believe there's a connection between the disappearance of our DS and all these shenanigans with Taranovsky."

"I do, but I can't prove it and without proof, Springfield won't entertain it. You heard her, when I suggested there was more to this case than meets the eye. She wants to focus on the evidence to hand."

"She does have a point and she's the boss."

"Tell me about it. Anyway, I'll have to go and do this pick up with Jackson, so can you manage Rivers on your own?"

"Sure, no problem." A wicked smile spread across McTierney's face. "I like a bit of pressure."

"Just stick to the rules. You're not the Lone Ranger. No funny business, we have precious little evidence as it is now.

We don't want some fancy brief throwing out any evidence you do stumble on because you've roughed up his client."

"Scout's honour, boss."

"You were never in the Scouts were you?"

"No. But I'll keep it clean."

"Good. And on that subject, when I bring this Gandapur girl back to our place, we can't have any talk about the Taranovsky case. I don't want to risk the possibility of his solicitor claiming that we've programmed her against him."

"No worries boss. I do know the rules. It's just sometimes you need to bend them to make progress."

Bee nodded. "One last thing, no matter how attractive this girl is; you don't hit on her."

"Would I?"

Bee rolled his eyes at his colleague.

"Now talking of women, I've got a suspicion that the evil queen is using Bishop as a spy."

Bee pulled a face at the accusation.

"She keeps popping up to our area when Bishop is alone and chatting to her, asking little questions about what we're doing. I think we need to be careful."

"I don't think Bishop would betray us and, anyway, Springfield is just doing her job."

"Maybe. All I'm saying is be careful."

"Your point is duly noted. Now go and ruin Rivers' evening, while I arrange a meeting place with Jackson, but be careful. Rivers is not a kidnapper. We've seen his place, he couldn't even keep a bike safe, he's not going to be able to keep a police officer locked up. But that doesn't rule him out as a killer."

McTierney's eyes widened, and he stepped back slightly.

"You think so?"

"Yes I do. At least I think it's possible. I can't imagine him as a kidnapper, as I said, he doesn't have the organisation, but as we know anyone can be a killer. If he and Itzkowitz had rowed, perhaps she found out about the other girl, who knows? But he might have seen it as a way out, and he's probably one of the few people who would know that she'd answer the call on Saturday afternoon and that she'd be on her own at the industrial estate. So, it's not a stretch to give him motive, means and opportunity."

"When you put it like that." McTierney nodded his approval.

"Just be on your guard, and I'll see you at the house later."

"Sure."

Bee moved to the door and pulled it open, but then pushed it closed again. "One final thought."

McTierney cocked his head.

"I think I know why we were sent to Exeter."

"Spill the beans."

"To get us out of the way and ensure that Itzkowitz answered the call."

McTierney smiled, "With both of us out of the county, there was no chance that either of us could step in and take the call instead."

"Precisely."

TWENTY-TWO

McTIERNEY WATCHED BEE leave the building, then turned to walk back up the stairs to the CID area. As he walked across the open plan office his mobile phoned beeped with the arrival of a text. He pulled it to his face to focus on the words, scanned through the text and then his face began to scowl as he understood the message. He mumbled the word "bastards" as he read the words. 'L.G. is still alife. Fix it.'

He spun around in the office, hoping no-one was watching him and thrust the phone back into his pocket. He walked to his desk, collected his leather jacket and set off for the hospital. The good thing about this job was that there was always an opportunity to take out your frustrations on someone else. On this occasion it would be Jake Rivers.

East Surrey Hospital is the primary accident and emergency centre for most of the county and several towns outside of it. As such it is a modern and well-equipped centre, but it has evolved over many years and has a mixture of buildings; some new and some in desperate need of maintenance and repair. It's always busy and exudes a bustling, yet professional atmosphere. Having spent a few days as an in-patient in the previous year, when he'd be felled by an iron bar after a chase through Reigate High Street, McTierney was no stranger to the site and readily located the administrative block. A manager was packing up and looking to leave as McTierney approached the door.

"Sorry, I'm just closing for the day. Can you come back tomorrow?"

McTierney looked the man up and down. He didn't deserve a taste of McTierney's anger generated by the text; he decided to play nice this time and flashed his warrant card. "Sorry, can't do that. I need some information, but it won't take long."

Five minutes later McTierney walked away, his bad mood had deepened. It appeared that Rivers's claim to be at the hospital last week stacked up. Of course, that still left the afternoon free and with it the possibility that he could have been at the industrial estate on the northern side of the town.

McTierney's new friend had directed him to the porter station, located somewhere between Haematology and Dietetics, where he bumped into a round, full-bodied man with a prominent belly and a ruddy oval shaped face, who explained that he was the porter captain. McTierney didn't want Rivers called to the main station. He preferred to track him down away from prying eyes, so he took some advice and set off into the bowels of the hospital.

He'd been told that Rivers was often found around the East Entrance, and it was here that McTierney caught sight of him, but when he called out, Rivers turned and walked away. McTierney didn't want to run through the hospital, but he wasn't about to let Rivers escape, so he jogged to the main corridor and turned right, heading back towards the café area. Rivers took an early turn off to the left, which was a stairwell to the floor above, but McTierney sensed this was a decoy and he headed on to the Porters' base and wheelchair station. Three minutes later Rivers cautiously pushed open the door and walked straight into McTierney. Realising that there was no escape, Rivers changed his act to a man greeting a long-lost friend. "DS McTierney! If I'd known it was you, I'd have stopped earlier. I didn't recognise you in the daylight."

McTierney eyed him with contempt, "Do you always run from people calling out your name?"

"Can't be too careful around this hospital, it attracts a lot of weirdos," Rivers paused then added, "case in point," and laughed. Rivers offered a flash of a smile and a pause as if he was a stand-up comedian expecting a round of applause or a big laugh. But McTierney wasn't in the mood for fun.

"Let's go for a walk. I've some questions for you. The boiler room will do, no one should disturb us down there."

The boiler room was a large airless hellhole with pipes and conduits running in every direction. It had high ceilings, brick walls, fluorescent lights and a row of noisy clunking boilers. Nobody in their right mind would want to spend long in there. McTierney shoved Rivers against the wall and grabbed him by the lapel. "You lied to me last night. I don't like to be lied to, let's see if you can do better this time."

"I, I, er I didn't mean to," stuttered Rivers.

"You told Inspector Bee and myself that the last time you'd had contact with Fran Itzkowitz was on Thursday night, but that wasn't true was it?"

"I don't know, I might have been mistaken. I can't think up against this wall."

McTierney released his grip. "Start talking."

Rivers dusted himself down, "Sorry I got confused. I think it was Saturday morning that I last spoke to Fran."

"Sure?"

"Yes."

As Rivers answered he turned away so McTierney couldn't see his face as he uttered the crucial word. Was that to disguise a lie? McTierney clenched his fist. "Just one more time, so I've got it absolutely clear in my mind."

"Saturday, it was Saturday," Rivers spat the words at McTierney. But McTierney smiled, he liked it when a suspect got riled; it meant they were more likely to lose their cool and make a mistake. He reached into the back pocket of his jeans and pulled out a small notepad. He licked the end of his pencil and pulled on a blank simpleton expression.

"Sorry Mr Rivers, but Inspector Bee can be a grumpy bastard at times, and he will want to have a full record of your response." He paused, "Did you personally choose to withhold evidence from a police investigation?"

Rivers glared at him.

"Shall I put 'Yes' for that?"

"No! I've just answered your bloody question." Rivers bared his teeth.

"No need to shout, I can hear you."

McTierney noticed Rivers had a sheen of sweat developing on his cheeks, chin and forehead.

"Let's talk money for a moment."

Rivers eyes darted from side to side as if looking for an escape from the conversation.

"You've been hassling Miss Itzkowitz for money. Why?"

Rivers exhaled deeply, "I owed some money to a bloke from Dorking for the amp I use in my gigs. Fran said she'd help me out, then changed her mind."

"Smart lady. But why did you have to get nasty over it

and start threatening her?"

"I didn't."

"I've seen the text messages."

Rivers fell silent. Then sheepishly added, "It was banter. I was disappointed. I didn't mean it, it's just…" He paused. "It was just that, I knew I'd get grief from Mick in Dorking."

McTierney grunted. "Hmm. Talking of Dorking, there's something else I want to check. You told us you met Miss Itzkowitz in a pub in Dorking. Would that be The Surrey Yeoman?"

"Yes, I think so. What of it?"

"Have you been back there lately?"

"No."

"Why not?

"If you must know I didn't like the acoustics there much."

"Nothing to do with you being barred from the place then."

Rivers nostrils flared "If you know the bloody answer, why ask the question?"

"I want to hear your answers; understand what you think is the truth and quite frankly, you don't seem to know what the truth is."

"Look, can't we go somewhere else, it's baking in here."

"No. I like the heat. Anyway, I thought you liked it out here with all the other rats."

"What is this? Another case of the police beating up the wrong guy?"

"Don't put ideas in my head."

Rivers shook his head in disgust, but McTierney had saved his ace.

"Give me the keys to your van, I want our forensic team to check it over."

"What! You can't do that." Rivers began to fidget.

"Oh yes I can, and you know what, it's much more fun than beating you up. The keys." McTierney opened his palm. "And where's it parked?"

"It's back at the house," mumbled Rivers.

"Thanks. You know the thing about murderers is that most of them are as thick as shit, if you'll excuse my language. Even the clever ones are never quite as clever as they think they are. I've met so many of them who think that they can get one over on me, but they still make mistakes. If you ask me what's the best thing about being a detective, it's that moment when I know that I've got them. When the mask comes off, when the whole thing is solved, and they crumble like sand in front of me."

"I'm not a murderer. I'm not." Rivers was almost screaming.

McTierney enjoyed it when a suspect began to break, "Is there anything else you should be telling me?"

"No. I haven't killed Fran or anyone."

"I'll be back when forensics have searched your van. Let's hope they agree with you."

MCTIERNEY WALKED BACK to his car. He didn't like Rivers. The man in him was offended by the cheapness of the man. The policeman in him was offended by his disdain for the truth of any kind and the human in him was offended by the casual disregard he had for life. He treated everyone with contempt. No McTierney didn't like him one bit, but he did believe him when he said that he hadn't killed Fran Itzkowitz. Although he would accept that the hospital boiler room in the bowels of the building was nicely out of the way if someone had a body or a kidnap victim to conceal.

TWENTY-THREE

JACKSON HAD ASKED Bee to meet him at the far end of the car park at the giant Tesco superstore at Purley Cross. The store didn't close until midnight, but Jackson thought that was too late for Gandapur, so they agreed to meet at nine-fifteen. Even at this time of the night, the store was far from deserted, but the far end of the car park had almost no traffic and Jackson had found a spot out of the arc of the floodlights. Bee drove slowly around the car park and pulled into a space alongside his friend with their windows aligned. They lowered them together, allowing them to speak without stepping out of their vehicles.

"Thanks for coming."

"Don't mention it."

"Look, I'm sorry to drag you into this affair, but I don't think there's any choice."

"Don't worry, you helped me on plenty of occasions at Hendon, I'm happy to return the favour."

"This is no walk in the park. It might only be for a few days more, but it won't be easy." Jackson's eyes continued to dart around the car park. "You'll need to be patient with Gandapur, she's a good girl but she doesn't trust anyone." He ran his finger around his shirt collar, "And for that matter, neither should you."

"Don't worry about me, I'm aware of the risks. I'll be okay."

"I hope so, and I've got something to help you."

Jackson turned away from the window and leant across to the passenger seat of his car. He returned to the window, cast a furtive glance left and right and passed a towel across to Bee, who frowned at the package as he took it in his right hand.

"It's a gun. You might need this. Don't worry, it can't be traced, if you have to use it, wipe it and dump it. Here's a box of bullets, it's already loaded but you never know."

Bee's eyes bulged and his mouth fell open.

"I presume you remember your firearm training."

"I do, but I'd hoped not to have to put it into practice."

"If we're lucky you won't, but we need to be prepared for anything."

Bee noticed his hand shake as he leant over and placed the gun in the glove box of his ageing Mercedes. He turned back to face his old friend.

"Right. Let's introduce you to our star witness. I'll just pull my car forward a yard to make this easier."

Jackson got out and opened the rear door of his midnight blue 5 series BMW and Bee's eyes fell on a vulnerable young Pakistani girl. She looked frail and frightened in equal measure. Gandapur wore no make-up, but her sad eyes shone brightly. She had comfortable, baggy clothes in dark colours and a black cap over a set of headphones, keeping the world out. She hopped silently between the two vehicles. Bee closed the rear door behind her.

"You need to treat her with kid gloves; she's scared out of her wits," said Jackson, as Bee joined him standing between the two cars, looking around to see if anyone else was taking an interest in them.

"As you'd expect."

"But she's determined to testify in court."

"That's good."

"Yes the guy that was shot, was a friend of hers. Well, a friend of sorts, he was the security guard in the building where she worked, and he would always speak to her in the morning. I don't think there was anything more to it than that."

Bee grimaced.

"She's not made many friends here, and he was someone who offered her a friendly face. I don't think it went any further than that, but she's got a strong sense of right and wrong and is committed to doing what she feels is her duty."

Bee nodded his approval.

"Do you know the back story?"

"No, not at all."

"Okay, well I guess you've got a minute."

Bee looked around the car park, nobody was paying them any attention. "Yes it would be good to know the background."

Jackson took a breath and launched into his story. "It seems Gandapur was working late, here in a bank in central Croydon," Jackson turned his head 90 degrees and nodded to the north. "She was trying to finish an important presentation for the following day, when Taranovsky and his gang broke into the bank and confronted the security guard on the front desk."

"Aha."

"Apparently Gandapur suffers from claustrophobia and

wouldn't use a lift if she was on her own, so this evening she had walked down the back stairs carrying her laptop and the presentation in her shoulder bag. The door at the bottom of the stairs had a glass panel in it and it was through this panel that she witnessed Taranovsky threaten the security guard and then shoot him in cold blood."

Bee's face crunched up and his eyebrows furrowed, no matter how many times he saw or heard about a murder, he couldn't accept it. "Ugh. That's not good."

"No. Evidently Taranovsky turned around like a peacock in front of his men, and that's when Gandapur got a good look at him. She stepped back from the door in horror and ran down another flight of stairs into the basement car park and hid amongst the few cars that remained, until the next morning when people began arriving for the next day."

"So, her testimony is central to the case."

"It is. The gang had cut the feed to most of the security cameras, but in their haste, they hadn't cut through all the cables and left a solitary camera in use. The CCTV footage from this unit had picked up the murder but the image of the killer was grainy and open to interpretation. The prosecution case is much stronger with a statement from a witness and Gandapur is going to deliver it. The trouble is Taranovsky knows this and is out to silence her."

"No surprise."

"Quite. The word is that he's offered one million dollars to the man, or woman, who pulls the trigger and kills this girl."

Bee whistled, "That kind of money is going to attract a lot of people." He turned to leave, he wanted to get Gandapur back to Outwood and far away from any prying eyes, but Jackson grabbed his sleeve.

"Going forward, I think we should use encoded communication."

Bee frowned. "Really?"

"If not encoded, then something discrete. Whenever we communicate start the message with a misspelling of the other's name, then leave a line and then go straight into whatever you want to say."

"Okay, so Ian becomes IAIN."

"Exactly, it's a simple mistake, no one would notice or copy. And you become SCOT."

"Got it. Okay can I go now? I'd like to get her home and settled."

"Sure, take care. But don't go directly home, take a circuitous route."

Bee frowned.

"Seriously, you never know."

"Okay. I'll drop you a mundane note tomorrow about something else and that'll be confirmation that everything's going to plan."

"Good, that's the way you need to think. I can't thank you enough for doing this. Anytime you need a hand, just ask."

The two friends shook hands and returned to their own vehicles. Back in his own car Bee passed a blanket through to Gandapur in the back seat. "I think it's best if you lay under this until we get you away from here. It won't be for long, but as you know you're in danger and there's some nasty people around here."

She took the blanket in silence and disappeared under it.

TWENTY-FOUR

BEE BEGAN THE journey and found his eyes constantly drawn to his rear-view mirror. His imagination starting gaming with his brain; any vehicle behind him for more than 500 yards became a tail, no matter what his intelligent brain said to him. The journey from Purley to Outwood is no more than 12 miles and follows a near direct north-south line along the A23, the main London to Brighton road. The first part of the trip is through the busy area of Purley, and, despite the late hour, there was a lot of traffic on the major roads. Within the initial couple of junctions Bee was convinced he was being followed when a Jeep-style vehicle accelerated through a set of lights and dropped in close behind him. The road was multi-laned at this point and Bee moved to the left and slowed slightly hoping to encourage the vehicle to pass, but it stuck tight behind him. Bee's heart rate began to climb but as he debated making a run for it the Jeep turned left. He sighed heavily and cursed himself for being so easily taken in.

With Jackson's advice bouncing around his head, Bee opted to leave the main road as soon as feasible and took the B276 across the countryside of Surrey. The road runs parallel to the principal arterial road but carries much less traffic. But this allowed his imagination to deduce that any car on this quiet road must be following him.

The narrow, winding roads were framed by high hedgerows which seemed to close in as his headlights carved a path through the darkness. The absence of streetlights should have heightened a sense of remoteness, but Bee didn't feel it. If anything, he felt trapped. The occasional small village appeared sporadically in the vast dark countryside, but the snaking roads meant Bee couldn't maintain a speed of even 30mph. He felt at the mercy of the gang who would inevitably be following him. Fields stretched into unseen horizons. He glanced up to see a distant canopy of stars, all miles away making him feel more alone than ever. He needed a companion.

"Carol. Hi, it's Bee here. I need some advice. I'm looking after a young Pakistani girl for a few days. But that's completely confidential. She needs a meal as do I. What do you recommend?"

"Don't go to McDonalds."

"No, I know that much."

"You could try a take away kebab or a curry. I guess the kebab would be quicker."

"Great, thanks. Can you do me one more favour? Call McTierney and ask him to get them. Thanks. I'll see you in the morning. Can you come over to my house and I'll brief you there?"

Bee drove over the M25 on a narrow bridge and began to feel more relaxed; there hadn't been a car in his mirror for any of the last four miles, if anything was going to happen, he believed that it would have done so by now. He slipped quietly past the Hawthorns School and reached the A25. He paused and looked both ways, there wasn't a car in sight. He turned right and headed west for a mile before turning south off the main road and re-joining his favoured minor roads. He was within reach of his beloved Outwood, and his home. He hoped that it would shine, that the quaint countryside would sparkle, the rural charm would penetrate and lift the spirits of his guest over the next few days. The wildlife was always a good bet, but then he arrived at Millers Lane on the edge of the village and saw a badger splattered at the side of the road. Then it started to rain. He made one last hope that McTierney had produced the goods in the food stakes. He felt the slightest twinge of disappointment as he pulled up outside his house.

It was eight years ago that Bee had bought the property; a secluded converted farm cottage three quarters of the way along a cul-de-sac; 500 yards beyond the nearest inhabited building and out of view of any traffic that might pass along the minor road that led out of the quiet village. It was as remote a dwelling as you could find and yet he was still within five miles of two major motorways and the town centres of Reigate and Redhill, and only 30 minutes from Gatwick airport. He leant towards his passenger and told her to stay under the blanket until he opened the front door leant of the house. He left the car, drew in a long breath, but the persistent drizzle cut it short. He scampered around the side of the house and opened the back door, before returning to collect Gandapur. She kept the blanket over her head, and he carried her solitary suitcase. McTierney was waiting for them in the kitchen, a bottle of Pilsner in his hand. "Good evening Mr Bond, and this must be the elusive Miss Moneypenny."

Bee scowled at him. "Very funny. Have you done anything about food?"

"Deliveroo is taking care of it as we speak."

"Good. And have you made a security check of the place?"

"Every room. All the windows are locked and secure. They wouldn't keep out a professional, but they'll stop most mortals, and I've set up a few tricks and triggers on the downstairs windows."

Bee nodded his approval. "Good man. Let me introduce you to Miss Lily Gandapur."

The young Pakistani stepped forward and offered her hand, McTierney shook it. "Ron McTierney, at your service." Gandapur offered a half-smile.

Bee took Gandapur on a tour of the house and left McTierney to handle the food delivery. Bee installed Gandapur in the upstairs guest bedroom, which had a southern perspective and would allow her to see any vehicle approaching along the only road that led to the house. He took her across the hallway to his study; "I'm arranging for someone to be here with you for most of the time, but I suspect there may be a few hours when you're on your own. If you like reading detective stories, there's plenty here to choose from. Philip Marlowe is my favourite." He pulled 'The Maltese Falcon' from the middle shelf and passed it to Gandapur. She smiled sweetly but didn't take it. "If you change your mind, you know where they are."

Bee stood in the centre of the room looking for inspiration; it came from an owl hooting from the woods. He stepped across to the window, outside the moon cast a silvery glow into the garden. "Outside there's a shed, a garage and a summer house." He paused, "I call them Tom, Dick and Harry," Bee wanted to laugh, but the joke was lost on Gandapur, and he slipped back into an uncomfortable silence. It seemed like a good moment to share a few house rules with her. Bee felt more relaxed talking about police matters.

"I'm sure you know the seriousness of the situation, so I don't want you to leave the house unless you're accompanied by either myself, or DS McTierney. He likes to lark about but at heart he's a good officer and he knows what he's doing." Bee felt himself questioning his own words for a second but felt comfortable with them and added a positive "mm-hmm."

Gandapur nodded her understanding and Bee decided to press on.

"I'm going to ask you to stay away from the windows. We don't get visitors here, but just in case, it would be better if you could stay upstairs as much as possible. I don't want you to make any phone calls, in case someone is tracking your phone. In fact, it's better all round if you can keep it switched off. Jackson believed that there was someone, maybe more than one person in the police force who was working for Taranovsky, the man who shot the security guard. It's safer not to use it at all. You might want to think about what you will be saying in court."

"I know who he is Inspector Bee, and I will not do anything stupid to risk my safety. I have every intention of going to that court and telling the judge that Taranovsky shot my friend. I can spend five days here not doing very much if that is what it takes."

Bee was taken aback by Gandapur's show of determination but quickly recovered himself. "Good. That's very good. I wish more witnesses were as resolute as you."

Gandapur smiled for the first time since she'd entered the

house. But Bee killed the moment.

"We do have to have an emergency plan. If you're here alone and something bad happens, someone you don't know approaches the house, call me at once. Here's my direct number, I'll call you now, so you've got my number in your phone. If you have to leave the house, you can escape across those woods. Bee pointed to the blackness out of the window. Trust me, there's open woodland for miles. If you can get in there ahead of a potential assailant you could hide for hours."

A look of fear darted across Gandapur's face. But McTierney saved the moment by calling up the stairs to announce the arrival of food. The combination of McTierney, Deliveroo and the local kebab shop provided a feast for the hungry trio and conversation was suspended for 20 minutes as they sat down in Bee's kitchen to fill their bellies.

McTierney took the lead in getting the conversation going as Bee cleared away the dinner plates. After a couple of false starts with pets and boyfriends he struck gold when he asked Lily about her family. Her mother and father were committed Muslims living in West London, but it was her brother who was to shape the discussion for the remainder of the evening.

"My brother is having an arranged, now called assisted, marriage, which will happen in Lahore next January."

"Do they still happen? Why?" asked McTierney.

Lily looked surprised by the question and took a moment to answer, "Because your parents know you better than anyone else and they can help you make a good decision. A decision which affects the rest of your life."

"But what if this person doesn't fancy you? Or worse you don't fancy this person."

Gandapur leaned away from the table to distance herself from McTierney's challenge.

"You'll have to forgive Ron; this will be an alien concept to him."

Gandapur winced at the idea, "No problem. Not many people without faith believe, and I suspect Ron is not close to his family."

It was McTierney's turn to be upset. He swallowed hard, "My family's fine but I don't need them to manage my life for me. I can find a partner for myself perfectly well, thank you."

"Family is not a good topic for this household; we've both experienced losses," said Scott quietly.

"Oh, I'm sorry." Gandapur lowered her gaze.

Ron wasn't to be subdued; "I can't get my head around the idea of agreeing to marry someone you've never met. It's a recipe for disaster. You need to know the person you're marrying. A 'try before you buy', if you like. It makes sense for both parties."

Gandapur rose to the challenge, "Oh no. Not at all. Do you know the divorce rate for western marriages?" She didn't wait for an answer. "It's 55%; more than half. But for arranged marriages it's 6%. You couldn't have a bigger contrast."

"But what about love? I can't believe I'm saying this, but you need a spark, a connection. Have you watched 'Four Weddings and a Funeral', or any romantic movie for that matter?"

Gandapur smiled at the idea, "Yes I have seen the film. I've lived in the UK all my life; I'm not from another planet you know. I agree that love is important, but you don't have to start with it. It's more important to be sure you can find it and it lasts."

McTierney shook his head, "So my friend Dean Grant is wasting all his money working through Tinder."

"He is. He won't find happiness there."

It was McTierney's turn to smile, "He might disagree with you on that, but I'll accept that it doesn't seem to last."

Bee attempted to bring the discussion to a conclusion; "Maybe we can all agree that human beings are the most adaptable species on the planet."

Both Gandapur and McTierney looked perplexed at the sudden change of direction for the conversation. Bee attempted to keep it going.

"Look at the different places we live and the challenges we are able to overcome."

Bee had lost his audience, and a silence wrapped itself around the trio.

"It's been an exhausting night; I think I'll go to bed now if that's alright."

"Sure. We'll be here all night, and I'll be here in the morning. Let me show you the upstairs bathroom."

When they reached the top of the stairs, Gandapur turned to Bee, "Thank you for looking after me tonight. You've been very kind."

"No problem. I fear I should apologise for Ron."

"That's okay. Your little friend is so funny. Is he for real?"

Bee smiled, "He means well, he just can't help some of the things he says."

When Bee returned back downstairs he found McTierney pouring himself a large whisky.

"How come she gets the upstairs room? I've been here for four years and haven't had a sniff of getting upstairs."

Bee looked upset, "She's a priority, and it's safer upstairs, if anything does happen." He looked over his shoulder to ensure that they were not being overheard. "Then you are our first line of defence."

"Thanks a bunch."

"You're welcome. Now, before you have too much to drink, there's been some developments tonight I want to share."

Bee recounted his conversation with Jackson.

McTierney's eyes bulged. "Shit, so now there's a thousand bounty hunters out there, all looking to make a fast million dollars and to counter that all we have is a little gun each."

"That's right, and I think we'll do well to get through this without using them."

TWENTY-FIVE

BEE WAS ALWAYS an early riser but this morning his phoned beeped before he'd made it downstairs. He looked at the screen then frowned in horror as he read the message; 'SCOT, Keep your head down the boss is steaming about the apparent loss of Lily Gandapor. I'm denying all knowledge, but he knows I visited her yesterday. Stay safe.'

Bee wondered about the wisdom of the plan Jackson had proposed. Maybe he should have tried to dissuade his friend, but it was too late now. Coming on top of his deception of Lisa Springfield, Bee began to worry if he'd taken on too much.

McTierney sauntered into the kitchen and began his usual routine; it took him a couple of minutes to notice that Bee was sitting quietly glued to his mobile screen. "You alright? Pass the milk."

Bee didn't respond. McTierney walked around and stood in front of him. "Boo"

Slowly Bee lifted his head, "I don't like the way this case is developing."

"Don't worry. Miss Star Witness will be gone in a few days, and Carol Bishop will never know you had another woman stay over in your house."

Bee blinked twice, "What?"

"I said Carol need never know that you've been entertaining behind her back."

"Is that all your brain ever thinks about?"

"No. Beer, football, and the occasional piece of police work sneaks in when I'm not paying attention."

Bee shook his head. "Just so we're clear, Carol Bishop knows that Gandapur is staying here for a few days. In fact, she's on her way over here now to take the morning shift. I'll cover the afternoon shift, and I'll need you to work from here for some of tomorrow."

McTierney smiled to himself, "I suppose I could make myself available tomorrow afternoon. Will you tolerate our guest being chaperoned in The Bell?"

Bee gave him a bitter smile.

"Oh well. Worth a try."

McTierney finished his breakfast and headed off to the Reigate station, passing Carol Bishop on the long drive leading to the house. Gandapur joined the party in the kitchen and Bee introduced the two ladies over the first of many cups of coffee. The two women bonded over Asian food and Bee quickly felt unnecessary, which suited him perfectly, as it enabled him to drift off to his police laptop. He returned 20 minutes later to find them engrossed in a discussion over spices and metaphorically patted himself on the back for a good decision.

"Ladies, apologies for the interruption, but I need to leave." He turned to Bishop, "Looks like Babylon has been identified as arriving at Gatwick airport last Thursday and is now being held at Bromley police station."

"No worries, I brought my laptop. I've got plenty of work to do checking on the list of Wembley attendees and the Guildford friends of Itzkowitz. Good luck with our American friend."

★ ★ ★

MCTIERNEY HAD ONLY been at his desk for 20 minutes when he had a phone call from Maria on reception. He felt it was time for a coffee so set off downstairs to collect the package she told him had arrived. A large rectangular cardboard box sat across the desk looking like it might topple over at any moment.

"Expecting a present? Somebody must love you; this came from a florist."

McTierney shrugged and spun the box around to read the label, 'FAO DS Ron McTierney.

"It's not my birthday until November," he joked as he pulled at the Sellotape holding the box together. He lifted the lid and froze. Maria was suddenly aware of the silence and abandoned her laptop. She stood up and walked around to the front of the desk and took a sharp intake of breath. Inside the box was a wreath in the shape of a cross. A card sat in the middle of the white lilies. It read, 'Goodbye to your career.'

Maria slammed her hand over her mouth as her eyes bulged. Slowly she recovered herself and turned to McTierney; "My God. What have you done?"

McTierney took a moment to reply. "Nothing. Well, nothing much."

His brain kicked into gear, "Who delivered this? Do you have a name or a contact of some sort?"

Maria was back in the moment; she returned to her chair and scanned her visitors book. The log had been signed by

Joe the Florist. She cursed herself for not being diligent. "Wait, I was intrigued by the delivery, and I watched the guy leave; he got into a white van. I'm sure it was a Willows van. That's the florist on West Street in Reigate, on the corner."

"I know it. Look, can you hide these? Bee knows what's happening, but the evil queen is not yet on board and now isn't the time to get her up to speed. I'm going to do some shopping in Reigate. I shouldn't be too long. If Bee turns up, you can brief him."

★ ★ ★

BEE SLIPPED INTO his Mercedes and was about to leave when his mobile pinged with a text message. He leant across the soft leather seat and grabbed the phone, but didn't like the message.

SCOTT, We need to talk. Can you meet me in the car park of Coulsdon South train station at midnight tonight? Do you know it?

The correct spelling of his name was an obvious red flag; it wasn't the kind of mistake Jackson would have made. But what did it mean? Had Jackson lost his phone or was it something more significant? He needed time to think about it, the drive to Bromley would help.

★ ★ ★

MCTIERNEY PARKED IN the small car park on Upper West Street and walked the 100 yards south to Willows Florists. The florist shop in mid-summer was alive with vibrant colours and sweet fragrances. Buckets of sunflowers, zinnias, and daisies lined the glass front of the store. McTierney stepped inside, a small bell rang, the air was heavy with the scent of roses. Bouquets of wildflowers wrapped in brown paper lay on the counter, while an assistant was busy preparing another.

McTierney decided to tread gently, given the sensitive nature of the case and his growing sense of insecurity over the path they were following. He flashed his badge, "Good morning, we had a delivery at the police station this morning, a wreath delivered to DS McTierney. Could you tell me if it came from here?"

The lady stopped her arrangement and bobbed down below the desk to search for their order pad. She flicked it open and brushed back a few pages. "I don't recall it; certainly, I didn't create it, but I wasn't here yesterday."

McTierney waited while she continued to talk and search.

"Ah, here we go. Yes. It was a call-on job from Croydon."

"What does that mean?"

"It means the customer visited a store in Croydon to place the order and they passed it on to us."

"Do you have the name of the original customer?"

"No, sorry."

"How about the shop in Croydon?"

"Yes, I can give you that. Shall I write it down?"

McTierney left with the name scrawled on the back of a business card. All roads seemed to lead to Croydon.

★ ★ ★

BEE ARRIVED AT Bromley police station convinced that the

New York connection would prove to be a red herring. But it needed to be investigated. The Bromley police had kept Babylon in a small interview room and left him to stew while Bee made his way east. As soon as Bee entered the room Babylon was on his feet to remonstrate with his detention. Bee assured him that it was a matter of routine and that if he answered a few questions he could be released that day. This appeared to calm the American.

Bee asked the standard questions about when Babylon had last seen Itzkowitz, when they had last had contact, what was the nature of their relationship and received the expected answers. He made a few notes and brought the investigation up to the present day. What was Babylon doing in the UK? – He had come to England to visit the grave of his grandmother – that would be easy to verify. How long was he staying? – Until the following weekend – again easy to verify and in fact Babylon showed him a Eurostar ticket to Paris. Had he been in contact with Itzkowitz since arriving in the UK? – No – not quite so easy to verify, but Babylon was prepared to share his mobile number and that would allow Bishop to make some basic checks. Could Babylon account for his movements on Saturday afternoon? – Maybe. He'd been sightseeing in London. Had been in Madame Tussauds museum in Marylebone during the afternoon – there should be some CCTV of visitors entering the building, something else Bishop could verify.

Bee had an uneasy feeling, Babylon had answers for every question, and perhaps a little bit too detailed. He wondered if he'd spent his time in the interview room preparing an alibi. But it wasn't going to be easy to hold him in the cells any longer. His thought process was interrupted by Babylon getting agitated.

"What's going on brother? Why am I being held?"

Bee took a sharp intake of breath and decided to tell him the truth. "Fran Itzkowitz, who you obviously know from your time in America, is missing and has been missing now for nearly a week. We're worried about what's happened to her. Your presence here in England at the time of her disappearance could be a coincidence or it could implicate you in her disappearance. Do you have any comment to make?"

Babylon hung his head, then slowly lifted it with a huge grin spreading across his face. "Ha! That'll teach the bitch! You don't expect me to feel sorry for her do you?"

Bee looked blank.

"Do you know what she did to Little Jimmy in New York? She murdered him. Cold blood, no justification. If someone's taken out that bitch, then that's karma." The smirk stayed fixed across his face, and he started to laugh heartily.

Bee pressed his lips together and his features tightened, "If you don't mind, this isn't a joke."

Babylon stopped laughing, but stared directly into Bee's eyes, "Oh it is. It really is. You've just made my day, my week, my year. Do you know what that bitch is responsible for? I hope you find her. In a ditch!"

"Before you get too excited, you're a suspect."

"Get real. I wouldn't know where to find her." Babylon sat up in his chair, crossed his arms and drilled his eyes into Bee's. "Prove it."

Bee knew he couldn't prove a thing. As much as he didn't like the American, he knew he'd have to release him.

"I'm going to let you go, but I want to know where you're staying while you're in England."

Babylon snorted loudly and stood up to leave, pushing his chair back across the floor, "I'll be on the Old Kent Road if you need me."

★ ★ ★

MCTIERNEY HAD THE same sense of uselessness as he drove to Croydon. He found the florist, spoke to a pleasant young lady behind the counter who told him precisely nothing. They'd taken the booking first thing that morning, a nondescript man of average build and average height had come into the shop, made the request and paid in cash. To cap it all they didn't have an in-store security camera that could give McTierney an image of the customer. The girl finished by adding her condolences to whatever loss he was suffering. McTierney stomped away and headed back to Reigate.

But if Bee and McTierney felt they had had bad mornings, the news that greeted them at the Reigate station made their afternoon a thousand times worse.

TWENTY-SIX

BEE ARRIVED AT the station, parked at the back, next to McTierney's car and headed into the old building, eager to catch up with his colleague. But he didn't expect to find him standing at reception. He screwed up his face in surprise, but something about McTierney's appearance looked wrong. He took a step forward but felt his attention drawn to the large TV screen on the far wall, which was tuned into Sky News. A red banner was running across the bottom of the screen repeating the words 'police officer found dead'.

Bee's mouth fell open, and he thrust out an arm towards the desk as McTierney walked towards him. His mind started to race, churning through the information that was crashing into it. "Oh no. Not Itzkowitz. I should have saved her. I should have found her."

McTierney reached him, grabbed his arm and led him to a chair. "No, it's not Fran. It's not her. Come sit down." He turned his head to Maria, "Can you get him some water?"

Bee sat down but instantly wanted to stand up again as his brain sent confused messages to his limbs. "Not Fran? But the news, it says police officer found dead. I must go and investigate. I must go to the scene. Where's Kelly? Call Kelly."

McTierney pushed him back down in the chair. "Sit

down. You need to stay here. It's not Fran."

"Not Fran?" Bee's eyes were bulging and his eyes blinked rapidly as he tried to process what he was hearing, "But it says so on the screen." He tried to push his arm up towards the TV screen, but McTierney pulled it back. Then he moved to stand directly in front of Bee, he grabbed his shoulders and shook them.

"Listen to me. It's not Fran. It's…" He paused, not sure how to say what had to be said. "It's DI Jackson. Your friend from Croydon. He's been found shot dead at a deserted warehouse on the edge of Croydon."

Bee slumped back in the chair and fell motionless for a few seconds then exploded, "What?"

McTierney pushed him back into the chair, "Keep it together. I know he was your friend, but we can't let Springfield know what's been going on."

Bee stared back at him, his hand slipped up and covered his mouth, then dropped away. He opened his mouth to speak, but no words appeared. His eyes darted between Maria, the TV and McTierney. "But I only saw him last night." His voice warbled with emotion.

McTierney took his hand, "I know. I know."

Tears began to fill Bee's eyes, "I can't believe this. I just can't believe it. Who would do this and why? Ian was a good man."

McTierney gave his colleague a knowing look, but Bee was too distracted to notice. "I think we can guess why this happened, even if we don't yet know who. The only good news here is that it shows they're rattled. Jackson must have been on to something."

Bee looked up through tearful eyes, "But he would have

told me."

"Maybe he didn't have the opportunity."

Bee's eyes shot up to meet McTierney's then he slumped back in his chair and pushed his hand into his chest, "Jackson was smart, he would've been careful who he trusted. This is terrible. I can't believe it."

McTierney looked left and right to check there was no one watching them apart from Maria, then slapped Bee around the face, "Sorry, boss, but we need to go. The evil queen was looking for you earlier and Kelly's left an interesting report on your desk."

Bee shot him a glance. McTierney smiled, "Yeah, I know, but I thought it might be important, so I opened it."

The forensic report that McTierney had referred to lay in a confidential envelope on Bee's desk. He lifted the packet and turned to McTierney, "This one." McTierney answered with a nod.

Kelly had examined the chocolate wrapper they found at the industrial estate but was unable to link it to Itzkowitz. He had slightly more information on the tracks they had found. The tyres were 150mm wide and commonly found on high performance cars. Since the car had been reversed onto the mud Kelly had been able to identify the tracks of all four tyres independently. The most interesting detail was that the driver's side rear tyre was excessively worn; the tread was bordering on 3mm, and therefore due for replacement. All four tyres had the same tread pattern and were made by Goodyear.

Bee looked unimpressed and tossed the envelope back on the desk.

"Turn it over, the next page is the best bit."

Bee looked like he couldn't care less but did as McTierney suggested. Kelly had also found time to examine the van of Jake Rivers, and it was these results which had excited McTierney. In the back of the van there were small traces of Itzkowitz's blood. Not enough to suggest she'd lost a lot of blood there, but definitely she'd been in the back of the van.

"That could be useful," said Bee.

"You're telling me. Let's get a warrant for his arrest and go pick up the bastard. I'm looking forward to wiping the smile off his smug face."

Bee offered a weak smile at his colleague but before they could get organised, Chief Superintendent Springfield appeared at the far side of the office and marched across the space. McTierney glanced over to check if Bee was composed and ready. Bee took a deep breath and nodded back to his colleague.

"You'll have read the news." Springfield ignored McTierney and addressed her question directly to Bee.

"Yes Ma'am."

"Maria informed me that DI Jackson was a friend of yours. You have my condolences inspector."

"Thank you." Bee paused momentarily, but he was back in the game. "Do you know anything about the circumstances of his death?"

"No, I don't."

Bee flexed his fingers and looked ready to speak but Springfield closed him down. "It's not our case, I know he was a friend but leave it alone. The Met have plenty of resources to investigate this. We have enough to do right now." She turned to share this message with McTierney. "Are we clear?"

Both officers muttered a response.

"Good. Of course, this does raise the stakes for our missing officer."

Bee nodded, but Springfield held up her hand to stop him speaking. "People are making links between the disappearance of Itzkowitz and the death of Jackson. Do you think it's credible?"

Bee tilted his head to think; "Unlikely, but not impossible."

"What makes you say that?"

Bee shrugged his shoulders, "One is dead, one is missing. I'm not aware that they knew each other, so any connection is tenuous."

Springfield pursed her lips and narrowed her eyes, suggesting that Bee had given the wrong answer. "Maybe we just haven't found the body yet. That's how Assistant Chief Constable Raven is thinking, and much as it pains me to contemplate the loss of one of our own, I tend to agree with him."

"I don't think we should be giving up on Itzkowitz. There's no evidence to suggest she's dead."

McTierney leant towards the conversation, eager to speak, but bit his tongue.

"And no evidence to suggest she's alive." Springfield lifted her volume, then turned around to ensure they were alone. "If I'm not very much mistaken we don't have any idea where she might be."

Bee dropped his head, "No Ma'am."

McTierney stood behind the chief superintendent, and he couldn't see Bee's face, but he knew from the tone of voice that he would be frowning, but then that was Bee's default look. A short silence developed, before Springfield brought their discussion to a close, "The assistant chief constable and the Met police commissioner are holding a senior heads meeting tomorrow. I've been invited to join them in London. Anything I should know before I attend?"

This was another question that would go by unanswered.

Springfield turned and marched away leaving Bee and McTierney standing by their desks. As she disappeared out of sight, McTierney let out a sigh of relief. "If the evil queen is out tomorrow, that'll make it easier for all of us to be out of here."

Bee looked up and shrugged his shoulders, "Maybe, but we need to find Itzkowitz, and I'd like to know what happened to Jackson. This case is spiralling out of control."

"Speaking of Jackson, now he's gone. What happens to Gandapur? Do you think we should tell Jackson's boss that we've got her?"

Bee pinched his lower lip. "The trouble is, we don't know which side he's on. Jackson was convinced that there's a mole in the Croydon team, but he didn't know who, and we certainly don't. If we reveal our hand, we could be handing Gandapur over to the very bad guys, we're trying to protect her from."

"We can't keep her indefinitely."

"No, but let's see how things play out over the next couple of days. An opportunity might present itself."

"Fair enough, it's not like we don't have enough to do. By the way when I was out I had a phone call."

Bee raised his eyebrows.

"It wasn't the lottery people, far from it. The voice was male yet sounded disguised, but the message was crystal clear.

It said 'you nicked the concert tickets from my friend's house. That's theft. A crime. Your career as a copper is over. You'll go to jail, and you know what happens to coppers in prison, especially bent coppers.' McTierney looked ashen as he recounted the call. "Then he finished with a laugh and said, 'you're mine'."

Bee stared back at his partner in stunned silence.

"I don't mind telling you, I'm getting scared."

"You're not the only one."

"And that's not all?"

"There's more." Bee's eyes were on stalks.

"Not long after the call, I received a text." McTierney opened his mobile and passed it across to Bee who read it aloud. "Why is L still alive? Don't fail me you won't like the happening. I warned you. You have three days to complete your task, or you lose another friend."

"Do you think they mean Itzkowitz?"

McTierney shrugged his shoulders. "That would fit. But it kind of implies that Jackson was my friend, and yet I'd only met him the once."

"Hmm," Bee went to hand the phone back to McTierney, but pulled it back and read the text again. "Yes it says another friend. Maybe the sender thought the text was coming to me?"

"Or maybe they simply didn't know that Jackson and I weren't friends."

"Possible. The other point about this message is the use of the phrase, you won't like the happening, that's strange English. I don't think our sender is a native English speaker. One of the other texts had a misspelling didn't it."

"Taranovsky isn't English, and he knows about the concert tickets so he could be responsible for both messages. But that doesn't fit with Itzkowitz's blood being in Rivers's van."

"No. If Rivers has killed her, why is Taranovsky threatening to kill her?"

The two men exchanged puzzled looks, before Bee spoke again. "You go rattle Rivers' cage, while I focus on our Russian friend. He feels like our best lead, even though he's in jail at the moment."

The two detectives contemplated the idea, before Bee spoke, "One way or another I think we're getting closer to the end game."

TWENTY-SEVEN

THE SUN HAD dipped, and the heat was fading from the day, but it would soon be replaced by heat from a different source, the food, and later the conversation. As the two detectives parked their cars outside Bee's house and walked towards the front door, Bee grabbed McTierney's sleeve, "Let's not tell Gandapur about the loss of Jackson. It'll only worry her."

"Sure. By the way, it worries the shit out of me."

"And me too."

Bee pushed open his front door and was hit by a tsunami of cooking smells. The aroma of a hot, spicy dish had escaped from the kitchen and was waiting to ambush them in the hallway. A sharp peppery kick tingled their noses. The two men exchanged happy smiles. McTierney spoke first, "Excellent, a curry, I only hope there's cold beer in the fridge."

Bee smiled, "Ever since you moved in, cool beer in the fridge is the one staple in my kitchen."

"And you say I never do anything for you."

"You're late," shouted Carol Bishop from the kitchen. "We nearly gave up on you and started without you."

Ron and Scott burst into the kitchen, "Sorry," said Scott, "We got stuck at work. You know how it is."

Carol smiled sympathetically. "No worries, you're here now and we've agreed there's to be no work talk tonight."

"Suits me," said Ron, as he pulled open the fridge and retrieved a bottle of Budweiser. He waggled one in the direction of Scott who reached across and took it. "What's for dinner?"

Carol reached across and grabbed Lily's hand, "This wonderful young lady has been teaching me to cook, so this is her treat. I think it's intended to be a thank you, but I'll let Lily explain it to you." Carol pulled Lily into the centre of the room and nudged her to speak.

Lily smiled weakly, then took a breath. "Yes, Carol is right. This is my thank you to you two gentlemen for taking care of me and welcoming me into your home."

"No worries, you're welcome," said Ron, smirking and taking a swig from his bottle.

Scott glared across the room at him, "You're very welcome Lily. I think I should be thanking you for putting up with Ron. Now what have you prepared for us?"

"It's called Nihari, I guess it's the national dish of Pakistan, a bit like your roast beef or fish and chips." She paused and looked at Carol, who encouraged her with her eyes.

"In simple terms it's a meat stew made with caramelised onions, tomatoes and a few other vegetables. I took a few from your vegetable basket in the kitchen, some peppers and a carrot, I hope you don't mind."

"Sounds like any other curry," said Ron.

"Sorry, ignore him. He's a neanderthal. It sounds extraordinary. How do you cook it?" asked Scott.

Lily blushed, "Oh, it's quite easy. It's thickened with some flour, and doesn't take long, although you should cook it slowly to allow the flavours to develop from the bones. I could teach you."

"Yes, I'd like that." Scott smiled across the room, "Even more so if you could teach Ron, but we probably don't have the time."

Ron was busy searching for a second beer from the fridge and allowed the comment to pass.

Lily continued "Although this one is made with lamb shank, and you should keep the bones in while you cook. Or you could change that to beef if you prefer it, and you can add whichever spices you prefer. I added turmeric powder, coriander, garlic paste and chilli powder. Nutmeg is good if you have it."

"I'll put it on the shopping list."

Lily offered a half smile, "It's served with hot naan bread straight from the oven and some rice. Again, I just took the rice from the kitchen, but I prefer brown rice because it contains the whole grain and has more fibre and is more nutritious for you, and I think is better for your blood."

Carol nodded her approval.

"To finish it off, I've served it with lemon slices, chopped green chillies and chopped ginger."

"It sounds fabulous. It was very kind of you to do this."

Lily offered a half curtsey.

"I think we should get stuck in, see what this curry tastes like," said Ron.

The four friends sat down in the dining room where Carol had set the table. Scott went to find a bottle of wine; Ron stayed with his beer, while Scott and Carol opened an Australian Shiraz, but Lily drank sparkling water. Ron took a large mouthful of the meat but an explosion of flavours in his mouth sent him reaching for Lily's water. "Wooah!" He waved his hand in front of his mouth. Sorry, I'll get you a new glass."

Scott was a little more circumspect with his fork, nodded his approval across the table; "It's delicious. I expect this is especially popular at the end of Ramadan."

Lily smiled at his understanding. "You know a lot about our culture Scott."

"Not really, I'm ashamed to say. Just a few headlines."

Dinner concluded with a chorus of approval for the meal and Scott suggested that they all move to the lounge to relax. Scott was careful to position himself in a single armchair where he leant back with his wine glass and felt himself relaxing for the first time that day. Ron took on the role of party entertainer and opened with one of his jokes.

"A couple of weeks ago I went sea fishing with a friend of mine. After six hours we'd only caught one small flat fish each. He says, 'I think we should cook one of these for dinner.'

'Fine,' I said, 'Your plaice or mine'?"

The joke fell flatter than either of the fish, but Ron wasn't perturbed. "I'm reading a book on anti-gravity – I can't put it down!"

This time Carol smirked, "I like that. I know I shouldn't but it's quite clever. For you!"

"Don't say anything remotely positive, you'll only encourage him," cautioned Scott.

But the advice came too late, Ron was on a roll, "I've just read a book, yes another book, this one was about Stockholm Syndrome. It was pretty bad at first but by the end I really liked it."

"Okay, that'll do. Not only are the jokes bad, but I can't relate to the idea of you reading books."

Ron offered a look of mock disappointment, but bounced back with an open question, "Instead of books, let's talk films; they're so much better than books anyway. Lily, what's your favourite film?"

Lily looked surprised to be asked a direct question but was determined to join in with the games. She tilted her head and bit her bottom lip, "Not sure. I do like a love story, so maybe 'Titanic'. Is that okay?"

"Oh yes, that was good," added Carol. "Kate Winslet was wonderful and she's in my favourite too. I'd pick 'The Holiday'. I know it's supposed to be a Christmas film, but it's a feel-good movie that picks me up any time."

"It would certainly feel good to be squeezed in between Kate Winslet and Cameron Diaz."

"Oh, you have to ruin everything," said Carol, throwing a mock slap in Ron's direction. He grinned in reply.

"Come on then, what's your favourite? Something with Angelina Jolie in it, I expect."

Ron screwed up his nose, "No she doesn't do it for me."

"I bet she's jumping for joy in relief," said Carol, turning to Lily and giggling with her.

"If you want to know, I'd choose 'Pulp Fiction', although 'Snatch' is a close second."

There was a general murmur of approval amongst the friends and then their eyes moved to focus on Scott. "And what about you inspector?"

"Oh, you don't want to ask him; it'll be some black and white detective caper featuring Sherlock Holmes or, who's that guy you like?"

"Philip Marlowe," said Scott hesitantly.

"Yeah him, there must be dozens of films featuring him," dismissed Ron.

Scott grimaced and took his time to answer. "Well, I do like a good detective movie, so I can happily watch Marlowe and most of the old Hitchcock movies are good."

"Get off the fence and make a decision," moaned Ron.

Scott held up his hand to hold off the criticism, "Okay, if I'm only allowed one choice, then it would probably be 'Avatar'."

"'Avatar?'" chorused Carol and Ron.

"What kind of film is that?" challenged Ron.

"A science fiction epic, a 3D masterpiece, visually stunning and the winner of three Oscars. Not that any of you lot would appreciate it."

With the evening gaining momentum, Carol suggested they introduce Lily to an English tradition, a game of Scrabble. Scott held his breath fearful that Lily may take offence but Ron, who was always competitive approved the idea before anyone could dismiss it. "I'll get it," said Carol, "I saw it this afternoon, when us girls were chatting." Scott waved his hand in acquiescence and got up to clear some space on the dining room table.

Ron began and after much delay he produced the word Tart.

Scott winced.

"What kind of tart?" asked Carol. "It's nice to know what you have in mind when you choose a word," she added.

Scott thought the game would disintegrate before it had begun.

"An apple tart," said Ron, making sure he caught Scott's eye.

"Very good," said Carol, "I like a tart."

Scott squirmed in his chair before he produced Trained, Carol played Bottom, and after careful consideration, Lily added Cow. Ron's second word was Bed and Carol asked, "Who's in the bed, Ron?"

Scott thought Carol must have had too much wine and waited for Ron to drag the conversation into a storm, but he offered a conservative reply of "I am. And I'm on my own." Scott breathed a sigh of relief. Maybe the evening would be enjoyable after all. He continued with Grain, Carol played Amber and Lily, after much thought placed, Qulurm.

"What's Qulurm?" asked Ron.

"It's a fruit," said Lily, to a sea of blank faces.

Scott was the first to respond, "Yes I believe it's a cross between a quince and a plum."

Ron jerked his head back and stared at Scott, who ignored him and continued to tot up the score. "And that's a Q on a triple letter score. You've got 36, Lily. Well done."

Ron looked distracted and struggled to make his third word, settling eventually on Rat. "Sorry it's rubbish I know, but I've got terrible letters."

"Not too bad," said Scott, who had found himself playing UN peacekeeper, "And a double word score. That gives you 6." He tried not to smirk, as Carol lapsed into a coughing fit.

Then Scott took the T from rat to create Truffle. Carol used the L of truffle to make Lean and Lily used the N of lean to form Zenoxiac. Another silence fell on the board, but Scott was determined to keep the mood jolly.

"Very good," said Scott, "X on a double letter score is 16, so your word total is 34, Z on a treble word score, 34 times 3 is 102, C also on a treble word score, 102 times 3 is 306, 50 bonus for using all your letters, that makes a grand total of 356. I've never seen such a score before, that's amazing."

Lily twisted in her seat, "Sorry, I guess it's what you call 'starters luck', is that right?"

Ron glared across the table and shook his head in disbelief. "What the hell is Zenoxiac supposed to mean when it's at home? Do we have a dictionary in the house?"

Carol touched her nose and looked at the ceiling, "I think it means containing foreign bodies, if I'm not mistaken."

Ron screwed up his face, "Phhw. How would you use it in a sentence?"

Scott chipped in, "If your beer was found to contain a dead mouse, I might say, Look out Ron, that beer's very zenoxiac."

"That would be such bad luck," said Lily.

"Yes, but he'd still drink it," added Carol.

Ron shook his head in disbelief.

"Shall we have a recap of the scores?" said Scott. He didn't wait for a response. "Lily is out in front with 425, I've managed 127, Carol is close behind on 119 and Ron is bringing up the rear on 32."

"Oh, dear Ron. I thought you'd be good at this game," said Carol.

Ron blew out a deep breath, "Normally, I am."

But the rest of his explanation was lost in a chorus of jeers.

"Sorry I can't keep this going any longer," Carol's face exploded with laughter.

Ron looked shocked, his head swivelled from Carol to Lily to Scott, but everyone was giggling, "What's going on?"

he demanded.

But nobody could reply as the room erupted with laughter. Eventually Scott pulled himself together, took a sip of wine, "Didn't you notice, you were being set up?"

Ron stared back at him blankly.

"None of Lily's words are admissible and when you left the room to do your security check around the house at the start of the game, Carol hand-picked your starting letters."

Ron acted out being hurt, "I used to like you," he said.

Scott continued his explanation, "Carol wanted to set you up with the letters to spell out 'wank' just to see if you'd use them."

Ron was incredulous, but Carol was lost in fits of giggles.

"You can thank me for restricting it to 'tart'."

"Oh yes, you've been a big help here. When did you know about this jape?"

"They briefed me during one of your many trips to the beer fridge."

Finally, Carol composed herself. "Sorry Ron. We thought of the idea this afternoon, when we were looking around the house and I was describing you to Lily. I did say you are someone who always likes a joke."

Soon afterwards Carol took a taxi home, Lily retired to bed and Scott and Ron began tidying up the kitchen.

"A good night tonight, but let's have a quick chat in the morning about what we're going to do tomorrow. We need a plan to tackle the threats you've been receiving."

"Sure. It's heating up a bit at the moment."

Scott nodded. "Yes, I'd like to think that Lily's hot dish is the only heat I'll be facing for the next five days, but somehow I doubt it."

TWENTY-EIGHT

As Bee came down the stairs he thought he could hear a conversation taking place in the kitchen. McTierney's door was firmly closed, and the sound of a snore told him that McTierney was still asleep, so he wondered, who could Gandapur be talking to? He tiptoed back upstairs to collect the gun Jackson had given him and slowly pushed open the kitchen door.

Gandapur was standing in a dressing gown talking to the kettle. She turned her head, smiled and offered him a coffee. Bee nodded his agreement and then looked for somewhere to stow his gun. Not finding anywhere suitable he laid it on the counter next to the toaster.

"Be careful. Don't point the gun at Tommy."

Bee looked perplexed.

"Tommy the toaster," said Gandapur, as if that explained everything.

Bee grinned, "You've given names to some of the appliances."

"I have. They work better when they have a name. Kevin will boil sooner now he feels he's loved."

A knowing smile played on Bee's lips. "I do the same."

Gandapur's face lit up with his response.

"But I don't think McTierney would understand."

Gandapur shook her head; the warm glow stayed on her face.

"How long have you been giving names to things?" he asked.

"Pretty much all of my life," she said. "I think it started with teddy bears and just grew from there."

Bee smiled, "Yes, Disney has a lot to answer for."

The pair traded notes on which appliances deserved names, which functioned better with a name, and which had no right to ever be christened. They moved to the kitchen window and stood admiring the garden. "It's beautiful," said Lily. "On days like these, you notice how colourful life can be. You look out here and it's every colour of the rainbow. It's never just green and brown."

Bee chuckled in agreement and then confessed to naming many of his garden plants and started to point to a few; Isaac the apple tree, Bertie the bird feeder, and a set of solar lights named after the Spice Girls.

Gandapur clapped her hands as she joined in, "Isaac after Sir Isaac Newton. Oh, that's so clever."

Bee smiled indulgently and Gandapur enthused excitedly when he explained that he often felt guilty about growing his own carrots when harvest time came around and he had to pull them from the ground. "It's a good job I'm not a farmer with a family to feed; I'd never be able to wring the neck of a chicken, or worse, fatten up a turkey for Christmas."

"I think you should become a Muslim; you have so many beliefs that would fit."

"I don't believe in any God," he said puncturing the atmosphere.

Gandapur screwed up her face and Bee felt compelled to

offer an explanation. "It's partly the science behind it and how the earth was created. I would like to have faith in something or someone, but there's just too much trouble and suffering in the world for me to believe that there could be any positive force out there orchestrating what happens." He paused hoping that Gandapur would meet him halfway, but she didn't. "I mean there's so much rage and anger in the world, and it's getting worse by the day."

"Is that why you're a policeman? To try to make the world better?"

"A bit. I do want to make the world better, but I'm under no illusion that I can make a significant difference. I'm not Superman."

Gandapur laughed.

"But I do hope that I can make a major difference to a few people. You are a case in point. If I can keep you safe, get you to the court next week and you can testify, that would be a good thing."

A soft smile played across Gandapur's face, "That's so sweet," she said, reaching up as if to kiss Bee on the cheek, but at that moment McTierney stepped into the kitchen.

"Oi, oi! What's going on here? Breakfast for two?"

Gandapur recoiled away from Bee who looked flustered. His eyes scanned the room looking for an escape. But he picked the wrong exit. "We were just talking about the phenomenon of Disneyism."

"The what?" McTierney frowned as he reached for a mug.

"The official name is anthropomorphism; it's where people give names to physical items and create personalities for them. It happens all the time in Disney films, hence the slang phrase. So, one might call the toaster, Timmy and tell him what had happened to you during the day."

McTierney shook his head in disgust. "Surely not."

"It happens. I used to think it was just Tom Hanks and me, so I'm relieved to find someone else, Lily, who does it."

Gandapur offered a weak smile.

"That's not a club to be proud of," said McTierney pouring hot water from Kevin the kettle.

Bee kept digging. "I frequently curse the electric toothbrush for having no charge left when I want to clean my teeth. three weeks ago, I berated the pot plant in the lounge, calling it a 'lazy sod' because it had hardly grown since I'd bought it two months ago."

McTierney shook his head and disappeared off for a shower, leaving Bee to tell Gandapur about a time last summer, when he struck up a friendship with a blackbird in his garden.

"Every day when I opened the back door I would hear the blackbird singing and spot him sitting in the upper branches of a tree just over the back fence." He moved to the window and pointed to the tree. "I convinced myself that he would appear whenever I entered the garden and, if he wasn't there, I would make a sound that didn't resemble a bird but, as far as I was concerned, represented a code known only to him and me, and he'd invariably appear."

McTierney was loitering by the kitchen door. "No. Stop. You shouldn't be having this conversation. For Christ sake's you're a detective inspector. People look up to you."

Bee looked a little crestfallen and McTierney wandered off.

"I think it's fine," said Gandapur soothingly.

Bee offered a weak smile, "Yes. McTierney's a great guy to have around, but he sees the world through blinkered glasses. It's his way or no way. He doesn't understand my autism at all. Social conventions can be hard for autistic people to understand, so practising with a blackbird can be a great help. Over the last few years, I have become more reclusive because I have been able to, but I recognise that it isn't always good for me."

"Personally, I think you're doing brilliantly. I feel safe and content here, and that doesn't happen often."

McTierney returned to the kitchen and went straight into practical mode, "Who's working today and who's babysitting?" He turned to Gandapur. "No offence."

"None taken," she replied.

Bee frowned at him. "What's urgent for you today?"

"I'd like to shake up Rivers again, and I'd like to have a preliminary chat with Itzkowitz's previous boyfriend. But I can leave that until tomorrow if you want to follow up on the Jackson story."

Bee glared at him for mentioning Jackson's name. "Yes, Rivers definitely needs a visit, and it would be useful to follow up on your wreath."

But in the end it was Springfield who settled the debate about who should be in the office and who could be on protection duty in Outwood, when she sent a text to Bee telling him to meet her in her office at 11 o'clock. The message was punctuated by four exclamation marks and Bee assumed he was in for another protracted cross examination by his new boss.

★ ★ ★

SPRINGFIELD'S OFFICE WAS unusually quiet, the faint hum of computers and the distant chatter from other departments did little to dispel the tension in the air. Springfield had drawn the blind halfway, casting slanted shadows across her polished desk. She sat behind it, jaw tight and fingers drumming an ominous rhythm against the arm of her chair. Her usual calm demeanour had been replaced by a simmering fury. Bee tapped gently on her half-open door.

"Enter."

Bee poked his head around the door, his face pale and strained. Before he could speak, Springfield's sharp glare froze him where he stood; a rabbit pinned in the headlights.

"You wanted to see me," he stammered.

"Close the door, inspector," Springfield's voice was menacingly low. "We need to talk."

Bee took a seat opposite the desk and felt like he'd been summoned to the headmaster's office for smashing his favourite vase.

"Do you remember our conversation from yesterday afternoon, when I told you I was going to London today to attend a high-level meeting with the commissioner of the Met and other senior officers about the current attacks on the police and I asked you if you had any information that I should be aware of?"

"Yes I do." Bee wondered where this was heading but kept his focus rigidly on Springfield.

"Good. What was your answer?"

Bee hesitated, "I don't think I had anything to tell you

A TICKET TO MURDER

Ma'am."

"No, you didn't." Springfield allowed a pause to develop. "Do you think that was the right answer?"

Bee's lip began to tremble as he searched for a clue for what was about to hit him. "Yes Ma'am."

"According to Detective Chief Inspector Cooke you paid a visit to Jackson two days ago. I thought you were dedicated to the missing Itzkowitz case, so perhaps you could explain to me why you thought it so important to slip off and talk to DI Jackson."

Bee squirmed in his seat; he felt his secret world was about to come crashing down. He needed to think fast. He reached for a glass and Springfield's water decanter to buy himself a moment. Springfield eyed him suspiciously, "Well?"

"Jackson asked for the meeting, because he felt threatened. We go back years. You probably don't know but we were at Hendon police training school together. There was a time when things weren't going well for me, and he helped me through some difficult times. I owed him. We held the meeting in daylight to make it look like a regular piece of police cooperation, but in reality it was personal stuff. I'll take the day as holiday if you want."

Springfield swatted away the idea, "I don't care about your time and your hours. But what I do care about is you bunking off from a major case involving someone from your own team to go and help out an old friend. How's that going to look to other members of the team?"

"McTierney would understand it."

"That's as maybe, but your team consists of more than just your lodger. You're an inspector in this station and a damn good one too. People look up to you. You have a responsibility whether you like it or not." Springfield eyed him suspiciously, "Trouble is, I don't know whether to believe you."

Bee looked up, convinced that his face was giving him away. Springfield paused and her eye caught the front page of the newspaper on her desk; the headline of 'Police Officer shot dead,' stared back at her. A knot twisted in her stomach. "But right now we've got too many other things to think about, so I feel obligated to give you the benefit of the doubt. But this won't keep happening."

"No Ma'am. Honestly, you can trust me," mumbled Bee.

"I bloody hope so." Springfield stared straight at Bee until he turned away in discomfort.

"So why did Jackson feel threatened?"

Bee twisted in his seat again; he was sinking deeper with every statement. "It was work related. He felt he didn't have the full backing of his team. I don't want to say more, because I don't have any evidence. But if I think about it, maybe I'm not surprised he's been killed."

Springfield raised an eyebrow at the suggestion but didn't say anything. Bee took the pause as an opportunity to go on the attack.

"Do you know what's happening to track down Jackson's killer?"

"Not in any detail. Cooke said something about them rounding up the usual suspects."

"That's a cop out," yelled Bee, louder than he would have wanted and releasing some tension.

Springfield jerked her head back. "I beg your pardon."

"They're doing nothing. That's all the standard stuff; there's nothing new there. Nothing to say that they're taking this seriously. It screams cover up." Bee was halfway out of his chair before he pulled himself together.

"Sit down inspector. It's not your case. I might say it's a pity you've not been so passionate about finding our own missing officer."

Bee bowed his head.

"It seems this unfortunate business with Jackson has clouded your judgement, inspector. You need to get a grip on yourself."

"But what about Jackson, it sounds like he's being hung out to dry."

"He knew the risks. We all do."

"Did he? Perhaps he thought he could count on his fellow police officers."

"You have no evidence for any of these outbursts inspector. You need to bite your lip, or you'll be on suspension!"

Bee mumbled an apology.

Springfield gathered her breath. Bee kept quiet waiting for her to speak, the pause seemed interminable. "But while we're talking about the Jackson case, DCI Cooke informed me that he would like to interview you in connection with his death. Why do you think he would want to do that?"

"I haven't a clue."

Springfield felt a pang of disgust at what she perceived to be a straight lie – so much for his 'Honest Joe' image around the office. "You'd better make arrangements to visit Cooke in Croydon."

TWENTY-NINE

CROYDON POLICE STATION is a modern building, a combination of bricks and concrete, designed with functionality in mind. It sits in the centre of the town on Park Lane and operates on a continual 24-hour basis. Bee left his car in the visitors' area and climbed the steps up to the main entrance, announced himself to the desk sergeant and waited for Detective Chief Inspector Cooke to come and find him. As he had expected, Cooke left him to stew for 20 minutes before he marched down to collect him.

Cooke was a tall, muscular man with broad shoulders, slicked back black hair and moustache to match. "You must be Bee," he said, thrusting out a hand and shaking Bee's hand vigorously. He turned back to the desk sergeant, "Dave, I'm taking Bee with me."

Bee noticed that Cooke didn't bother to sign him in, as would have been protocol. Cooke didn't waste any time on chit-chat as he led Bee away from the entrance, up two flights of stairs, along a corridor and into the DCI's office. Nor did he offer Bee a drink. Cooke felt within his rights to rough up any fresh meat who crossed his path and didn't show sufficient deference. This bumpkin detective from the woods fell haplessly into that category.

Cooke had the traditional large office with an equally

large desk on which stood a dual screen computer. The room had a row of filing cabinets along one wall, a white board on another and a long window which looked towards Park Hill Park. Bee couldn't see a single book anywhere in the room. Bee was keen to get to know the man a little and seized upon a photo on the corner of Cooke's desk. The photo was of a young footballer wearing a red and white striped top. Bee leant across to admire it.

"Who's the future England captain?"

"Oh, that's Mikey, he's my nephew. That's from a few years ago when he made his debut for Exeter City."

Bee felt his blood run cold; his eyes locked onto those of DCI Cooke. At that precise moment he felt both he and Cooke knew that the DCI was involved in the Taranovsky gang and the disappearance of Itzkowitz. But he needed to speak to keep the conversation going. "Is he the next Harry Kane?"

"No, I doubt it. He's a centre-half, but he's not a bad lad. Hopefully he'll make the grade."

Bee nodded his response, and Cooke took advantage of the slight pause.

"Take a seat inspector, this needn't be a long conversation and then you can get back to your patch. I believe you have a missing DS to find."

Bee's posture stiffened by the reference to Itzkowitz, and he adopted a defensive position, "Is this going to be recorded on tape?"

"No. I don't go in for all that faffing about." Cooke dismissed the idea with a sharp wave of his arm. "This is an off the record chat between two police colleagues."

Bee crossed his arms and nodded his acceptance, but

scarcely had he done so, Cooke opened, "What were you and Jackson doing at Taranovsky's house when you dropped by there on Tuesday?"

Bee's head jerked back, "I'm sorry. I thought I was here to discuss the demise of Ian Jackson."

"You are. And you can start by telling me what you and he were doing at Taranovsky's house."

"I don't see how it's relevant to the investigation."

Cooke felt his body temperature rising, "I'll decide what's relevant, now answer the damn question."

Bee twisted in his seat, "I wanted his advice on my missing detective sergeant."

"Bullshit."

Bee shrugged his shoulders, "That's what we were talking about."

Cooke looked at Bee, as a boxer might look at a punchbag, before launching an attack. He pursed his lips then tried a different tack.

"Jackson was looking after some valuable property. I think you know who I mean. But she seems to have disappeared. Do you know where she is?"

"I don't know what you mean. You're talking in cryptic riddles. You'll need to ask a straight question, if you want a straight answer."

"Don't fuck with me Bee. No excuses. You'll be the one who loses." Cooke was close to shouting.

"I'm just here trying to help you. I'm keen to do anything that will help bring Jackson's killer to justice." Bee was speaking quicker than normal, and he pinched himself to slow himself down.

"Is that so?" There was menace in Cooke's voice. "If I

discover that you're meddling in this Taranovsky case or that through some misguided loyalty to Jackson you've helped to move Lily Gandapur I'll be down on you like a sledgehammer. Your little career will be over. Gone."

Bee leant back in his chair, adding distance between the two men.

"I'll give you one more chance to tell me what you know about Taranovsky and this Gandapur girl."

"All I know is what I read in the papers. Taranovsky is a Russian gangster who's due to appear in court next week, when with any luck he'll be found guilty of murder and sent to prison for the rest of his days."

"I wouldn't put too much trust in what you read in the papers, inspector." Cooke smirked and allowed the conversation to drop.

Bee picked up the gauntlet, "What's happening with the investigation into Jackson's death?"

Cooke looked surprised at the question, "We're pursuing several lines of enquiry."

"Would you mind sharing those with me please? He was a friend and I'd like to know how the investigation is proceeding."

"Yes I would mind, inspector. The Jackson case is nothing to do with you. Unless of course you have some information about Jackson's movements on Wednesday and Thursday that you'd like to share with me."

Bee remained silent.

"Have you?"

"No."

"Then I think we're done here." Cooke stood up. "I'll show you off the premises. I don't want you snooping around the place. I'll escort you to the front door."

Bee hesitated to get up; he was struggling to think straight. He'd become convinced that Cooke was somehow implicated in the murder of Jackson. His mind lurched back to the black tattoo that he and McTierney had identified. He began obsessing that Cooke might be hiding a tattoo of a black hammer on his right wrist. Cooke was wearing a long-sleeved blue shirt and Bee couldn't see beyond the back of his hand. He looked away, trying to think of something else, but his mind wouldn't release the idea.

Cooke stood impatiently glaring at Bee, who finally got up to leave and offered his hand to Cooke, as they shook hands Bee twisted his hand over. Cooke looked surprised but then something clicked in his mind. His eyes locked on Bee.

"Were you expecting to see something inspector? A tattoo perhaps?"

Bee blanched, "No not at all." He moved to release his hand, but Cooke had different ideas and yanked Bee across the desk and glared into his face. "You need to be careful inspector, you're not as clever as you like to think."

As they retraced their steps back to the front desk, they walked in silence. *Damn* thought Bee, *I've revealed my suspicions, and I've got nothing to show for it.* As the pair arrived at the front entrance a young man in overalls was standing by the desk with a clipboard in his hand. The desk sergeant tapped him on the shoulder and pointed towards DCI Cooke, "This is the gentleman you'll be wanting."

The young man in the overalls took a step towards Cooke but hesitated in the wake of his quarry; a man striding with purpose.

"What is it?" demanded Cooke.

The young man wavered but then found his voice. "I'm returning your car, sir. It's had the gold level valet service as requested."

Cooke offered a curt, "Thank you, I'll be with you in a moment."

But the young man had a message, he seemed compelled to deliver, "My manager told me to advise you that the driver's side rear tyre is excessively worn; it's due to be replaced, in places the tread is below the minimum of 3mm. The other tyres are all okay. My manager said we could do it for you this afternoon, we have several premium tyres in stock if you want me to take it back now."

"I said I'll be with you in a minute. Just wait. No excuses."

Bee looked at Cooke, he seemed unduly vexed over the delivery of his car. A nasty thought shot across Bee's mind, and he made his exit quickly. He sat in his car pretending to listen to a message on his phone, while silently he berated himself for the handshake fiasco. How could Cooke have had a black hammer tattoo? If that was so, then surely Jackson would have seen it and would have told me.

The vulpine Cooke and the young man were still in conversation, then after a couple of minutes Cooke disappeared back into the station. The young man walked back to the white Audi Q5 vehicle and pulled out of the station car park. Bee followed him out of Croydon and west on the A232 to a valeting garage on the far side of Carshalton. Bee stopped to note the address and contact details and placed a call to Carol Bishop.

THIRTY

BEE HEADED BACK to the station and the planned team review that Springfield had demanded two days earlier. It was a meeting he wasn't looking forward to. He knew Springfield would ask him about the interview with Cooke and that she'd expect a full answer, and there was virtually nothing of the discussion that he felt he could share with her.

Hence, he was disappointed to pull into the car park and notice that her blue Range Rover was sitting in its usual position next to the main building. But his mood improved instantly when Maria told him that Springfield had been ambushed by Itzkowitz's mother who had flown in from America and immediately demanded to see someone senior in the force. Springfield had tried to palm her off with a regular officer, but when the mother had threatened to go to the US embassy, the chief inspector had capitulated and had agreed to see Mrs Itzkowitz. It transpired that Itzkowitz's parents had separated a few years ago, and, as the only child Fran Itzkowitz had become the apple of her mother's eye. So, despite a fear of flying, she had made the journey across 'The Pond'. After that a candid police chief superintendent was no match for an obsessed and worried Jewish matriarch.

Maria had taken tea and biscuits into Springfield's office and didn't expect to see her superior before she left that afternoon. Bee smiled at the information and began to tiptoe away from the desk and upstairs, but Maria's second piece of news stopped him in his tracks.

"In view of what's happened with Jackson on top of the disappearance of Itzkowitz, Springfield has launched a major police hunt for our missing DS. It might get overshadowed by the hunt for Jackson's killer, especially as the focus is much the same area. But it's the number one story on the news."

"Yes, I heard it on the radio coming here. I can't say I'm surprised and it's probably the right thing to do. The challenge we'll face is sifting through the hundreds of sightings we're going to receive. I suspect there'll be some overtime this weekend if you fancy working."

Maria shook her head, "Sorry. I have plans."

BEE ENTERED THE makeshift operations room, where Kelly and Bishop were waiting for him, as well as the new recruit Rockford, while McTierney was on the phone from Outwood. He opened the meeting with the news that Maria had just relayed. The team had already been briefed but were still talking about the news. The key question on everyone's lips was voiced by Carol Bishop, "Do you think Itzkowitz is going to be okay? It's been nearly a week"

Bee sucked the air over his teeth, "Yes," he said, as definitively as possible. "Fran Itzkowitz is an experienced officer; she's been through a lot in New York City, probably more than most of us. She'll know how to make contact with her captors, she'll know what to say, what to do, and more importantly what not to say. I'm not saying it'll be easy, but she's probably better placed than any of us to survive this ordeal."

He looked around the room and the general silence told him that the team had bought his explanation. Unfortunately, he himself wasn't so easily convinced. But it allowed him to change tack.

"It's great that you're all here, because things are heating up and we don't have much time."

"I agree that there's not much time," said McTierney. "I've had another threatening text, telling me, that my friend has 48 hours to live unless I do as I've been told. I'm interpreting my friend to be Fran Itzkowitz."

"That seems to fit with what we know, and the timeframe would tie into the forthcoming court case featuring Taranovsky. All of this seems to point towards Tuesday morning."

There was a general nod of heads around the table.

"What was DCI Cooke like? Pussycat or Tiger?"

Bee shuddered as he answered the question, "Cooke has an ego and an arrogance beyond his payslip, and that itself must be considerable. But firstly, I need to share my suspicions with you from this morning. DCI Cooke didn't have any interest in talking to me about Jackson. He wanted two things; one, to ask me about my recent meetings with DI Jackson and if they involved Lily Gandapur, to which I denied any knowledge."

"Did he believe you?" asked Bishop.

"I don't think so, but he didn't really have much choice. That led into his second thing; he wanted to put the frighteners on me and make sure that I knew that if he found any reason to question what we were doing, he'd be after me."

"But you don't scare easily, do you boss?" It was McTierney down the phone.

Bee chuckled, "Not any more, not after two years of living with you. Anyway, the interview provided us with two key leads."

The group around the table became animated. "Number one, we have an Exeter connection, albeit a little tenuous, which is that Cooke has knowledge of, and affection for Exeter, through his nephew." Bee held his hand up, "Not rock solid, I will grant you, but it's a start and when I tell you the next one it takes on greater significance."

"Get on with it, then," said McTierney, "The anticipation is killing me."

"As I was leaving, a valet service man arrived to return Cooke's car. It sounded like he's had it deep cleaned, which is interesting in itself, but the ace in the pack was when the young lad told him that he had one nearly bald tyre." A spark of interest flickered across Kelly's face.

Bee turned to him, "Yes. It sounded exactly like the set of tyres you described as being from the car that we believe abducted Itzkowitz last Saturday."

Kelly whistled, "Sounds like an ambitious appeal to the umpire."

"It might be, but also it might be exactly the break we're seeking. Now, Carol, did you make the two calls I requested?"

Bishop smiled across the table. "I did and I think it worked as you'd suggested."

"Good. Can you share the details with the rest of the team?"

Bishop looked around the room as if she was going to

enjoy her moment in the spotlight.

"Yes. Initially I posed as Cooke's secretary and called the valet company who'd taken his car and told them that Cooke had forgotten to mention that he would be away for a day or two and therefore he would send a Mr Kelly to collect his car early on Saturday morning." She grinned across the table at the pathologist, who looked surprised.

"Me?"

Bee chipped in, "Yes. Sorry I didn't have time to discuss it. I trust you'll be okay with what comes next."

"There's more?"

Bishop licked her lips and continued, "Then I called Croydon station and spoke to Cooke and told him that the wheel balancing machine had developed a fault. As you predicted, he didn't take it well." Bishop turned to smile at Bee. "I apologised and said we'd ordered the part, and it will be delivered and fitted in the morning. Once that's done, his will be the first car we work on, and it will be delivered back to him early afternoon. He had a rant about incompetence, until eventually I manged to squeeze in that there will be no charge for the tyre. That seemed to placate him."

"Perfect," said Bee. Then he turned to Kelly, pausing to find the bridge of his glasses with his forefinger and pushed them gently back into place. "In case you haven't guessed, you're the delivery driver, but in between you'll have 3-4 hours around Saturday lunchtime to search the car for anything the valet missed during his deep clean."

Kelly offered a faltering smile at the plan, "And what exactly are you hoping I'm going to find?"

"I'm not sure, but hopefully something that proves Itzkowitz was in the car last week."

Kelly nodded his acceptance.

The slight pause was broken by a question from McTierney, "Can I ask something else about the Jackson investigation? Did you learn anything new? Are you going to try to get involved? I'm sure you want to know what happened to him."

"Your assessment is spot on, but there's a problem, in a word DCI Cooke. And before anyone tells me that's four words you all know what I mean."

Bishop smiled across the table.

"Anyway, Cooke is all over this investigation and explicitly told me to keep my nose out. I'm afraid I won't get far snooping around."

"Too bad," said Bishop.

"However, I do have one idea." Bee looked around the room at his colleagues.

"Not me," said Kelly. "I'm fully loaded."

"Quite. No, I was thinking of someone else in our team, someone who has a unique set of skills."

Bishop and Rockford exchanged nervous glances. But Bee shook his head at them. "I'm looking for social skills, the type DS McTierney has in spades."

"Uh oh. This line's gone funny," said McTierney.

Bee laughed, but carried on, "It's scarcely a week since you were seconded onto the Croydon team to help with the search of Taranovsky's house; I'm sure you would have chatted to a few fellow officers while you were there."

"Probably asked one of them for a date," added Bishop.

"Maybe," said McTierney.

"Good. Can you call her back and find out who was the first officer on the scene after Jackson's murder was called in?

Once you've done that I'll give you a list of questions for you to ask."

"I guess I walked straight into that one," said McTierney.

"While we have your attention, did you make any progress with Rivers?"

McTierney tutted, "No, not really. I dropped by his house, but he wasn't there or, at least, wasn't answering the door, and he must have been awake because the curtains were all open and I made a racket. Both of his neighbours claimed that they hadn't seen him for a few days, but apparently that's normal. After that I called into the hospital, but he's not on shift either today or tomorrow. They don't expect to see him until 2pm on Monday. What they don't know is that I'll intercept him in the car park."

"Good plan but make another home visit tomorrow. We need to work out if or how he fits into this case."

Bee turned his attention to officer Rockford who had been grinning along with the stories as they were repeated. "Now, Rockford, you're going to have a part to play in this too."

The young officer puffed out his chest, "I'm ready to help, sir."

"Forget all the sir stuff, just call me Bee. What I need is someone to review all the traffic cameras that were tracking vehicles leaving Reigate on the day of the abduction. We've not done much of a job trying to find Itzkowitz, so let's change our approach and see who we can find."

"I'm on it."

"Good. Start with DCI Cooke's car. I'll give you the registration when we finish."

Rockford beamed across the table; he looked delighted to

be involved.

"Two more topics," said Bee. "First up, Carol, can you trawl back through that list of Wembley concert attendees and see if you can find either Cooke or any other officer's name from the Croydon station. We always said there must be two kidnappers, so if I'm right and Cooke is one of them, he still needs an accomplice."

Bishop signalled her agreement.

"And lastly an open question to everyone here. Where does Rivers fit into all of this?"

"I don't like him," said McTierney. "Every time we speak to him he seems to be lying. It tells me that either he knows something he ought to be telling us, or he has something to hide. I want to keep the pressure on him."

"Agreed. There's something not quite right with Rivers." Bee paused. "Do we know of any link between him and Cooke or him and Taranovsky? If not, can we find one?" He paused. "I guess that falls on your plate too, Bishop."

"No problem."

THIRTY-ONE

FRIDAY NIGHT FOR the Lily Gandapur protection team took place at Carol Bishop's flat in Redhill. Gandapur welcomed the change of scene and, although not his idea, Bee was quick to support the plan, believing that maintaining a routine as close to normal as possible would help everyone deal with the pressurised situation. Once McTierney knew there would be beer in Bishop's flat he was committed to the plan.

Bishop's apartment was on St Anne's Rise, part of the sprawling St Anne's development which had been built in the summer of 1992 on the old site of the St Anne's Society school. But that was long gone, the only remaining feature was the clock face, which had been saved when the tower was demolished and now stood in the Belfry shopping centre in central Redhill. The development stood to the north-east of the town, squeezed in between the London to Brighton railway line and the Carrington school, which had been built a few years earlier.

Bishop rented a first floor two bedroom contemporary flat. McTierney climbed the stairs, walked through the front door and requested a tour. Bishop left Gandapur in the kitchen and duly obliged; she could do the whole thing in less than a minute. The door opened into a small hallway which ran the length of the flat and provided a spine to the layout. On the left side were the basic facilities of toilet, bathroom, airing cupboard and kitchen, while on the other side were two good sized bedrooms and a lounge diner. McTierney pushed his nose into each room, nodded and grunted and returned to the kitchen. "I couldn't see the beer fridge anywhere. Is it hiding in here?"

Bishop tutted, as Gandapur moved to the fridge / freezer unit and fetched a beer from the back. She passed it to McTierney along with an opener and a knowing smile. He nodded his approval. "Good to see the training is coming along well. I'm in the mood for a long beer tonight."

"Where's Scott?" asked Carol Bishop.

"He's scampering around the outside of your building, checking this and that, making a security sweep. I told him if we're on the first floor, the only risk is the front door, but he wouldn't listen."

Bee's reconnaissance didn't take long, and he soon joined everyone in the kitchen. "I brought over a couple of bottles of wine." He placed them on the only free surface he could find in Bishop's petite kitchen.

"Did you find anything to cause you concern?" asked McTierney.

"Plenty," said Bee with a sigh. "Not least the fact that this neighbourhood, as modern as the blocks may look, still has a great number of residents who can't judge space."

"What?" challenged Carol.

"Don't get him started," said McTierney taking a long swig from his bottle, "I know where this is going."

Bee looked hurt. "It's simply that this block of flats has 12 large black wheelie bins with names or numbers on the lids, and almost without exception, the people never leave enough space and have to squeeze in the last couple of letters."

"I'm glad I put a number on mine," laughed Carol.

"Good job," added McTierney, "Otherwise that would be a deal-breaker for our inspector." He swayed out of reach of Bee's mock punch, as he tried to restore order.

Now he was in the kitchen, Bee's eyes wandered across from one window sill to the other. Carol anticipated him making a mental note of all the pot plants she had placed there; two geraniums, an anthurium and a fern.

"It's because I don't have a garden, well not one of my own. There's a large communal lawn with a few rose bushes at the back, but I don't think anybody ever ventures down there for pleasure."

"Still, no mowing the lawn," said Ron.

"And what would you know about mowing a lawn?"

"I did it once when you were away."

Scott shook his head and turned his attention back to Carol, "Is there anything I can do to help?"

"No. I think us ladies have got dinner covered. Lily has been teaching me some new ways to cook curry, so you've got a similar meal to last night, but with a few different spices. Oh, and we're using lamb tonight instead of beef."

"Sounds delightful. How about I lay the table?"

"Yes, good idea. We're eating in the lounge / diner, it's the only big room in the place. You two need to leave us alone while we cook. But before I forget, I contacted Madame Tussauds today and Babylon's alibi checks out."

"Excellent, thanks," nodded Scott.

"Before I leave you, I must share my latest joke with

you," interjected Ron.

"There's no need," said Carol, but it was too late.

"I once read the biography of the man who invented the elevator; he started at the bottom and worked his way up."

Scott pushed Ron into the lounge, "Have you been overdoing the sugar intake today?"

"No," grinned Ron in response. "I just like a party. But while I think of it, 500 hares escaped from London Zoo this morning."

Scott looked puzzled.

"The police are combing the area."

Scott groaned, "I know it's Friday and the end of the week, but…"

Ron waved away the protest, "I'd never eat in a restaurant where I could get in."

"What?"

"It's a joke. A modern take on Groucho Marx. His grave is in Highgate cemetery."

"No that's Karl Marx. Oh my. This is going to be a long night. I wish I'd come by taxi."

Although Ron had overplayed the idea of a party it was amazing how quickly some good food and wine cheered up the group. The early tension of the day dissipated as the second and third bottles of wine came and went from the dining table, the conversation became lively and there was laughter, and no more Ron jokes.

The conversation ranged from teenage posters on bedroom walls; 'The Spice Girls' for Lily, 'Black Beauty' for Carol, 'The Clash' for Scott, not Sherlock Holmes as Ron insisted it should have been and to no one's great surprise, 'Buffy the Vampire Slayer' for Ron himself. Next the chatter lurched to the left and touched on the dexterity of master criminals. This conversational cul-de-sac had its origin in a harmless remark from Scott, who mentioned that DCI Cooke had been left-handed and perhaps he had his black hammer tattoo on his left wrist. But that was enough for Ron to initiate a debate about most left-handed people having something to hide.

"I presume you're referencing the Latin word 'sinister'," said Scott.

"No, I'm just saying most lefties are crooks."

Scott shook his head, "But the idea of that comes from the Latin word sinister which means left sided and has been adopted into English with an extended meaning of underhand or malicious."

"Whatever. I'm thinking about Jack the Ripper, he was a leftie, and so was Voldemort."

"Voldemort is a character from a book, not a real person," said Scott.

"If we're talking movies, then I think Anthony Perkins is left-handed in Psycho. That should have been in my list of top films last night, but I forgot it," said Carol, reaching for the bottle of red.

"Oh no," shuddered Lily, "too scary for me. I can't watch that."

"Hang on," said Scott, trying to bring some sense to the discussion, but as the only sober one around the table, he was fighting an uphill battle. "You can't include fictional characters in this debate. Not if you're trying to have a proper discussion."

But it was too late for that.

"I remember reading Dr Jekyll and Mr Hyde, and in that

the doctor is right-handed, and the murderous Mr Hyde is left-handed," added Lily.

"Good point," said Ron pointing across the table. "And all the stormtroopers in the Star Wars films are left-handed."

"All of them?" asked Scott sarcastically.

"Yes," said Ron dismissively, "Everyone knows that."

"And Darth Vader," added Carol excitedly.

"Perfect. That clinches it," said Ron leaning back in his chair triumphantly.

"Why don't we ring up Putin and see if he wipes his backside with his left-hand?" said Scott in disgust.

"Don't be silly, Scott," said Carol, "but I do think our upbringing plays a big part in what we become."

And with two short sentences Carol brought the debate to a halt. Ron tilted his head, thought about the premise hanging over the table and laid down the gauntlet for his host. "How so?"

Carol took a deep breath, "My mother used to tell me this story. It's about a mother's love for her daughter. I think she always hoped it would encourage me to give her a granddaughter, but that hasn't happened yet." She threw a sly look in Scott's direction, but he didn't respond.

"It's the first day of school and you're there at the gates with the other mums when your little one comes running toward you clutching a painting they've done in class that afternoon. You grab the painting, take a look at the awful daubs on the page, unable to make head nor tail of what it's supposed to be; wondering if it's a giraffe or a man with three legs holding a very large stick."

Her audience chuckled.

"So, you say, 'Goodness me, what a wonderful picture,

aren't you clever?' And there it is, a seed is sown in the mind of the child that a connection exists between what they do and how much they are worth." She paused and took another sip from her wine glass. "But if, on the other hand, you push aside the dreadful painting and give the child a big hug, look into their eyes and say, 'I'm so proud of you. Now then, let's have a look at this painting,' Then the story might turn out differently because the child is validated simply because they exist without reference to anything they've achieved."

Gandapur clapped her hands excitedly, "I love it. Oh, you'd make a wonderful mother!"

Carol bowed her head and ignored the compliment, "Of course, this simplistic example isn't the only reason we might grow up thinking we're only worth something if we get an A* in our maths exam or go on to become a detective inspector." She avoided looking at Scott, who shifted uncomfortably in his chair and the table fell silent.

"Achievement is, for some of us, the best and sometimes the only way of getting attention in a chaotic or emotionally arid childhood environment," he said.

"Well, that killed the conversation," said Ron. "Personally, I've had a great time, but perhaps it's time we headed home."

THIRTY-TWO

AS THE THREE friends approached Bee's house, he sensed something was wrong. He slowed his car down, cut the engine and gently rolled onto the driveway. He turned to McTierney, "We might have a problem here, are you okay?"

McTierney tapped the gun under his jacket, "Ready and waiting."

As Bee's Mercedes rolled to a stop, he could see that the front door was swinging open. "We've had visitors. I wonder if they are still waiting? Stay here while I go to the door."

Bee pushed the car door open, turned his ear to the nightscape; somewhere in the darkness a fox screamed, and Bee pulled his gun from his pocket. McTierney nodded his approval. Bee looked over his shoulder to see a frightened face in the back seat. "Don't worry, we can handle this, but keep your head down, and stick close to McTierney."

Gandapur's eyes widened, and she started breathing heavily but nodded her head rapidly at the instruction. Bee drew his revolver, tiptoed from his car, and nudged the door open, a dull shaft of light spread across the driveway, and he disappeared inside. McTierney slipped across to the driver's seat while peering through the darkness searching for any kind of movement.

McTierney shuffled across to the driver's seat, then

stretched a hand into the back of the car, he fumbled for Gandapur's hand. He felt her trembling and gave her hand a squeeze. "All okay so far?"

She didn't reply. He glanced into the back and found a pair of frightened eyes. "Keep your head down but be ready for anything."

Then Bee re-appeared at the door and beckoned for the pair to join him. Together they scurried across the gravel driveway and into the house, slamming the door behind them.

"Downstairs seems okay, and I'm inclined to believe that whoever paid us a visit has gone, but stay here with Lily, while I check the other rooms. If anything happens, get her away from the house, don't worry about me."

Alarm raced across Gandapur's face, but McTierney switched gears and nodded his understanding, his earlier alcoholic slumber quickly forgotten. Two minutes later, Bee returned to the kitchen, "No sign of anyone upstairs, but clearly we've had unwanted guests."

"People coming here to get me?" spluttered Gandapur.

"Probably," admitted Bee, moving across to touch her arm.

"But we're here now. They won't get through us," added McTierney. He walked across to the kitchen table and picked up a large potato which had been left on the table with a kitchen knife sticking out of it. "Lovely," he said.

"I think a potato is a slang term for a police officer in parts of Russia. I'd guess that's another in the series of not-so-subtle messages," said Bee, taking the potato from McTierney's hand and extracting the knife.

Gandapur joined them, staring at the vegetable. "This is

your friend who they are threatening just to get at me. Maybe I should tell someone that I'm not going to speak in court. Maybe that would bring your friend home safe."

Bee grabbed Gandapur by the shoulders. "No. Absolutely not. It wouldn't change a thing."

Gandapur half screamed in response to Bee's reaction. McTierney had stepped back in shock at Bee's statement but added his own thoughts. "He's right. It's too late to call it quits; all the bets are laid."

Gandapur's jaw fell open as she digested what the men were saying. McTierney ploughed on, "If all this is Taranovsky, or one of his gang, as seems likely, then you'll always be a risk to him. He's not going to stop until you're dead or he's in jail. As far as he's concerned it's you or him."

Bee had calmed down a touch, "He's right. There's no way back for Taranovsky. He would always be afraid that you might change your mind and testify against him some time in the future. No matter what you said now, he'd never believe you."

A shot of helplessness flashed across Gandapur's eyes. "But don't worry," said Bee, "they're doing this to scare us, but we've both seen this before. We don't scare easily. Three more days and you'll be in court, and this will all be over."

Gandapur's head dropped, and she began to mumble, "But what if they kill your friend? I don't think I could live with myself knowing that I'd caused the death of another person."

Bee turned on her again, "Now listen. You are not responsible for what happens to her. Whoever has taken Fran is fully and solely answerable for whatever happens to her."

Gandapur avoided his face, so Bee pulled it up, "Do you

hear me? None of this is your fault, and don't ever start thinking that it is."

Bee let go of her and stepped back a pace. McTierney gave him a knowing look. "I think we're all getting a bit tense tonight. Perhaps we should try to get some sleep."

"Yes, good idea," said Bee.

McTierney nodded to Bee to move away from Gandapur and took advantage of the space to whisper in his ear, "Do you think there's still someone out there in the woods watching this place?"

"No. I think they've delivered their message and they've gone. But we need to think about how we're going to manage the next few days. This house isn't as secret as we'd hoped."

McTierney inclined his head. "Look, while you get Lily settled upstairs I'm going to take a walk around outside and set up a few bottle booby-traps outside under the windows."

"Good thought. At last, we've found a use for all those empty beer bottles you create."

Fifteen minutes later the two detectives were reunited in the kitchen. "Did you see any killers; Russian or otherwise?" asked Bee.

"Just the odd fox. But anyone trying to get in through the windows will make a lot of noise, so we should get a warning if anyone comes back in the early hours."

"Good. From what I can see, it looks like they simply kicked in the glass in the back door to gain entry. Nothing sophisticated, so in its own way that's encouraging. I'm always happy confronting thugs rather than villains, who can think as well as shoot."

McTierney smiled, "Yes, I've been thinking about how we solve our little problem here. Putting aside your classic speech from a few minutes ago, I think it's time someone died."

Bee nodded. "I think you're right. I'll get it organised."

THIRTY-THREE

THE ATMOSPHERE IN Bee's house had changed overnight; the light frivolity of Thursday night had been replaced with a dark mood of apprehension. Bee was in the kitchen eating a slice of toast by the window when Gandapur came in. She flicked on the kettle and joined him at the window. "What's up?"

"Nothing much. I was watching a blue tit bravely resisting a great tit's bullying on the bird feeder. I always find myself cheering for the underdog."

"Your blue tit should be grateful he's not taking on a blackbird. They are so territorial."

Bee smiled at the comparison.

"Am I an underdog?"

"Yes, no, well maybe." Bee smiled at his own indecision. "No. Someone who stands up for what is right, shouldn't be called an underdog. You're a champion of justice."

The pair stood watching until the blue tit was vanquished, Bee sighed and turned away from the window. "Did you sleep?"

"No, not much. How about you?"

"Only fitfully."

"Come on, I'll help you tidy up the kitchen."

"Thanks. Once McTierney is back in the land of the

living, we'll pick up Bishop and head into town."

★ ★ ★

WHILE MCTIERNEY SLUMBERED, Bee headed into the office to check on a couple of items that had disturbed his sleep. Considering it was a Saturday he was surprised to find the ops room a hive of activity; Springfield had cancelled leave for everyone and was using the room to direct operations to a band of new recruits that she was about to send out into the field to search for Itzkowitz. Bee put his head around the door but was too slow to withdraw it and found himself pulled into the limelight.

"Ah inspector, good timing. Would you like to offer some encouragement to our newly mobilised team as they embark on a full-scale search for DS Itzkowitz?"

Bee thought that there was nothing he wouldn't rather be doing, but realised that it had been an instruction, not an invitation. "Of course." He walked slowly to the front of the room, while racking his brain for something to say.

"Hi. Thank you for giving up your Saturday to join the search." He paused and caught Springfield's eye, the initial smile had left her face, and he felt sure that her blood was starting to heat. "Fran Itzkowitz is a very resourceful officer and I'm confident that she will have developed a rapport with her captor and still be alive." He glanced to his right and Springfield seemed to have relaxed slightly. "But I believe she is being held by someone with intimate knowledge of how the police operate and therefore they, and it will be more than one person, could be dangerous, so you should expect and investigate the unexpected."

"Thank you inspector." Springfield had heard enough. Bee escaped towards the door, stopping only to nudge Rockford to follow him. Bee led Rockford away from the CID area to a quiet corner.

"How have you been getting on with that different angle I gave you?"

"Not had much time to work on it. When the chief arrived, she wanted me to join her task force."

"Consider yourself rescued. I'll deal with Springfield, and you focus on the traffic leaving the industrial estate last Saturday. Let me know if you find any interesting drivers, especially the driver of that white Audi, but keep an eye open for any car registered to Croydon police."

Rockford's eyes widened at the suggestion that the police might be involved in the abduction but took Bee's instruction without comment and found himself a quiet office in which to review the traffic camera footage.

With his new team fully engaged and the chief busy with the mass search, Bee had taken the opportunity to slip out of the building and allow himself some thinking time. He walked along Wray Park Road juggling a few ideas around his head. His face alternated between frowns, squints and smiles as he sifted the pieces of the jigsaw. How far did Taranovsky's network stretch? How did someone discover his home address? Where was Itzkowitz being held captive?

He was lost in his own world, staring into space, scratching his head and muttering to himself and didn't see the three youths walking towards him until they were right on top of him.

"Watch out mate."

"Look where you're going Grandpa, or you'll be back at

square one."

Bee stumbled off the path into the road and mumbled an apology, but his mind was gone and didn't register the abuse that followed. Square one, of course. That's where he should have started.

Bee found his own discreet spot and searched through the calls submitted to the station. He wanted to replay the original call that Itzkowitz had taken; it had only occurred to him that morning that he hadn't heard the call himself. Being away in Exeter, he had left others to recount the events of that day. Whenever he was faced with a murder he made it a priority to absorb the murder scene as a way of entering the mind of the killer. He didn't know why he hadn't done this before now, it had been a manic week, but it was a mistake on his behalf.

It didn't take him long to find the recording and although it was short and distorted, deliberately so he thought, he was sure he recognised the voice. Could it be that of DCI Cooke? There was no emotion in the voice. The call referred to a suspected robbery and yet the voice was calm and efficient; there was no fear, no excitement. It was rehearsed and cold, it didn't sound like a member of the public seeing something for the first time. He couldn't match the tone decisively, but the speaker had used the phrase, 'no excuses,' and that was something that Cooke had said yesterday. Bee noted that it wasn't conclusive evidence, nor was it the sort of theory to put in front of Springfield, but for him it was another step in the right direction. He decided he needed to hear it again; he rewound the tape.

Rockford left his desk and walked around the makeshift station searching for the inspector. How could he ever hope to make the grade as a detective if he couldn't find an inspector in a police station? He was about to abandon his hunt when he heard someone talking in the temporary interview room; slowly he turned the handle, opened the door and pushed his head around the frame of the door. Bee was at the desk listening to a tape recorder. He held up his hand to silence the young officer, let the tape play and then beckoned him into the room. "Come here, listen to this."

Rockford sneaked across the room and tilted his head towards the speaker. Bee played it again.

"Tell me what's your immediate impression of the speaker?"

Rockford's mouth fell open. "Er. It's a man. Although he says it's an emergency, he doesn't sound panicked."

"Good. Anything else?"

"Sounds like he might be reading from a card. It's measured and controlled."

"Yes. Good. Anything more? Think."

Rockford shook his head, "No, sorry. Do you know who's speaking?"

"I'm convinced I've heard that voice before, I think it's DCI Cooke from Croydon, but the voice is disguised, so I can't be sure."

A pregnant pause enveloped the two men who exchanged hesitant looks, before Bee broke the silence. "You were looking for me. Tell me you've found Cooke's car."

Rockford wavered, then said. "Probably best if I show you."

They returned to Rockford's desk, and he re-started the tape. "I'm sorry sir, but I don't think DCI Cooke's car is here."

"It must be. I'm sure he made the call into the station to lure Itzkowitz away."

Rockford shook his head. "Sorry, not seeing it."

"Focus on the A23 north out of the town on Saturday afternoon. That's the most likely route. Can you run the tape on the screen?"

Rockford did as requested and soon the two men were staring at a screen watching a line of cars snake out of the town. Bee began to fidget, "come on where's that damn Audi?"

And then it appeared, not an Audi Q5, but Itzkowitz's VW Beetle. "Stop!" shouted Bee. "That's Itzkowitz's car, we need to follow that and see where it goes."

Rockford hit the stop button, and the image of the pale blue VW was frozen on the screen. Bee reached across the desk and grabbed Rockford's hand. "Do we have any cameras which give us a front facing image. It might show us who's driving, because I very much doubt it's Itzkowitz herself."

"No. At least not here, the camera is set up to capture rear plates, generally they are easier to read than the front ones."

Bee tutted. "Okay, before we lose this, get a copy of this still. We may need it as evidence. Then let's log the five cars ahead of the Beetle and the five cars which are following it. This was a two-man job so the accomplice will be close."

Rockford did as Bee asked and then when the tape began to play again, there was the white Audi Q5, two cars back. Rockford stopped the image and compared the registration plate to the one given to him by Bee, the previous evening. "The numbers are different; they're not even close. It can't be your crooked DCI, sir."

Bee nodded his head gently, "Oh it is. He's using false plates. I bet that plate doesn't exist in our database."

Rockford took a few minutes to cross-check the new plate against the Police National Database, which takes its data from the DVLA register in Swansea. Bee's eyes watched him, but his mind was elsewhere, whirring through the machinations of how to confront a DCI. Suddenly he realised Rockford was waiting for him. He looked down at the screen.

"Here it is sir. It does exist; it's registered to a Mrs Eleni Thomas from Newport."

"Clever bastard."

"Do you still think it's DCI Cooke?"

"Of course it is. This merely proves, he knows how to cover his tracks. It'll make it a bit more difficult for us, but we'll get him."

Bee walked away to stare out of the window. Rockford watched him cogitating. Bee pulled his lip, stared into space and eventually spun round, and pushed his glasses further along his nose. "Okay, this is what I want you to do."

Rockford wrote down the three things, then looked up to ask Bee a question, but by then the inspector had gone.

THIRTY-FOUR

MEANWHILE SOMEWHERE ON the outskirts of Carshalton Dr Kelly was starting to perspire in the rear seat of the VW Golf he had booked as an Uber. The driver, a middle-aged man from Horsham continued in his attempts to make conversation. Kelly continued to parry his efforts and wondered why the man didn't take his less than subtle hints that he didn't want to talk. On most days Kelly would be happy to chat with anyone, especially if he could twist the conversation around to cricket, but not today. Today he was uncomfortable. Uncomfortable with the subterfuge; uncomfortable with the heat; uncomfortable with being chauffeured. It was a new experience for the medical man who liked to be in control. Control of himself and the situation around him; he dealt with science, with facts and with certainty. He didn't warm to casual drivers who spent too much time looking over their shoulder trying to make chit-chat and too little time looking at the road.

Kelly liked the curious American detective, she always put him at ease, and he wanted to help, but he was unconvinced that this was the best use of his talents. In his own mind he believed he was about to steal a motor vehicle and McTierney's reassurance that any case would be dismissed once a judge knew the full facts didn't assuage his fear. Once again he began rehearsing the conversation he knew was coming. His driver looked up thinking he was being invited to speak. "Just rehearsing a speech," said Kelly abruptly. "Please focus on the road."

Kelly exited the car, ignored the man's offer of a business card and walked smartly away, dragging a black pull-along suitcase containing his gloves and coveralls, a magnifying glass, a selection of swabs and evidence bags and a camera. Time for the show to begin.

★ ★ ★

AFTER BEE HAD left, Rockford allowed his imagination to wander. What would he do if he wanted to lose a car between north Reigate and Croydon? He'd seen enough TV crime shows to know what the bad guys did. It was a short distance from the site of the probable kidnapping of Itzkowitz to the main arterial road out of Redhill to the north. No opportunity to dump the vehicle there. He opened Google Maps on his phone and started to follow the line of the A23 towards London. The first part ran through Merstham passing a few shops, a pub and plenty of houses. It felt a bit too busy. Then the road crossed over the M25 and entered a green area, plenty of trees and open land but still a few houses, although most were set back from the road. Within a couple of miles, the road merged with the M23 grew into a dual carriageway and became much too busy. Rockford switched his focus to the periphery of the road. For a main road running into London, which he knew to be regularly congested, the neighbouring areas were rich with possibilities: lakes, forests, dead ends, deserted cul-de-sacs. He pulled back from his phone. No. Any vehicle abandoned in plain sight would have been reported by now. He scrolled on, moving closer to London. Coulsdon; a full-blown suburb of houses, shops and businesses, complete with thousands of pairs of eyes and hundreds of potential witnesses. He scrolled on. Purley. Coulsdon, but worse. Maybe he'd been kidding himself that he could help the inspector. With Purley in the centre of his map, Carshalton came into view a few miles to the west, and there between the two was the answer. SF Scrap Cars, a little out of the way, the perfect place to hide a car, in amongst other cars, where it would look at home and not attract any suspicion.

Rockford was having a debut to remember. On the back of their previous discussion, he felt emboldened to share his latest discovery with Inspector Bee. "Yes, sorry to bother you, boss, but I was thinking about what I would do if I had to lose a car somewhere between Redhill and Croydon and I found something you might want to see."

Bee watched Rockford show him the potential route from Redhill which he had plotted on Google maps ten minutes earlier. Bee's eyes began to sparkle as Rockford clicked on to the website of SF Scrap Cars and panned through some of the photos. With each successive photo, Bee tapped his foot. The scrapyard was out of the way; it looked dated; wasn't a major commercial operation; it was a perfect hiding place. Before Rockford had finished Bee was on the phone to McTierney.

★ ★ ★

WHILE ROCKFORD HAD moved the investigation from

Holmethorpe to Purley, Chief Superintendent Lisa Springfield had assembled her search team at Holmethorpe. She was at her commanding best; feet set apart, mouth, eyes and face focused on the task, no hint of amiability. In front of her stood 12 officers all in hi-vis jackets, above three drones buzzed overhead scanning the ground, and four dogs strained at leashes eager to begin the search. There was a tense hush in the air broken only by Springfield's sharp tone as she briefed the team on their mission. The team was to fan out in a semi-circle and cover as much ground as they could in what Springfield called a spiral search. Every officer had been issued with a map and a photo of both Itzkowitz and her car; three ground teams had been established plus an aerial team which was to direct the ground resources to likely points of interest. Any unusual item was to be logged and bagged. Any item of significance was to be reported to Springfield.

On her command, the drones rose, and set off in different directions, the respective operators glued to their screens. The dog teams each gave one of Itzkowitz's tops to their dog and let them run. The walking teams followed close behind pushing their way across the terrain with long sticks. The first team worked through the industrial estate, the second crossed into the mobile home park which bordered one of the nearby railway lines, the third searched through a playground and school. Every wisp of fallen tissue, each thread, all fragments of scrap metal were meticulously examined, photographed and logged. Despite the occasional shout of a name or the crackle of a walkie-talkie, and the marking-off of an area as 'searched', no significant finds were reported to Springfield. The scene was one of efficient teamwork and tireless effort but the whole operation was tinged with a deep, underlying desperation.

Even Bishop, who tried hard to maintain a sensible work life balance had sacrificed her Saturday morning and was trawling through that list of Wembley concert attendees. Just as Bee had predicted, there on the list was a Cooke. This one was a Sharon Cooke but that would suffice as the credit card address matched the home address of DCI Cooke on the police database. Bishop felt a buzz of electricity surge through her veins, as she circled the name with her red pen. She knew this one would count.

McTierney also tried to avoid working on Saturday, although for different reasons, but he too joined the working club. He flicked through his phone to find Mel's number. Although she was surprised to hear from Ron, once he rolled out some of his best patter, she relaxed and chatted away and without noticing she offered the name of the first officer on the scene after Jackson was murdered. But ten minutes later he found a different response. Someone had forewarned the officer about the Reigate station attempting to ascertain inside information on the shooting of Jackson. McTierney received a frank rebuttal. Each of Bee's questions went unanswered. Then, believing his work was done for the day, McTierney treated himself to a cold beer from the fridge.

THIRTY-FIVE

THE DOOR WAS opened by a swarthy man who looked like he hadn't cleaned a car in his life. He looked Kelly up and down before speaking. "What do you want?"

"I'm here to collect Detective Chief Inspector Cooke's white Audi car."

"News to me. We provide a full collection and delivery service to the chief inspector."

"I believe it was agreed yesterday. The chief was called away and didn't want to inconvenience anybody, so he sent me to collect it."

"What? Cooke didn't want to inconvenience anybody?" The man frowned at the statement. "Are we talking about the same bloke? I've never known him to give a shit about anyone but himself."

Kelly felt himself starting to sweat, "I'm not sure the chief would appreciate your tone."

The swarthy man leant towards Kelly, pushed his tongue around his mouth. "He ain't here is he, so what he don't hear, won't hurt 'im."

"I wouldn't recommend upsetting the chief."

The man looked Kelly up and down and shook his head. "It's not gonna be me who upsets him. You'll be the one who winds him up."

"In what way?"

"For a start, you're black."

It was Kelly's turn to frown. "I am. All of me."

"Cooke hates your sort. If he knew you were driving his car, he'd send it back to me to have it cleaned again."

The answer hit Kelly like a piledriver to the face, and he stepped back, before pulling himself together. "Mr Cooke needs to be educated."

"Are you for real?" The swarthy man narrowed his eyes and drilled them into Kelly's face as if committing his appearance to memory.

"Indubitably."

The swarthy man shook his head. "Hang on, I need to check this. This is all a bit weird." He stepped inside the shopfront and left Kelly outside with his blood pressure racing.

Kelly was on the doorstep for a couple of minutes, but it felt like an hour. With every passing second he convinced himself he was going to be exposed. Why hadn't Bee told him that Cooke was a racist. Kelly's mind began to race, thinking of an escape plan. If Cooke's thug returned having exposed their plan Kelly would need to escape without drawing attention to their suspicions. Kelly spun around to examine his surroundings; a non-descript industrial estate, no bus stop, few people, no big shops, nowhere to hide, nowhere to run. He began to fidget and exhaled deeply. Suddenly he was aware of someone standing behind him. He turned back to face the same swarthy man.

"Daphne in the office says your story checks out." He looked disappointed.

"Good." Kelly avoided catching his eye. "Good. Can we

get on with it. Only I've got a lot to do."

The man took his time to move but pointed to the left side of the building and began walking. It was then that he noticed Kelly was dragging a large case. "What's in the case?"

Despite all his preparation Kelly was unprepared for the question, "Oh, nothing."

"Looks heavy for nothing."

Kelly ignored the remark and, having entered the rear of the property he hastened towards the only white Audi he could see. He stopped by the boot, but the man put his hand on his shoulder, "I asked you a question."

"I'm sorry, what?"

"What's in the case?"

"I'd tell you but then I'd have to kill you," laughed Kelly, but his audience wasn't laughing.

"Seriously, it's private and personal and belongs to Mr. Cooke, so I don't think I can share it with you. Not without his express permission."

"Hmm. He can be a difficult man, but he's a good customer. Here's the keys."

Once Kelly was in the car and driving away from the valet company he recalled the single piece of advice Bee had given him for the operation. He had cautioned against trusting another police station and had instructed Kelly to hide in open sight. He had proposed taking the car to the entrepreneurial team washing cars in the car park of the giant Tesco at Purley Cross, which Bee had noticed three days earlier. Kelly was sceptical but to his relief he discovered that it worked. He handed over £500 in cash to the team to borrow their canopy for a couple of hours. For Joe and his crew, it was the easiest money they'd ever earned, and they were delighted to slip off to the store's coffee shop.

In normal circumstances Dr Kelly would follow a systematic and meticulous process to ensure no evidence would be missed or contaminated, but mid-morning on a Saturday in the middle of a retail store car park and with a clock ticking in the back of his mind, Kelly had to improvise. But he didn't compromise; full protective clothing was the order of the day as Kelly pulled on a white coverall, protective shoes, gloves and a mask.

He began by taking photos of the car from all angles but quickly tightened his focus to the interior. If Itzkowitz had been in the vehicle at all it was likely that she'd been in the rear or the boot. He used a spectrometer to scan the seats with an ultraviolet light looking for hair, fibres and blood. The top surface of the seats offered nothing. No problem, Kelly smiled to himself, valet companies clean all the obvious parts; they do all the headlines. But blood, and fluid seeps down into the recesses and bowels of the car. Gravity is the enemy of the slip-shod cleaner and the silent accomplice of the diligent forensic scientist.

As he'd hoped, once he delved further down he found a few hairs; he used a combination of tweezers and tape to lift the hairs out of the seat cracks and into the waiting evidence bag. He lifted the floor mats, but here the valet company had earned their money: no fibres, no blood. He began taking swabs from the seat belts; they were often a gold mine of trace evidence. He completed his search of the car by swabbing the parcel shelf and the air vents. Without a microscope he couldn't quantify the material he was collecting but he felt positive. He opened the rear door, at first glance it looked clean, but had the valet people removed the parcel shelf? It seemed not. His first swab came back rich with residues. The next looked like it had found blood. Bingo. He'd enjoy watching Bee arrest the swarthy man, there must be enough material here to make a case for an accomplice to kidnapping.

THIRTY-SIX

McTierney used the morning to follow up on Itzkowitz's first boyfriend, James Fisher who lived in Dorking. McTierney hadn't wanted to go, muttered about futility of the visit all the way along the A25 to Dorking and ranted all the way back, once he'd established that Fisher had just returned from a business trip to Vienna and had been out of the country at the time of Itzkowitz's abduction.

He followed this visit with a second fruitless trip to White Bushes in search of Jake Rivers; despite knocking out the opening chords to 'Smoke on the Water' on Rivers' front door, he couldn't entice anyone to answer it. He tried the same trick on the back door but louder as his frustration grew, but with the same result. Hence it was mid-afternoon when McTierney met up with Bee in central Reigate.

They dropped into Beryl & Pegs coffee shop on Holmesdale Road for a coffee and a cake – it was Bee's first food since breakfast, and he demolished a generous slice of carrot cake in four bites. Even McTierney, ranting in his ear about the time he had wasted driving over to Dorking, failed to spoil Bee's enjoyment of the cake. He pushed the empty plate across the table.

"Time for some action," he said and the two men left the café. Bee began striding towards the railway crossing on the main road, but McTierney dawdled a few yards behind him. Bee waited outside Reidy's Barber Shop until his colleague arrived. "That's where I get my hair cut. The barber is a nice guy; he doesn't make me feel like I need to say anything."

McTierney looked at his hair and into the shop through the long glass front. "I guess short all over isn't too complex. I'll keep it in mind. Do we have to do this?"

"We do. Now come on, we've only got ten minutes."

As Bee and McTierney stood talking they watched a middle-aged man stride out of Reidy's Barber Shop. The man with the new haircut crossed the road and stopped outside a food shop to look at his reflection. He began trying to brush his hair forward with his hand.

McTierney smirked, "Too late now mate."

The man walked on and tried another window, a woman inside stared back out at him and the haircut man scuttled away.

"Do I have time for a courage building swift half? There's a pub just down the road."

"I thought you never drank halves."

"I don't. But I thought there was more chance of you agreeing to a half."

"No. Come on, let's walk."

It had been a sunny afternoon, but a cloud slipped across the sun as Bee and McTierney walked over the level crossing and headed down to the Tunnel Road, which ran under Reigate Castle Grounds and was closed to traffic. Walking towards them were Carol Bishop and Lily Gandapur. Bee's face lit up at the sight of the two women but was soon screaming in horror as a gun was pulled, two shots fired, and Lily Gandapur fell to the ground.

McTierney raced back the way they had come and a few minutes later a doctor came running from the private GP clinic on Castlefield Road by the roundabout they had just crossed over. The doctor bent down over the prostrate body, checking for signs of life. Bee cleared some room, while Bishop phoned for an ambulance. The doctor's movements became more frantic as he searched for a pulse and then began trying to resuscitate Gandapur. On his knees he spread his hands across her chest and began a series of chest compressions. He pressed down rhythmically for three minutes as sweat began to form on his forehead. He alternated between compressions and breaths into her mouth, stopping frequently to check for signs of recovery. But to no avail. Lily Gandapur died before the ambulance arrived to whisk her away.

THIRTY-SEVEN

IN THE MINUTES after the shooting Bee's team swung into action; Bishop had left with the ambulance and McTierney had chased off in pursuit of the unknown shooter. Bee took command of the scene and began working through the protocol for the aftermath of a shooting. Quickly, he assessed that there was no ongoing risk to the public, and had the immediate area cordoned off by the time the first police car arrived. Kelly and a forensic officer arrived shortly after the police car and began examining the scene. Bee stationed an officer at each end of the tunnel to restrict movement of the general public and to preserve the crime scene. He took the details of the few people who were in the vicinity and could potentially be witnesses. Then as more officers arrived he left them to take full statements from each of the six people. He took a moment to work out where the gunman would have been standing.

Springfield arrived on the scene sooner than Bee had hoped and any thinking time he might have enjoyed evaporated. "Inspector, I heard the headlines, but in your own words tell me what the fuck happened here?"

Bee swallowed hard; he'd known this question would come. He recounted the key moments that had led up to the shooting. Springfield stood listening intently, concern etched across her face. "So, three of my team were here at the time of the shooting but you're all okay?"

Bee nodded his agreement.

"Thank heavens for small mercies. I can't afford to lose any more of you." She sighed heavily. "Do you happen to know the victim?"

This was the bit Bee wasn't going to enjoy, and he looked around and noticed that neither McTierney nor Bishop had hurried back, not that he expected them to. He blew out his cheeks. "Yes. I do. Did. She was Lily Gandapur, the lead witness for the prosecution in the Taranovsky case."

Springfield's eyes burst out of her head. "You're fucking kidding me!"

Bee dropped his head to look at the pavement and mumbled a weak, "No. I'm not. Looks like Taranovsky got her, despite all the precautions. we've been taking."

"Holy shit! The chief constable will be apoplectic. What were you doing meeting with Lily Gandapur in public two days before the biggest trial we've had in years is scheduled to begin?"

Bee sucked the air over his teeth. "DI Jackson asked me to help out. He was worried that someone was going to eliminate Gandapur. He didn't trust any of his colleagues. I've been looking after Lily Gandapur since Wednesday evening. I suspect Jackson was killed when he wouldn't give up her location. Not that he knew it anyway."

"What the fuck were you thinking?" Springfield leaped from concern to anger and grabbed Bee by the shoulders. "Presumably you recruited McTierney and Bishop and the rest of your little gang into this caper."

"No. It's all my doing. Obviously McTierney and Bishop

knew about the plan, but it was my idea, they were just following orders. McTierney even argued against the plan."

Springfield raised her eyebrows, but Bee continued, "If you want to blame anyone, you should blame me. If you want me to resign, I will." Bee paused hoping that Springfield would dismiss the idea, but she didn't. "Jackson was my friend. I did it to help him." He paused. "And because I thought it was the right thing to do. There had already been two attempts on Gandapur's life. She wasn't safe in Croydon; something had to be done."

Springfield inhaled deeply, "It seems she wasn't safe here either."

"No. These people are ruthless and have connections everywhere."

Springfield frowned at the suggestions; Bee sought to explain. "I've been searching my brain trying to work out how they would have found us. There must be a mole in the Reigate team somewhere, probably the same person who was involved in the set-up to have Itzkowitz abducted. We glossed over it in the last team review but a spy in the camp would help to explain a few things."

"Seriously? You think there's someone on our team working for this Russian. Do you have any evidence?"

"No. None at all. But that itself is evidence for me. It's all too clean, too simple. There are too many details which an outsider wouldn't have access to, wouldn't know about. They've all fallen into place for whoever is behind this."

"That's some accusation."

"I realise that. But I'm convinced of it."

Springfield looked uncomfortable to be having the conversation in the open. "Until you have some evidence, you better keep that thought just between us. Now, did you see the killer?"

"No. I think the shot came from behind me. I know it's a cliché, but it all happened so fast."

Springfield stared at him like a disappointed school teacher. Bee took a breath, then closed his eyes and started to recount his story. "McTierney and I had walked down from the station area, we'd crossed the roundabout and were ten, maybe 15 yards into the tunnel approach. Bishop and Gandapur were walking towards us from the town centre; they were ten feet in front of us. We were just exchanging hellos and all that and then I heard a single shot, maybe two, and Gandapur fell to the ground. Bishop went to her aid, I called an ambulance, McTierney raced off to get help. All over and done in ten seconds."

"Is that it?"

Bee looked startled to be asked for more. "I don't think we'll find a witness worth the name. There didn't seem to be anyone around at the precise moment."

Springfield turned around to familiarise herself with the geography of Bee's statement. A thought bounced across her mind, and she turned back to Bee, but he had stepped away and a traffic officer came running towards her.

"Ma'am we've got a log jam of traffic both ways on the A25. The town centre is at a standstill, the road out to Dorking is blocked." He gestured to the traffic behind the chief super, "And that queue goes all the way back up to the motorway and will be affecting the junction by now. We need to do something; either re-open the roads or set up a major diversion."

Springfield looked back up the hill and could see cars

bumper to bumper all the way, the town was in gridlock. She beckoned Bee to join the discussion, "Do you think we need to keep these roads closed? Will the traffic have a bearing on your investigation?"

Bee looked left and right and made a quick decision. "No. Release the traffic. Kelly's in situ and we've logged the details of any witness who might be able to help."

THIRTY-EIGHT

IT WAS 8 p.m. before McTierney arrived back at Bee's house in Outwood. He dropped his rucksack by the door, walked straight to the fridge and took a bottle from the middle shelf. He sprung the cap and drank the contents in one slug. "That's better," he sighed, standing the bottle on the kitchen counter and reaching for a replacement.

"Tough afternoon?"

"I hate witnesses. I only made it through the last statement by promising myself that I would soon be rewarded with a cool beverage brewed from the majestic crystal-clear waters of the Colorado River."

"I think it's brewed in Northampton."

"Don't ruin the image."

Bee smiled, then tilted his head inviting an explanation. "Tell me about the witnesses."

"Three hours I've spent listening to idiots, who haven't seen anything useful." He took another gulp of beer. "Half of them claiming to have seen something, were young men with a few drinks inside them." Bee fought the desire to point out the irony in what McTierney was saying. "The rest, sad individuals or attention seekers looking to get their name in the paper."

"I'm guessing we don't have any leads to follow."

"No, we don't. Not one."

"Excellent. A job well done."

"Thanks. What's for dinner? And I need a long beer."

"I thought you'd have your beer head on, so I'll knock up a chilli con carne, and hopefully the rice will absorb some of that beer."

★ ★ ★

THREE HOURS LATER and both men had a belly full of chilli and beer; Ron turned his attention to a bottle of whisky that he'd had his eye on for a few months. They had avoided any discussion of the case all evening but as they stretched out on the sofa in the lounge, Ron asked the question that both of them had been considering but hadn't wanted to face. "Do you think Taranovsky's hoodlums will come back again tonight?"

Scott blew out his cheeks; "I hope not. Now there's no need for them to eliminate Lily Gandapur, I'd hope that they would consider themselves to be out of the woods and take the night off."

"Ha! Out of the woods. I like it. I wonder if that's where they came from?"

Scott screwed up his nose. "I doubt it. If you don't know your way around the woods here, you can easily get lost. Plus, they seem to apply crude brute force wherever they go. I imagine they drove straight down the lane, guns at the ready."

"Good job we weren't at home."

Scott took a sip of his whisky and nodded.

Ron let the topic lie for a few minutes then added, "What

you need to do is invest in a bunker in the garden."

Scott frowned but it didn't deter Ron. "There's plenty of space out there, or you could get rid of that small patch of grass in the back yard that you don't know what to do with. You're always saying it's a pain to mow." Ron began to get animated and sat upright. "You don't need a big entrance, so no one would see it. Then once you get a few feet down you start to burrow. You can go far, and wide and even deep. Out here there's nothing to stop you. It wouldn't take long; you can spread all the earth over the fields. Build a few pillars for support, set up a generator for your power and you're halfway there."

"You're not selling it to me."

"Use your imagination. It'd be perfect for you. You wouldn't have to talk to any of the neighbours."

Scott lifted his head. "I don't talk to them now."

"I know, but this would take your isolation to a whole new level. Of course, you'd need a fridge down there for food and beer."

"I wondered how long it would take you to consider your beer supply."

Ron laughed, "Well it'd be a long tunnel to get to The Bell. Be easier to have our own. Then next time you upset a Russian gangster you'll have somewhere to hide."

Scott shook his head, "There must be an easier option, but I might agree to upgrading the first aid kit. Although I hope not to be under siege in my own home again."

The conversation lapsed and each man took a further slug of whisky. Ron got up and refilled both glasses. As Scott held up his glass he looked up to his friend, "I must tell you, I'm always amazed by your capacity to find happiness in any situation."

"What do you mean?"

"Your happiness is relentless no matter how much shit we're in."

Ron stared back at him, as if he didn't understand the words. Scott lifted himself up on his elbows, "Come on, you must be aware of it. You never let anything knock you off your stride."

Ron still didn't reply.

"Last night we were maybe half an hour from a gun fight with a Russian gang, which probably wouldn't have ended well. We've lost a close colleague who we're struggling to find, a close friend was shot dead two days ago. We were involved in another shooting today and when the chief finally catches up with what we've been doing over the last week, we'll probably both be out of a job, and yet you can sit here and talk fancifully about building a giant beer cellar in the garden. I don't know how you do it?"

Ron looked stung by the words as if they were an accusation. "I don't see the value in worrying about things I can't change. If the evil queen wants my badge so be it. Until then, I'll do my best to find Fran. If I have to fight a couple of mad Russians on the way, then that's what I'll do. But I wouldn't say I was happy all the time. I'm not especially happy at the moment, but I'm not unhappy. All I would say is that the happiest people don't have the best of everything, they just make the best of everything they have."

Scott pursed his lips, "Good philosophy if you can live it."

"I'll give you a case in point. Monday I'll be back on the case giving it 110%, but as soon as this case is over, I'll be dusting off my schoolboy French and making a date with the young mademoiselle I met on the train to Exeter."

Scott sat bolt upright. "You've got her phone number?"

"Of course," smiled Ron.

A look of incredulity spread across Scott's face, "I don't know how you do it. You find happiness in everything. It's a gift. It really is. I don't think I know how to be happy. All my life I've focused on getting things done. It's what I was taught as a child. It's all I know," he paused, "but it's not real happiness."

Ron turned to face Scott and put on his interviewer face, "Are you someone who feels more valuable when you're getting things done, achieving your objectives, ticking items off your to-do list?"

Scott's face flushed red. "Yes, I guess I am, although I won't phrase it in such a mealy-mouthed way."

"You're a slave to the classic 'things to do' list. You need to forget doing things and start enjoying things." Ron sent his point across the lounge with a broad sweep of his arm.

"Much easier said than done," said Scott, pointing his finger at Ron.

"Is it? I don't feel the need to achieve." Ron puffed out his chest, "I do what is expected of a policeman, because I want to. You know the story of my brother's early death. Ever since he died and I couldn't save him, I've wanted to make amends and I do that by helping people, and I do that by being a policeman. I don't care what society demands of me. I do it for Derek and for me. But I look for the positive in what's around me."

Scott waved away the story but let the comment pass.

"But what happens when you have a low patch? When

you're not achieving much. Like now, for instance. I know you've been busting a gut trying to out think Taranovsky, Rivers, and Cooke and co. But if you don't find Itzkowitz are you going to feel worthless for the next week?"

A look of resignation fell across Scott, "Yes probably. If I don't save Itzkowitz I'll blame myself and I'll be on the floor for the week that follows, maybe longer."

"And what happens when the next case drops on your desk two days later? There'll be another Fran somewhere needing your help." Ron raised his voice.

"I see the weakness in my argument. I just can't do anything about it. It creates an intolerable pressure, and quite frankly, you're not helping."

Ron dismissed Scott's concern and pressed on with his point, "One way of keeping this burning desire to achieve at bay is an idea I got from my old station chief in Norwich, Des Mayers. "He made a habit of keeping a 'have done' list as well as a 'to-do' list. When the day doesn't pan out as you'd expected you can still take credit for what you did instead."

Scott slunk down on the sofa, took a large gulp of whisky and tried to shut out the noise coming towards him, but to no avail.

"While your original plan might have included, 'lock up a killer', if you fail but you have 'paid the council tax', is that any less worthwhile?"

Scott raised himself back on his elbows and saw a chance to attack, "That's okay to a point. So long as you don't put 'drink a beer' on your list."

"As if I'd ever give myself such a low target." As if to prove the point Ron took a large swig of his drink and finished the glass. He was on a charge now. He reached across the floor for the bottle. "The only success worth talking about is doing what you want, when you want, where you want, and for as long as you want."

Scott squirmed on the couch.

"Ah, I should've added; and to whom you want."

"Just so long as it's legal and you don't make a mess on my sofa."

"Ha. While I'm on a roll, happiness is not a destination – it's a journey, and I have a seat in the first-class compartment. Come and join me."

"Would that be next to you and Miss France?"

Ron laughed. "Yes! But seriously life is not a rehearsal Scottie. Look, good stuff happens, bad stuff happens, that's life. You've just got to make the best of it. What's that Monty Python song?"

"I don't know, but I've had enough philosophy and whisky for one night. I'll see you in the morning."

★ ★ ★

LATER THAT NIGHT there was ample evidence across the Surrey Hills of Ron's theory. In Outwood, Bee struggled to find any meaningful sleep and three times he awoke from bad dreams where he had stumbled on the dead body of Fran Itzkowitz. A few miles away in Reigate, Chief Superintendent Lisa Springfield endured a difficult night; she had worked until midnight, but something troubled her about the reports of the killing of Lily Gandapur. Further south Dr Kelly had spent the evening watching a Denzil Washington detective movie and his sleep was fitful as he played out a dream with himself in the titular role being shot by a swarthy man.

Whereas on the ground floor of Bee's cottage McTierney had fallen asleep the moment his head hit the pillow, and his snoring resonated around the bedroom.

But for all of them the morning came too soon.

THIRTY-NINE

IT WAS A late start in Outwood for Bee and McTierney; the combination of beer and whisky from the previous night had taken its toll. But their respite didn't last long. At mid-morning there was a sharp knock on the front door. The men exchanged worried looks; nobody ever came calling at Bee's house. It was so far off the beaten track, that even the locals barely knew where it was and that was why Bee has chosen it. "Did you see anyone approaching?" McTierney shook his head. "Where's your gun?" Bee opened the cutlery drawer in the kitchen and picked up the weapon. McTierney crept to the window and tried to sneak a look out towards the drive, "I can't see a vehicle."

"Shit. It might be Taranovsky's mob paying a second visit."

The caller knocked on the door again.

"We'll have to open it," said Bee and he took the gun with him as he stepped towards the front door. Bee returned a minute later; a smile had replaced the gun. "It's our favourite pathologist,"

"You mean that bloke Booth, who worked on the Cave case with us," said McTierney loud enough so Dr Kelly could hear him.

"Sergeant McTierney, you're up before 11 o'clock in the

morning. What's going on? How are you progressing with your one-man campaign to save every pub in the county from closure?"

The three men took seats around Bee's kitchen table each fortified with a cup of coffee. Kelly's eye was drawn to the four coloured strips of paint on the far wall. "Are you thinking of decorating? I'd go for the apricot colour if it was me, but do you really need to bother, the place looks good as it is?"

"Yes!" McTierney clapped his hands in delight.

"Oh sorry, I've said the wrong thing," said Kelly.

"No matter," said Bee. "He doesn't have a vote."

"Back to the matter in hand, I bring a declaration," said Kelly, "And as we no longer trust anyone in our station, I thought it would be smart to deliver it by hand, rather than send an e-mail."

Bee nodded his approval of Kelly's approach.

"I come bearing two gifts; feedback on the murder of DI Jackson and the results of my examination of Cooke's white Audi." The two detectives leaned in. Kelly took a deep breath; "I spoke with the pathologist who attended the crime scene of the late detective. It appears that he wasn't under the same code of silence as the police officers under Cooke's sway."

"The Hippocratic oath is mightier than the inspector's curse."

Kelly smiled, "Yes, maybe. Key points from Drummond, my colleague. It was an execution style killing, two shots to the head. The weapon was a Russian made pistol; a 9mm Makarov. Quite rare in the UK, but actually the most common handgun in Russia. They pop up frequently in these conflicts in the Middle East and more recently in Ukraine. Mercenaries visiting those areas are known to bring them back home as a trophy."

"Yes, although our high-profile Russian is in jail awaiting trial, so has the perfect alibi," said Bee, before adding. "The use of a Russian gun will allow the police and the media to put the blame on a gang, or a Russian, and the investigation will follow one path and any possibility that it was somebody else will be forgotten." He shook his head. "If it was Cooke or one of his cronies, he's pulled a masterstroke here."

"Don't give up yet, inspector," said Kelly as he pushed a sheet of paper across the table. "Despite the efforts of the owner to have his car valeted, there was still some interesting residue to be found in the rear of the car and around the base of the seat belt fixings."

"Yes, yes, get on with it," said McTierney.

Kelly looked across the table and frowned, "Patience my friend." Then he broke into a smile, "What the hell, you won't listen. Yes I found blood. I ran it through the police database as Bee suggested, and we have two matches."

"Two!" said Bee and McTierney together.

Kelly nodded slowly, enjoying his last moment of power. "One for Itzkowitz and one for your friend Jackson. Both people have been in the rear of that car in the last couple of weeks, and both have lost blood there."

McTierney clapped his hands. "Brilliant. A step forward at last. Now we can nail that bastard."

Bee sucked the air over his teeth and his two colleagues looked at him. "Yes, it's great news. Good work Dr Kelly. But let's face it, we won't be able to use this evidence in a court of law. Not the way we acquired it."

The mood around the table dropped 20 degrees and a silence enveloped the trio. But Bee retained a positive frame of mind. "We're getting closer to solving this case. We know the guilty party even if we can't yet prove it."

McTierney looked up at his boss, "Can we clarify, who we think is the guilty party here? Is it Taranovsky or is it Cooke, or even Rivers? We seem to have a partial case against each of them."

"I believe DCI Ryan Cooke is our villain and responsible for the kidnapping of our colleague. Taranovsky is undoubtedly a criminal, but I don't think he's directly involved in the plot this time. As for Rivers, I doubt he has the capability to organise something of this magnitude."

McTierney nodded at the assessment, then changed the debate. "Maybe the thing we should be focused on is the kidnapping. I hate to say it but we're running out of time to save Itzkowitz. I don't think Springfield's big search turned up anything new yesterday."

"We need a break from somewhere," said Bee, and just as he finished, McTierney's phone pinged with a new message. He flicked the phone over and his eyes raced through the text.

"This might help. Someone, possibly Taranovsky, or one of his gang, has just acknowledged the news about Lily Gandapur."

"What do they say?"

"It says, 'Great work yesterday Sergeant. What took you so long?'"

"Send them a reply, see if you can engage them in a conversation. Ask them about releasing Itzkowitz."

McTierney began typing feverishly and put the phone

back on the table. Three pairs of eyes sat and watched the unit, but it remained silent. The seconds dripped by like minutes, until Kelly pushed back his chair, "I have to go, Springfield is demanding a report on the killing of Miss Gandapur. I've promised her a declaration by 5 o'clock today. She's another who doesn't believe Sunday is a day of rest."

"You're always happiest when you're working," offered McTierney, "Just like my landlord."

Kelly bowed his head and glared back across the table. "For your information, I am happiest when watching the West Indies batter either Australia or England. But until that happens again, I spend my time in the lab. Good day, gentlemen."

Kelly's movement sparked Bee into action. "I want the pair of you to visit the scrapyard that Rockford found yesterday. It might be the place where they dumped Itzkowitz's car, so search every inch of the place and see what you can find."

"First thing in the morning?"

"That will do, I doubt it's open today and anyway McTierney and I have a busy afternoon ahead of us."

"We do?"

"Yes. We need to understand why Itzkowitz has not been released."

"Because the kidnappers are bastards."

"Probably. But all along you've been receiving text messages about a trade. You kill Lily Gandapur, and we'll release your DS. Now everyone knows Lily Gandapur is dead, the story is all over the news, but there's no mention of Itzkowitz's release. Why?"

Two blank faces stared back at Bee waiting for him to

answer his own question.

"Because she was targeted. The kidnappers wanted us out of the way so they could capture her. There was a reason why they wanted her, and we have to find it. And it won't necessarily be logical, at least not to us. But it will be to the kidnapper."

The frowns on the faces of Bee's colleagues told him, that more explanation was required.

"We need to search through all of Itzkowitz's case history and see who she might have pissed off. You can do that."

"Oh thanks."

"I'll work through the murky history of Taranovsky, and we'll see if we can make a connection."

"Didn't Bishop do this earlier in the week?"

"She tried, but I don't think she knew what she was looking for."

"I'm not surprised, I don't know what I'm looking for."

"No, nor do I. That's why we'll do it together. You follow Itzkowitz and I'll follow Taranovsky, and we'll go through their pasts chronologically. Come on, get your laptop out and let's get started."

The two detectives sat opposite one another in Bee's kitchen and began calling out key words and dates to one another as they sifted through the histories of Taranovsky and Itzkowitz.

"March 2017 – a burglary case in Godalming. Looks like Itzkowitz's first arrest in the UK."

Bee didn't reply and McTierney looked up over his laptop, "Hello. Calling Planet Bee. Are you there?"

Bee looked ashen faced as he turned to face McTierney, "This is disgusting, I hope it's not true, although it probably is."

"What? Tell me."

"I don't know how to phrase this, it's hideous."

"Just read it."

Bee paused, blew out his cheeks, then read the extract aloud. "When Taranovsky was learning his trade he was asked to prove his loyalty to Kuznetsov, some other gang leader, and he did so by sucking the blood from the face of one of his victims. This leader loved it and promoted him to a lieutenant immediately."

"That's in-human."

"It gets worse. Not long after, he stabbed someone so ferociously that they drowned in their own blood."

"Can that be true?"

Bee shrugged, "Well it's not in The Times, but it's not the kind of thing you make up. He's human evil personified."

McTierney shook his head, but Bee was on a roll. "Says here that as a child he watched his drug addict father beat his mother to death."

"Here we go again, another psychopath blaming his childhood for his behaviour."

"He might have a point."

"No, not in my book. What else has he been up to?"

Bee scrolled down a few pages, "Taranovsky set up a company called Bolshevik Consultancy in November 2016. Says here that it specialised in shipments between Russia and the UK."

"Who were the Bolsheviks?"

"They were the creators of the Communist party, so a million miles from what Taranovsky seems to be doing these days. The very name is a contradiction; it's odds on a front for something else."

McTierney continued to scroll away. "Armed robbery in Guildford June 2017."

"I remember that. I think one of the bank workers was shot."

"Assault in a nightclub. July 2017. A couple of low-grade driving offences. Youths causing a disturbance. Nothing to get too excited about."

"Taranovsky is cautioned in Croydon in September 2017. Investigating officer is our late friend DI Jackson. Reading the report is looks like Taranovsky and some of his pals smashed up a bar in South Croydon. Jackson and others arrested the group, but Cooke intervened at the station and the gang was released without charge."

"Sneaky. So, five years ago, there's a strong link between Cooke and Taranovsky."

"It appears so, and back then Cooke was a lowly Detective Inspector."

"So, if he was the same rank as Jackson, how did he swing it to get Taranovsky off the hook?"

"Good question. I'm sure Jackson was as straight as the day is long, so I can't believe he would've accepted anything untoward."

"Does that mean we have another dodgy copper involved in this?"

"It's possible. There's no other name listed here. Let's keep looking."

"October 2017 a minor fraud case in Guildford."

"Does the company have a Russian or Croydon connection?"

"No. It's automotive; resetting the mileage on cars in one of the industrial estates on the edge of the town. What's our favourite Russian been up to?"

"Not much over the summer of 2017. Maybe he was out of the country. He doesn't make another appearance at Croydon station until December."

Slowly the coffee cups piled up as the two colleagues continued their searches through the recent past. A pair of bacon sandwiches were eaten and the plates pushed aside. 2018 morphed into 2019 and the advent of COVID dampened down criminal activity across the globe. Even Taranovsky seemed to take a break. Itzkowitz's police career jogged along but, if anything, Taranovsky's criminal career was outpacing it; six months of solid policing in the county town of Surrey didn't match rumours of drug trafficking and failed cases of armed robberies.

McTierney let out a heavy sigh. "I'm bored. Itzkowitz doesn't have a link with this Russian or any Russian for that matter. I'm nearly up to the point where she leaves Guildford and joins us and there hasn't been a sniff of a connection.

"I know. I was hoping Taranovsky would expand his drug trade down into Surrey, but he seems to have gone North and East instead. Largely unchecked, although he did have some bad news last October; his nephew Anatoli was shot dead during a police operation in Belgium."

"Ha! Best way to deal with some of these scumbags. The police in Europe are far quicker to use a gun. It's what they should do here, give us all a gun."

Bee lowered his gaze at his partner, but ignored the comment, then suddenly sat bolt upright. "This might be interesting. The police officer who shot young Anatoli was called Frida Ishberg."

"How's that interesting?"

"Female, same initials and I'd guess also Jewish."

"I know it's a connection, but it's going to get torn apart by any defence attorney worth his salt."

Bee nodded, "Yes you're right. Even I'm not convinced by it. Although I can easily believe Taranovsky is anti-Semitic."

"But you did say at the start, the connection might not mean much to us but would mean a lot to Taranovsky. It's clear he loved his nephew, he doesn't strike me as the sort of person who would accept bad stuff, he likes to have someone to blame, no matter how tenuous the link."

"It's certainly that."

"Let's take a break, I need some food."

FORTY

LATER THAT EVENING there was another sharp rap on Bee's front door. On this occasion the pair were sprawled around the lounge, although this time without the whisky bottle for company. Bee raised his head meerkat style. "Who on earth is calling now? I chose to live on the outskirts of a small village for a reason. This shouldn't be happening. Certainly not twice in the same day."

McTierney moved to the window but couldn't see who was outside. "Looks like there's a car out there, something big. There's not enough light to see, you need to install an outside light. But why don't you open the door and see who it is? They're probably lost."

Bee plodded to the front door and pulled it open, then jumped back in surprise, "Aargh. Ma'am, sorry. What are you doing here?"

Chief Superintendent Springfield strode across the threshold, not waiting to be invited in.

"I have some questions for you, and they can't wait until tomorrow."

McTierney had heard Bee's cry of surprise and rushed into the kitchen to see the source. Springfield took advantage, "Ah McTierney, make me a strong tea, milk no sugar."

Springfield didn't wait to be offered a seat, pulled back a

chair and sat down, then invited Bee to sit opposite her. A slow-motioned Bee obliged. McTierney put the kettle on, then began to tiptoe back to the lounge. "Wait. You're probably part of this, so you should hear it as well."

McTierney stopped, forced a smile onto his face and took the third seat at the table. Springfield spread her arms across the table, "Let me tell you what I'm thinking."

Bee and McTierney exchanged nervous smiles.

"I was reviewing the reports of yesterday's killing and I'm troubled by what I've read. I'll summarise for you. Tell me if I've got something wrong." Springfield looked from Bee to McTierney and back again, then flipped open a notebook. "The Gandapur shooting occurred on a pedestrian area, no traffic, no shops, no houses, the only witnesses anywhere near the incident are you two and Bishop, suspiciously all members of the same choir." Springfield paused to allow the point to register and looked from one to the other before continuing. "The others coming forward can't offer anything material. The medic and the ambulance both arrived within five minutes. Do you know where the closest ambulance station is to the scene?" Springfield was met by two blank faces. "It's East Surrey Hospital; that's 15 minutes away on a Sunday afternoon. I know because I just drove it."

McTierney opened his mouth to say something but thought better of it and closed it again quickly. Springfield raised her hand to silence any future interruptions.

"So, you have a near miracle in medical support, but despite that, they can't save the victim. The body is packed up and gone within ten minutes. The only official police photo of the actual crime scene with the body is one taken by you, inspector, on your mobile. Most of the police officers are yet to arrive at that point, but when they do, the body has gone."

Bee began to fidget but couldn't take his eyes off Springfield.

"But someone does get there in time to see our victim, Russell Jakes, a photographer from the local newspaper. He gets a single photo of the body and posts it online telling the world that Lily Gandapur is dead."

Springfield paused and looked again at the two detectives. Each began to squirm until the kettle boiled and McTierney hopped up to make hot drinks for everyone.

"Are you suggesting it was staged?" mumbled Bee.

"No. I'm not suggesting it was staged. I bloody know it was." Springfield thumped her fist on the wooden table and hot coffee splashed across it.

Bee blanched at the accusation and his pause conceded the accusation.

"What I want to know is why?"

Bee avoided Springfield's eye and looked across towards McTierney for inspiration but found none. He pursed his lips as he struggled to find the right place to start.

Springfield tapped her fingers on the table, "Now, would be good."

Bee took a deep breath and dived in. Springfield listened intently to Bee's explanation and his theory about a conspiracy between Taranovsky and DCI Cooke. Her face contorted when Bee described the attempted attack on his house on the Friday night.

"I'd dismiss that out of hand, but for Dr Kelly's evidence, which tempts me to believe it, but none of this is admissible in court. Great endeavour but ultimately worthless,"

Springfield exhaled sadly. "Worst of all, there's a strong possibility that this boyfriend of hers, Jake Rivers killed her and that this conspiracy stuff with Cooke and Taranovsky is nothing to do with us. Our murderer might be sitting right under our noses while you're rocking the apple cart in Croydon. I understand that Jackson was killed with a Russian pistol, which might suggest a gang related killing, but it's a weak link."

"You're right to mention Rivers, because I think he has a part to play, and I don't know what that is, but if he killed her, where's the body?"

"Not all murder victims are found inspector, as you should know."

"I know, but if Itzkowitz was in Cooke's car as we believe she was, then how does she end up dead in Rivers's van? There's no connection between them." Bee paused. "There's no logic there."

"Maybe you haven't found the connection yet."

Bee shook his head, "I don't think so, Rivers is small time and petty crime. Taranovsky is big time, and if Cooke is involved he wouldn't mess around with a low-life villain like Rivers. It's too risky for him."

"I tend to agree, but I don't like to ignore the evidence found by Kelly. It must fit somewhere."

"Yes, but I don't know where." Then an idea crossed Bee's mind, "I've had a thought about why we can't find Rivers." His colleagues looked at him waiting for the revelation. "He's probably dead. At least that's a strong possibility. If he was involved with Cooke or Taranovsky, he's out of his league, and they'd kill him as soon as look at him. From what we've seen so far, they don't leave loose ends or loose lips to talk."

Springfield nodded at the logic, "That would fit. But for now, let's talk about you." She stopped to make her point. "You need to learn to trust people. Me, for starters!"

Bee flinched at the words. "I know," he acknowledged, "I'll do better." He paused, "All we need is something on Cooke, and I think we can crack this case."

"You really are convinced it's Cooke."

"Actually, I think we've been looking at this case all wrong. It's not Taranovsky or Cooke who is behind this. They're both involved. They are in it together."

"How does that work?"

"I'm not sure, but I think Cooke is the key. He's the one on the outside, making the moves. If we can nail him, it all falls into place."

"That won't be easy. He's a professional and he knows what he's doing. But first things first, where's Lily Gandapur?"

Bee looked at the floor, but knew he'd have to provide an answer, "She's staying at Bishop's flat."

"Is she safe?"

"I believe so. Certainly, as long as Taranovsky and co believe that she's dead, they're not going to try to kill her."

Springfield nodded at the logic, "Fair enough. Is she still willing to testify in court?"

"Oh yes." Bee relaxed for the first time since Springfield's arrival, "You'd have a fight on your hands trying to stop her."

"Good. That's one thing in our favour. Now let's get back to our missing DS. She's our priority."

"Agreed," said Bee recovering his mojo, "If we can find Itzkowitz, hopefully she can identify Cooke, or Taranovsky or someone as the kidnapper."

"Great, but where is she? We've been looking for her all week and haven't got anywhere close."

"I think she'll be in the greater Croydon area, but that's a big pond to fish in."

"And we need her alive. If your theory is correct and let's assume that it is, then once the trial is over and either Taranovsky goes to jail or even if he walks, they have no more need for Itzkowitz, she becomes a liability, a big liability. The obvious option is that they kill her and dispose of the body. I reckon you've got 36 hours in which to find her."

Then Springfield asked the question that everyone had been avoiding, "Do you think she's still alive?"

Bee hung his head and mumbled, "The chances are dropping by the hour. In fact, it's now more likely than not that she's not going to be found alive."

There was a long, uncomfortable silence. McTierney broke the hiatus, "He has been known to be wrong. Not lately but it does happen – especially if it's a question from a pub quiz."

Springfield scowled at the interruption. "It sounds like we don't have a plan."

Bee raised his finger, "I do have an idea, that might just work. But it's risky."

FORTY-ONE

East Croydon railway station is a major transport hub, bringing together rail, tram and bus services. The railway element is made up of six platforms spread across three major concourses connecting trains from all over the south east of England. They are connected by a new steel and glass structure which straddles the six platforms and houses the ticket office and a few retail outlets; coffee vendors, newsagents and the like. It's also a useful meeting place for hoodlums, gangsters and senior members of the police force.

This morning was to be no different. The early morning commuters had disappeared, but the platforms were far from empty. CS Springfield alighted from her train walked up the long sloping platform into the ticketing area and back down onto Platform 6. The railway platform stretched endlessly; a long expanse of concrete decorated with several large glass houses masquerading as waiting rooms and railway offices. Rows of uncomfortable metal benches lined the edges. Overhead a weathered canopy provided shelter, its beams adorned with peeling paint and multiple signs pointing in every direction of the compass. A short stubby coffee shop occupied the few passengers further down the concourse. Springfield walked briskly past everything to the deserted northern end of the platform and waited. The air carried a mix of metallic tang, and the hazy echo of engine oil, offset by the warm aroma of coffee. The platform's surface was dotted with faded yellow safety lines, slowing eroding under the thousands of footsteps which traipsed through the station every day. A station announcer informed the few scattered travellers that the 09:35 to Reigate had been delayed and was now expected at 09:50. For everyone else on the station it was a regular Monday morning, but not for Lisa Springfield. She turned and noticed a female figure on Platform 1 suddenly duck out of sight. Springfield checked her watch, he was five minutes late, her sense of vulnerability crept up another couple of notches. This didn't feel like a foolproof plan.

A sudden clamour caught her attention; Springfield's eyes were drawn to the far end of the platform; two tall men in overcoats marched towards her; their boots echoing on the concrete as passengers stepped aside. Behind them walked a silhouette, his face hidden under the brim of a fedora, he oozed towards Springfield. She knew it must be DCI Cooke. His movements were slow and purposeful, daring anyone to interrupt his progress. Nobody would doubt who was in charge here. As he reached the end of the platform a thick black cloud passed in front of the sun, the temperature dropped a couple of degrees and Springfield felt a shiver run down her spine. One of Cooke's goons gestured towards the solitary waiting room at that end of the concourse and pressed the button to open the door. Springfield stepped inside; Cooke followed.

"I was surprised to get your call yesterday evening. You made an interesting if outlandish, offer."

"I thought you should know."

"No. You wanted to make some money for yourself."

Springfield smiled. "And friends. Don't forget that."

"There are no friends in this business, only mutual interests."

Springfield offered a wan smile but no reply.

"What has your intrepid DI discovered that might be worth me paying £250,000 to make it disappear."

"He has evidence that will send you down."

"Evidence for what?" sneered Cooke.

"The abduction of a police officer, specifically DS Fran Itzkowitz who was bundled into a car, your car, last Saturday."

"You're bluffing. There's no evidence." But the early bravado in his voice tapered away.

"You were careless. You dumped her car at the SF Scrapyard. Trusting some minions to finish your work. That was sloppy; they're not as thorough as you might be. Our senior forensic officer visited the place. He has DNA samples which are about to enter the judicial system, and I'm willing to bet that once he's done that, he'll find a match between those and yours."

Cooke's mouth twisted in frustration, but he said nothing.

"Your money will ensure that I remove that evidence, and it never sees the light of day again."

Cooke turned away and snorted his disbelief.

"Let me guess what's going through your mind? You're wondering which part of her car you touched and whether our forensics man can find anything. Let me tell you he's the best in the business. If it's there, he'll find it."

Cooke sighed heavily and allowed his eyes to wander around the station.

"I don't think you realise how badly this could end for you. Not only will we have evidence to send you away, but we also have enough to ensure Taranovsky goes away too. All of this will come out in the near future when your boy, or is he your boss? Takes the stand tomorrow. He might be in the dock, but you'll be the one getting caught in the crossfire. Taranovsky doesn't strike me as the kind of man to go down without a fight. If he's got anything on you he'll use it. So, this is your last chance to save him and yourself. You have one hour to deposit £250,000 into that account or it'll be too late. Out of my hands." Springfield pushed a small business card into Cooke's hand.

"No." Cooke let the card fall to the ground, then clenched his fist and slapped it into his other hand, "I'm thinking it would cost a lot less than £250,000 to eliminate both your DI and this so-called 'forensics expert' of yours." The glint was back in Cooke's eye; he saw Springfield hesitate and seized the initiative. "You are making some very unpleasant assertions, chief superintendent." Cooke raised his voice. "I hope you know what you are doing. This could end very messily for you. Let's see, for a start, I could have you arrested for blackmail."

Springfield leant forward into Cooke's personal space, she spoke calmly, but her demeanour was of someone expecting an uncomfortable conclusion. "You and Taranovsky can't continue to murder people, police officers, anyone who takes a stand against you. This isn't Russia. We have laws. There will be outrage in the press. People will demand action. There will be consequences."

Cooke offered a yawn which rolled into an aggressive snarl. "The public don't understand how these things work.

Any furore will pass. People disappear all the time."

"You're playing with fire, and you'll be the one who gets burned."

"Is that it? Is that all you've got, some ridiculous, ill-conceived threat?" It was Alpha male time for Cooke. He clenched his fist in triumph and allowed himself an extended smile, he wasn't out of the woods yet, but once that bastard Taranovsky was gone, life would become a lot easier. "I think we'll take you with us, just for the duration of the morning, then if one of your cowboys wants to try something, you can tell him not to."

"Kidnapping a police officer. You've already tried that. How is that working out for you?"

"Save the smart remarks. Nobody's listening to you anymore. Now, follow Boris and you won't be harmed."

As Cooke stepped out of the waiting room he spotted the elusive woman on Platform 1 taking pictures on her phone. He clicked his fingers at the biggest of his two goons, "Get her." Cooke turned and looked across the tracks towards the woman, twisted his fingers into the shape of a gun and mimicked firing it at her. Panic spread across the face of Carol Bishop as she watched goon number one turn and charge down his platform towards the bridge that linked the platforms. The station exit was behind the bridge; it was a 100-yard dash that Bishop had to win but she hadn't run 100-yards since she was at school in the third form and the goon already had a 10-yard head start.

She started to run. She passed the first pillar, but the goon was running faster, he was 25-yards ahead. He would get to the central concourse first, which would block her only exit; she'd be trapped. Her heart was pounding fast. She looked around but there was nowhere to hide; a coffee bar, a toilet, a waiting room – all hopeless. She'd be waiting for the goon to find her, – he'd make mincemeat of her. The Tannoy announced that the 10:05 to London Victoria had pulled into Platform 1, the goon sprinted up the incline to the central area. The 10:06 southbound train to Horsham arrived at Platform 2. Passengers began to alight and to get in her way; Bishop's progress slowed to walking pace. The goon charged around the top concourse and clattered into a young woman. He yelled abuse at her and thundered down the concrete ramp onto the first of the three platforms. He paused at the start and walked steadily along the concourse, checking in waiting rooms, looking over shoulders into the café. Bishop was nowhere to be seen. The guard for the London bound train looked up and down the platform, put a whistle to his mouth and blew. The doors closed. It was the goon's turn to panic. He thumped the auto button on the door, jumped onto the train and began to walk menacingly down the carriage. As he did he spotted his prey. Bishop stood up and waved to him from the Horsham train.

FORTY-TWO

Dr Kelly had heard about McTierney's exploits behind the wheel and insisted on driving on the Monday morning. Together they pulled into SF Scrap Cars at a little after 9 o'clock.

"Careful where you park this, Doc," said McTierney. "Don't want anyone thinking that it's been abandoned and ready for the crusher."

Kelly gave him one of his dark looks.

The scrapyard was a rugged, industrial space filled with the remnants of discarded machinery, battered vehicles and worn-out domestic appliances. Located on the edge of town and away from any houses, with its own metallic architecture it stood in its own time zone, looking like nothing had changed for 50 years.

Kelly pointed to a sign proclaiming, 'No Unauthorised Entry.' McTierney touched his police warrant card. "Doesn't apply to me."

Kelly touched McTierney's sleeve, "Before we go any further, I should tell you that as a God-fearing medical man I don't condone violence."

"I thought you only prayed to the great God Vivian Richards."

"Don't take Sir Viv's name in vain, and don't mock me. I

mean what I say, if you can't apprehend him lawfully perhaps you shouldn't be doing it at all."

"Don't worry Doc, I'll play a straight bat, if only for you. But before we begin I have a question for you. The evil queen dropped by last night to give us the benefit of her wisdom. Your name cropped up."

Kelly's head twitched.

"How easy will it be for you to replicate your discovery on DCI Cooke's car? Assuming we can make it legit and tow it into your lab?"

Kelly nodded, "Should be possible. If we don't get everything I think we'd get something."

"Good. That's what I thought."

The two men began to walk towards a metal cabin, which offered itself as the only possible office on the site. A crow circled overhead scavenging for a scrap of food as the men crunched across a mud and gravel path littered with shattered glass; the early sun glinted on the fragments. The air was thick with the scent of oil, metal and damp earth while the sound of clanking steel power tools, and the occasional crashing of scrapped materials echoed through the yard. Towering heaps of scrap; old washing machines, broken bicycles and stripped-down cars formed a strange metallic landscape where workers in high-visibility jackets, yellow hard hats, and heavy gloves drifted through the maze dismantling, sorting and cutting metal with oxy-acetylene torches. The yard was a mess of tangled pipes, dented bonnets, and shells of every imaginable car. A thousand untold stories lay hidden amongst the debris.

From nowhere a large black dog raced from behind a tower of rusting cars and barked at the approaching men. "I hate dogs," said Dr Kelly, stopping in his tracks. "Especially ferocious ones that look like they haven't had breakfast."

A man stepped away from the bonnet of a Ford Sierra with a missing front door and yelled at the dog, which stopped a few yards short of McTierney and Kelly and traded his bark for a growl.

"You don't wanna be walking around here, Jasper won't like it."

McTierney reached inside his jacket for his warrant card, but before he could present it a familiar face stepped out of the cabin to see what was causing the commotion. McTierney switched his focus. "Well, well, well, look who it isn't, Jake Scumbag Rivers. What are you doing here?"

"I work here, DS McTierney, not that it's any of your business." Rivers cast a nervous glance in the direction of the Sierra man, but he'd lost interest and returned to the car.

"Oh, but it is my business Jakey boy. All your misdemeanours are my business."

Rivers offered a weak smile and walked over to McTierney and Kelly.

"Let me introduce you. Jake Rivers: sometime hospital porter, occasional musician, one time friend to Fran Itzkowitz and now murder suspect. Meet Dr Kelly: pathologist with the Reigate CID team and the man who identified the blood in the back of your van as that of our missing colleague – the aforementioned DS Itzkowitz."

The two men exchanged nods.

"Let's start with that, shall we? How do you explain the presence of blood from DS Itzkowitz being found in your van?"

"What? I can't. I didn't know there was any blood in the

back of my van."

"Clearly. When was Itzkowitz last in your van?"

"I don't know. A couple of weeks ago? Last time I played a gig probably."

"Different question. What are you doing here?"

"I told you; I work here."

"What does that mean? You work, what sort of work?"

"I know a bit about engines, so I help the men strip down an engine when we get a new vehicle in. Sort out the stuff that can be sold and leave the junk to be crushed."

"Or in my terms, stolen vehicles get delivered here; you strip them for parts, and then the shell gets crushed and hidden in the bowels of the scrapyard."

Rivers smiled at the accusation. "You've been watching too much TV."

It was McTierney's turn to smile, "Do you know who owns this place?"

"Gerry over there's the boss. You already met him. He's alright."

McTierney looked at the ground and kicked a stone across the gravel. "Are you sure about that?"

"Yes. Like I said, he's cool."

"Do you know who his big boss is?"

Rivers didn't seem to understand the question, so McTierney re-phrased it. "We have reason to believe that Dmitri Taranovsky has more than a passing interest in this place. Ever heard of him?"

Rivers shook his head. McTierney tilted his head slightly and squinted one eye, as if rehearsing his response. "A word of advice. Always understand who you're working for. You won't find Mr Taranovsky quite as cuddly as the NHS. He's one of the biggest international gang leaders there is. He killed his piano teacher when he was 12 and has graduated since then into extortion, drugs, robbery and all of them laced with outrageous violence. His trademark is to blast the kneecaps off his victims, so they're screaming in agony, then he talks to you, makes you listen to a recording of his piano playing before he shoots you. It's a long and painful way to go."

"You're making this up," said Rivers, but the colour had drained from his face. He turned to Kelly. "That can't be true, he's making it up."

Kelly took a deep breath, "I'm afraid to say that I've known pathologist colleagues spend hours examining a corpse, trying to work out which wound has killed their victim, such is the ferocity of Mr Taranovsky. I would echo DS McTierney's words of advice."

Rivers shuddered, made to challenge McTierney, but it was clear he was in two minds. Kelly took the opportunity to nudge McTierney and pointed to a battered blue car three-quarters up a tower of other battered vehicles. "Do you see the bumper sticker on that VW? I think that might be the car of our missing DS."

McTierney squinted at the wreck, "You might be right."

McTierney turned back to Rivers, "Can you get that blue car with the US bumper sticker down here? I want to look at it."

Rivers raised his hands in mock surrender, "Not me. That's way beyond my pay grade. I'll get Gerry for you."

A couple of minutes later Gerry had sauntered over and joined the conversation. McTierney repeated his request.

Gerry shook his head, "It's not for sale."

"I don't want to buy it. I want to confiscate it."

Gerry looked stunned by the request, "It's not available for examination."

McTierney yanked his overworked warrant card from his pocket and thrust it at Gerry. "I think it is. Get it down here now, or I'll arrest you for obstructing the police."

Gerry took a step backwards. "Hey calm down. No need to get feisty. All I'm saying is that the car you want is at the top of a pile of cars. It needs a fork truck to lift it down and I don't have anyone here qualified to shift it." He paused, then added with a smile. "It's a health and safety issue."

"Find someone who can move it and do it now!"

"It needs to be Stan, and I haven't seen him all morning." He turned to Rivers, "Have you?"

Rivers shook his head.

McTierney clenched his fist and pressed his lips into a tight line. "Call Stan, or anyone else you need to. Get him down here pronto and get that car on the ground sharpish. Or I'll do it." He looked at Kelly and rolled his eyes. Then turned back to Gerry, "We won't be leaving here until we've seen that car up close. But while we have a spare few minutes I'd like to look through the registration documents and purchase records for every vehicle on this site, starting with that VW. I've reason to believe that this site is a haven for stolen vehicles."

A smile crept over McTierney's face. He switched his focus back to Rivers, "Jake can make us both a coffee while we're reading. I hope you've got some good biscuits, because my mood needs to improve rapidly for everyone's sake."

Gerry laughed, "What do you think this is? The Ritz?"

McTierney ignored the remark, focused on Rivers and

gestured for him to move towards the cabin. "And my colleague will have the same."

The cabin, a makeshift office, was a small cluttered, greasy affair, offering a row of metal cabinets, a desk, two plastic chairs, a modest fridge, an overworked kettle and a tin of tea bags. While Rivers attended to the hot drinks, McTierney whispered to Kelly to step outside and call into the station to let Bee know the situation and ask him to drop into the yard if he hadn't heard from either of them within the next two hours. Kelly looked alarmed at the suggestion but did as he was asked. Rivers plonked a mug of brown liquid on the desk and slung a packet of chocolate digestives in McTierney's direction. McTierney checked they were alone and pulled the door shut.

McTierney had gone into the cabin to poke about and make a nuisance of himself. He wasn't looking for anything in particular, but he did it because he could, and because he was pissed off with Gerry's prevaricating about the VW. Worst of all, the excuses made sense. Confrontation is McTierney's default mode of operation; when he's stuck with a problem he hits it with a hammer until something happens. Either the hammer breaks or whatever he's hitting breaks. This morning it was the office desk that took the brunt.

"Let's make some space." With a single brush of his arm, he swept all the papers and the phone off the desk onto the floor.

"Hey!" shouted Rivers.

"Before you get all narky with me, let me explain something. Odds are that car out there belongs to Fran Itzkowitz, and you've already told us that you work here. That connects you to her disappearance. As each day goes by without her safe return, it's looking more and more like a murder case."

McTierney paused to allow the point to register. Rivers began fiddling with a pen on the desk, as McTierney continued. "Murder. That will mean prison, the only question will be how long."

Rivers jerked his head up to looked at McTierney but didn't respond.

"Could you survive thirty years? Cooped up in a little cell. The plaything of the gangs."

"Don't play games with me."

"I'm not playing games, Rivers, I do that on the football pitch on a Saturday afternoon, and this, I believe, is a Monday morning. The day you go to jail. The prisons like a bit of fresh meat. You'll go down a storm. So, you'd better start talking. While you still can."

Rivers lifted his coffee mug to his ashen face. As he took a sip McTierney hit him with his killer question. "Did you abduct Itzkowitz and bring her here?"

Rivers didn't flinch; he finished his drink and returned the mug to the empty desk. "No. Maybe I haven't been the best boyfriend to her, but I'd never hurt her."

"Are you prepared to help us find her?"

Rivers ran his hand around the back of his neck and let out a nervous chuckle. He flicked his eyes up to meet McTierney's and inhaled deeply. "Listen."

But before he could complete his sentence, Dr Kelly pushed open the cabin door and Rivers froze. McTierney turned and scowled at Kelly, but the moment was gone. A few seconds later Gerry arrived in the cabin, "I heard a crash. Everything alright?"

McTierney's scowl deepened. Rivers replied to him, "Yes,

we're fine."

Gerry looked at the mess on the floor and back at McTierney, his demeanour began to darken. "Doesn't look fine."

"We're just making some space to review all these documents that you're going to present to us."

Gerry's jaw tightened and his fingers curled into a fist as he assessed the situation. His voice became sharper, "Look there's a clue in the word 'scrap'. People come here to dump vehicles they don't want anymore. There's not a lot of selling goes on. This ain't fucking Sainsbury's."

McTierney relished the fight in the man. "And there's also a clue in the word 'police', now fucking do it before I arrest you."

The two men stood facing each other and McTierney sensed Gerry was weighing up his options, he was relieved that he'd asked Kelly to alert Bee to what might go down, but Gerry backed down from the standoff. He turned to Rivers, then pointed at the middle cabinet, "Anything we have will be in there."

Rivers nodded and moved towards it.

"I came in to tell you that Stan will be here shortly; we should have your car on the ground within the hour."

"Excellent," said McTierney. "It's amazing what can be achieved when you ask nicely. Now is there anything else you should be telling me?"

Gerry left the cabin, and Rivers began sorting through the cabinet, dropping a few files on the desk. McTierney stepped over to Kelly and whispered in his ear. "This looks like a good place to hide a kidnap victim. Private, out-of-the-way, not many passers-by. Can you have a wander around the place and see what you can find? It wouldn't surprise me to find a lock-up of stolen or smuggled goods. Or even, the remains of a dead body."

Kelly didn't look amused at the suggestion but did as he was asked. It took Rivers only three minutes to empty the contents of the cabinet on the desk.

"Is that it?" asked McTierney, looking with disdain at the paltry selection of papers on the desk.

"I guess."

McTierney flicked through the assortment; there was nothing relating to a VW Beetle, or a Miss Fran Itzkowitz. He tossed the papers back on the desk. "I wonder if Gerry was being overly helpful, sending us off in the wrong direction?" He got up and walked over to the first cabinet and pulled it open. A bottle of vodka, a few packets of cigarettes, a couple of passports, both Russian, a mobile phone, a map and a few crumpled receipts stared up at him. He moved to the third cabinet. A small bag of white powder, probably amphetamine, a roll of duct tape, a couple of knives and a pistol presented themselves for inspection. "Quite the Aladdin's cave. You really should choose your friends more carefully, Jakey boy."

Rivers lifted his hands in surrender, "None of that stuff is mine. I told you I only work here and most of the time, I'm out there taking bits off the cars."

"Talking of cars. The blue VW. Were you here when that came in?"

Rivers shook his head.

"Do you know roughly when it arrived?"

Rivers screwed up his face, "A week ago maybe? It's near the top of a pile so it can't be old."

"Are you ready to help yourself? Tell us anything more?"

But again, Kelly broke the moment as he returned to the cabin. McTierney swung round ready to shout at the interruption but paused when he recognised the pathologist. "The chap with the forklift is in the process of getting the VW down. By the way no obvious cache of stolen goods or dead bodies."

"Pity."

McTierney, Kelly, and Rivers exited from the cabin and watched Stan, and his forklift deposit the blue VW on the ground in the middle of the yard. The once proud Beetle looked very sad; one of the headlights was cracked, all the windows were smashed, the engine had been ripped out and the registration plates had disappeared, but crucially the rear bumper was unscathed. McTierney glanced at the interior, "Same beige interior."

He pulled open the passenger door and opened the glove box; a Hershey bar fell out; he looked at Kelly and smiled and walked to the rear and focused on the US sticker. "I think this is Itzkowitz's car."

"We'll need the chassis number to confirm it. 17 digits stamped on the chassis somewhere. I'll start my search."

"I'll call into the office and get Bishop to confirm the original, and I'll get Rocky and a couple of officers up here to cordon off the site. We're going to need to sift through the evidence up here."

Two hours later Kelly's Audi pulled out of the scrapyard, leaving two patrol cars behind. Kelly turned to his passenger, "I'll say this much, a day out with you is exciting. A bit like a ride on an Alton Towers rollercoaster; exhilarating, scary and rousing, and should only be considered before eating a meal and not to be repeated more than once a year. Where do you get these ideas?"

McTierney smiled "I was watching a Steven Seagal film last night before I went to sleep."

FORTY-THREE

With Springfield, Bishop, McTierney and Kelly all occupied around the county Bee drove over to St Anne's Rise in Redhill and took a turn providing protection to Lily Gandapur. The pair sat in Bishop's lounge, Gandapur reading a novel and Bee reading through the case notes and press stories on Taranovsky. With the Russian due in Croydon Crown Court on the Tuesday the media was getting into hyperbole about the case. Bee read an account by a journalist from 'The Guardian' that appeared to be uncomfortably close to the truth. He wondered who might be the source. The author suggested a connection between Taranovsky and the recent murders of Ian Jackson and Lily Gandapur. He looked across at the sofa and allowed himself a small smile of relief that at least this aspect of his plan was still intact.

He took a call from an excited and yet nervous Dr Kelly, tried to reassure him that McTierney was more than capable of handling a scrapyard and promised that he would send reinforcements if they didn't speak again within the hour. His phone rang again ten minutes later, and Bee wondered if the scrapyard investigation was over-delivering. But his mind was scrambled when the caller announced himself.

"Inspector Bee, this is Dmitri Taranovsky. It's too long

that we speak."

A sudden coldness hit Bee's core, and his jaw dropped. He looked around the flat as if expecting Taranovsky to be behind him. "Excuse me I thought you were in custody."

"I am, so what of it?"

"Just surprised that you're able to call me. And that you should have my number."

"I do what I want. This cell is small problem to me."

"You might think yourself clever to be using a phone in prison, but I'll get that taken away from you. One way or another you will learn you can't go around killing people. You're going to be in prison for 25 years to life. Minimum."

"Don't be ridiculous. People tell me you're smart. Start acting so. You know there's no evidence to hold me."

Bee bit his tongue; he didn't want to say anything that might suggest Gandapur was still alive. He switched the focus of the conversation. "Did you order the kidnapping of Fran Itzkowitz?"

Taranovsky allowed the question to pass unanswered, so Bee tried again, "Tell me is Itzkowitz still alive?"

"The ends justify the means."

"What's that supposed to mean? Are you telling me you're guilty?"

"Guilt is for the stupid."

Gandapur sensed it was Taranovsky on the phone. She put her book down and a flash of fear raced across the face. Bee signalled frantically for her to remain silent. Then turned his attention back to Taranovsky, "So what's that? Are you telling me you're guilty and stupid?"

It sounded to Bee as if Taranovsky had snorted at the suggestion. He allowed himself a quick smile, before

Taranovsky replied "I've done nothing wrong, the Croydon police are watching my every move, how could I do anything?"

"But you do know where Itzkowitz is, don't you? You could tell me."

Taranovsky offered a heavy sigh, "You intrigued me. People told me you were different, that you were intelligent. No one haff ever challenged my organisation. I thought there might be role for you in team, but I see you are just a clumsy policeman. I tell you something. Something you need understand. You are boy here and I am man. I be out soon and if you defy me, I destroy every person you care about and make you watch their pain."

"Sounds like that cell must be affecting your judgement. I don't think you are going anywhere."

"Friend of mine tell me that you haff some evidence that might interest Croydon police. You need make it disappear. While you can."

"I can't do that sort of thing. It's not in my mentality."

"It's your decision. You want powerful friends who look after you or you want powerful enemies who destroy you?"

"I don't think you're in any position to make threats. You're nothing but a bully, and a killer."

"It sounds like you try make name for yourself. The trouble is that name will be on your tombstone." Taranovsky began to laugh at his own joke. "You should take leaf out of the book of your dog. He did his job; you should do yours."

"How about your dog; DCI Cooke. Does he work for you? Or do you do his dirty work?"

"Sound like you floundering around in the dark. You haff no idea what happening. I'll give you advice, when I look for inspiration I read Dostoevsky. You try it, inspector."

"I'd be inclined to start with 'Crime and Punishment'. How about that? A chance to confront your misdemeanours. No doubt you consider yourself superior to others."

"Seems you haff read Fyodor. But you haff misunderstood him, or maybe you do that deliberately simply to vex me. It's time to go. I enjoy watching your demise."

The line went dead, and Bee turned his attention to Gandapur. Nodding his head he said, "That was Taranovsky, allegedly calling me from his prison cell. I don't know how he managed to do that, but it's clear he's not aware of your status."

"We will surprise him tomorrow."

"Yes. We certainly will. I'm looking forward to seeing his face when they call you to the witness box."

"He's not your friend."

"Most certainly not. But I have to admit, I don't think it was Taranovsky who made the call to the station last Saturday which lured Itzkowitz away to Holmethorpe. The voice is too different. Taranovsky has that harsh, dark Russian accent with lots of Zs. The voice on the tape is more westernised."

Gandapur titled her head. "I wish it would hurry up. The time is going so slowly Every time I look at the clock it's hardly moved."

Bee smiled. "Don't worry. It will come. We're very close now."

★ ★ ★

LATER THAT EVENING the whole gang had assembled in Bishop's flat to run through their plan for the following day, although no one was expecting to be called to speak apart from Gandapur. A sense of expectation engulfed the group, and they enjoyed another special meal from the expanding repertoire of their in-house Pakistani chef. It was only after they had eaten that Bee checked his police email and found an item to rip the wind from their sails.

"Shit! I can't believe this."

The group turned to face Bee as he continued to read. Realising he had an audience; he looked up and announced. "Cooke's white Audi has been stolen. At least that's what he's claiming. It was reported on Sunday and added to the police list this afternoon."

"No way! Yelled McTierney. "That's a crock of shit."

Bee continued to read through the report, then whistled. "This is good. The vehicle is reported as being stolen from outside Croydon police station. And here's the best bit. Police want to speak to a man of West Indian origin who was seen collecting the car from a valet company on Saturday morning. Then there's a detailed description of Kelly. Cooke is asking for full support from all Surrey officers to apprehend the man."

Everyone turned to look at the pathologist, who mumbled "Terrific. I lend you guys a hand and look what happens. You turn me into a criminal."

McTierney chipped in, "You have to admire Cooke. I know he's a scumbag, but he's clever. He's prepared to dump a £75,000 car to avoid jail. I guess it's an easy choice, but he doesn't mess about."

The comment hung in the air for a moment, before Bee hammered another nail into their coffin. "With the disappearance of Cooke's car, any hope we had of having

Kelly run a repeat of his forensics masterclass on the car to find more incriminating evidence has vanished."

The group fell silent.

"I fear that now it all rests on finding Itzkowitz."

FORTY-FOUR

BEE AND MCTIERNEY had returned to Outwood on the Monday night with the expectation that they would meet up again with Kelly, Bishop and Gandapur at Croydon Crown Court on the Tuesday morning. McTierney had assumed that this would allow for him to have a gentle start to the day, not rising from his bed before eight-thirty. But Bee had other ideas.

He had continued reading through the case notes the previous night after returning home and had stumbled across an 'Exeter connection' that he considered to be too much of a coincidence. Hence he hammered on McTierney's door at a quarter to seven telling him that he had worked out where Itzkowitz was being held captive. There was no response, so Bee pushed open the door and regretted it immediately; it looked like the room had been visited by the Israeli Defence Force, who'd emptied a full can of Lynx Africa to cover their tracks. McTierney rubbed his eyes and staggered to the door, still half asleep and oblivious to the excitement in Bee's voice.

"This better be good."

"I think I know where Itzkowitz is being held. There are several Exeter-related addresses around the Croydon area, two of which appear to be owned by Taranovsky. Cooke's nephew plays football for Exeter City, and we were sent down there. It wasn't random at all. It was their little joke."

"Hmm. A joke that isn't funny before seven in the morning."

"This is important, get your clothes on, we're leaving in five minutes."

"I haven't had any breakfast!"

"Five minutes. I'll buy you a McDonalds from the drive-thru in Earlswood."

As McTierney slurped on his strawberry milkshake, Bee explained for the third time that Taranovsky owned two other properties in the greater Croydon area, besides the house they had visited with DI Jackson the previous week.

"First, there's a residential house; Number 71 Exeter Road, in the Addiscombe district of Croydon. It's not far from the IKEA. To the northern side of East Croydon railway station. Classic commuter belt."

"Do we know who lives there?"

"No. Second up is an office building by the name of Exeter House. That's on Orchard Way, Beckenham. It's three or four miles further east, but well within the remit of greater Croydon."

"Do we have a search warrant for either of these?"

"No. I only discovered them in the early hours. This trip is primarily reconnaissance. If we need it we'll get a warrant during the day."

"Good. Can I go back to sleep until we get there?"

With little early morning traffic on the roads at 7 o'clock, McTierney only secured a short nap before Bee turned into Exeter Road. It was a regular street in a regular neighbourhood characterised by a variety of terraced and semi-detached houses, many of which dated back to the late nineteenth century. As luck would have it, there was a space immediately outside Number 71 and they could see a light on in the house.

"It looks nicer than I was expecting," said McTierney.

Bee ignored the comment, "Doesn't look like your typical kidnappers' lair, but maybe that's the clever part. Hiding in plain view." He scanned the property as he spoke. "Now we're here and with the invitation of a kitchen light we may as well do this properly."

"Does that mean I've got to move?" moaned McTierney.

Bee answered with a glare, and the pair took up positions; Bee at the front door and McTierney covering any potential escapee charging out from the side gate. Two minutes later the colleagues returned to the car satisfied that Derek Packstone was a mortgage broker about to travel into central London and not Derek Packov, master criminal and kidnapper keeping a police officer locked in the basement of his house or in the garden shed.

It was a short hop across Croydon to the east to reach Orchard Way. A short road running north to south. The building they wanted was a three-storey office affair, two doors along from a primary school.

"This looks a bit innocent," said McTierney, still eager to make a judgement.

Bee nudged his car into the visitors' car park and he and McTierney walked up to a rotating door entrance. Immediately inside the foyer stood a large reception desk, behind which sat a grey-haired security guard wearing a standard blue security suit with the nametag 'Graham'. Bee flashed his badge and gave a brief summary of their interest, omitting all the key details. Graham, who looked surprised at the intrusion, explained that all the employees of the American company who leased the building, had left by eight the previous evening, and as yet no one had returned for the morning shift. "First chap in is normally Dave; he comes by tram, but he won't be here for another 12 minutes." Graham looked up at the large traditional clock on the main wall to check his timings.

"All the same, could we take a quick look around?" asked Bee.

McTierney rolled his eyes, but dutifully volunteered to check the top floor, while Bee scouted around the two lower floors. The two colleagues left empty-handed five minutes before Dave arrived.

"Looks like your Exeter theory is blown. Still, you can't be right all the time, you'd be unbearable."

Bee looked at him, but didn't bother to argue.

"But you can make amends and buy me a proper breakfast in the town while we wait for the others to arrive."

★ ★ ★

CROYDON CROWN COURT is situated on Altyre Road in central Croydon, not far from the famous Fairfield Halls and close to the bustling East Croydon station. Primarily, it handles serious criminal cases such as murder, rape, and robbery. In 2009 it was the scene of the case of taxi-driver John Worboys, convicted of multiple rapes. As befitting a major court, it resides in an imposing building with bold architecture, featuring an asymmetrical façade of buff stone and a polygonal tower.

Bee and McTierney met Bishop and Gandapur in a

coffee shop just off St George's Walk. Bee hoped it offered a good combination of anonymity with a short walk to the court building. Gandapur sat silently sipping her black coffee in their booth at the rear of the shop. None of the group looked comfortable, but Bishop was the first to break. "What do you think is going to happen when we get to court?" She asked while looking at Gandapur, feeling that they could all do with a shot of reassurance.

Bee shifted in his seat; he wasn't sure of the answer but felt he should offer some encouragement. "There is a set process for court cases, so once everybody is inside and settled, the first thing will be the formal arraignment of Taranovsky." He looked directly at Gandapur who had lifted her head from her coffee.

"That's when he's asked if he did it," interjected McTierney, before returning to his chocolate muffin.

Bee sent him a look of reproach and continued. "He's obviously going to plead 'not guilty'. Then they select a jury. We have opening statement from both counsels. The prosecution sets out its case. Then the defence makes their argument. You get a closing speech from each side; the judge makes a summary of what he's heard. The jury deliberates and then comes back with a verdict and hopefully Taranovsky gets sentenced."

"And we all live happily ever after," laughed McTierney. "There's a bit more to it than that. That's the basics, but the first bit of interest will be when Taranovsky spots you sitting in the public gallery."

"Yes, when that happens I would expect the defence counsel to request an adjournment; they won't have been expecting you and it may unsettle them. So, I doubt you'll be called upon to make a statement today."

A flicker of fear skimmed across Gandapur's face. Bishop drilled her eyes into Bee, urging him to be more supportive.

Bee coughed "By now Springfield will have briefed DCS Harris on your dramatic return from the dead. She doesn't think that he's been corrupted by Taranovsky, but we couldn't take the chance." He began to warm to his task. "Inevitably there will be a lot of media outside the court, probably a TV camera crew. One of them is bound to recognise you and then the media will announce your presence, and the prosecution will have to call you whether Harris wants to or not." Bee sat back with a look of satisfaction, then remembered one more point; "On your way into court, answer every question with 'No comment'."

It didn't take long for Bee's supposition to be put to the test. The case was scheduled to start at 10 o'clock and Bee insisted that they should enter the court before nine-thirty with the intention of avoiding most of the media, but that plan fell short.

Bee and McTierney escorted Gandapur from the coffee shop with Bishop walking twenty yards ahead of them on the lookout for journalists. As they turned the last corner and the court came into sight, Bishop froze, and the threesome caught up with her. Outside the main building there was a swarm of journalists patrolling the steps searching for witnesses, the occasional flash of a camera signalled the arrival of someone relevant to the case, and pride of place was taken by a TV camera crew hunting for a celebrity. Bee gulped, slid his arm around Gandapur and said, "Remember, 'No comment'. Now let's walk quickly but don't run."

As they marched heads down towards the court building

one of the reporters spotted Gandapur and began shouting. "It's Lily Gandapur. She's not dead!"

Instantly the journalists flooded around the small group, like vultures to a kill. A couple of reporters began running alongside the group shouting Gandapur's name and random questions. Everywhere people were jostling for position, with microphones being thrust at Bee's group. The court had stationed extra police outside the building, and they stepped forward to create a human funnel through which Bee led the team. When they reached the top of the steps, the group turned and Gandapur recalling Bee's advice, gave her first 'No comment' to the sea of reporters massed below them. They stepped inside the court building, which was cordoned off from the tide of reporters, they all breathed a sigh of relief. McTierney turned to Bee with a smile, "Give it five minutes and everyone will know Gandapur's here. The first part of the plan has worked."

FORTY-FIVE

BEE, McTierney, Bishop and Gandapur took their seats in the front of the public gallery at the back of the room. There was thirty minutes to go before the case opened but the court was beginning to fill up. Bee checked his phone and saw a message from Springfield.

Harris on board. Wants Gandapur to testify.

The décor was simple, the court administrators were diligently preparing the room, and a bailiff stood ready to ensure order if required. Although the judge was yet to appear, the large high-ceilinged room had a formal atmosphere. The team had a clear view from the public gallery, looking towards a largely symmetrical layout of the wood-panelled room. At the front, the judge's bench was elevated and in front of this were two further benches, which Bee explained were for the court clerk and court reporter. Off to the left was the witness stand, where Gandapur would be giving her evidence, opposite this was the jury box with 12 vacant seats. Back in the centre of the court were two wooden tables each facing the judge: one for the defence and one for the prosecution.

As the clock ticked around the key players assembled in the arena, last to appear was the Honourable Justice Stephenson, who would be hearing the case. Bee was largely correct in his predictions, although he had under-estimated the impact that Gandapur's appearance in the public gallery would have on certain members of the court. Taranovsky couldn't take his eyes off Gandapur for the first five minutes. When he did, it was to glare at Cooke, who seemed as surprised as everyone else. Irina, who was also in the gallery, sitting two rows behind Bee, McTierney, Bishop and Gandapur, looked aghast and appeared to trade signals with Taranovsky.

Although Bee had correctly predicted that the defence team would request an adjournment, he was wide of the mark with the judge's response.

The judge looked over his glasses at the defence counsel; "This is Miss Gandapur, who was allegedly shot on Saturday afternoon in Reigate, but seems to have made a startling recovery."

"Yes m'lord."

"Presumably you had prepared your case last week. I don't know many counsels who work Sundays; therefore, you must have prepared your case with the possibility that there would be testimony from Miss Gandapur. Did you not?"

The counsel stammered a reply, "Yes, I did your honour."

"Good. Then I see no need for a long delay. We'll take a short recess and reconvene at 2 o'clock. But I will say that this is most irregular, and I trust that it's not symptomatic of what is to follow. I will not tolerate gamesmanship of any sort in my court. Both counsels have been warned."

A tremor of excitement rippled around the court, at the judge's decision, as spectators gasped, and reporters typed furiously. Bee pinched himself in delight, then watched

Taranovsky signal something to Irina. Bee swung his head around and felt convinced that whatever the message was, it had been received loud and clear as Irina was bending to gather up her bag.

The clerk of the court left his chair and walked to the exit, stopping to speak to Bee as he did, "Well done inspector, very dramatic, we don't get a lot of excitement here. You clearly keep a tidy house. You should be proud of your work."

Bee smiled, shook his hand and followed him to the door, then stopped and repeated the words; "Tidy house." His mind began to whirl; the Hershey chocolate wrapper, the long train journey, the smart house in Kenley, taking Gandapur to the safest place, the Exeter football shirt. It was that gestalt moment, it was suddenly all clear.

He turned to McTierney, "That's it, why didn't I think of it before?"

McTierney looked surprised, but didn't reply.

"It's obvious. We need to get to Taranovsky's house and get there quickly before Irina gets back and kills Itzkowitz."

"Irina kill Itzkowitz?"

"It's the obvious thing to do. Everything has just changed for Taranovsky, it's so obvious, I should have seen it. In fact, it's so obvious it's exactly what we did."

McTierney looked lost and grabbed Bee's sleeve, "Explain. What did we do?"

Bee stopped, grabbed him by the shoulders and looked directly at him. "We had a valuable asset, Lily Gandapur in this case, also a young female as it happens. We wanted to keep her a secret, so we took her home, to my tidy house. And that's exactly what Dmitri Taranovsky did. He took her, in his case Fran Itzkowitz, home, but to his tidy house, so he could keep an eye on her."

"Dangerous to have her on the premises."

"Maybe but he'd been let down by his supporters, that's why he was in jail in the first place, so he was taking no chances. Itzkowitz was critical to his plan. Why would he trust her to anyone else, especially when he believed his friendly judge would release him, so he'd be free to keep an eye on her?"

"But no more friendly judge."

"No." Bee shook his head as he spoke. "That rather messed up his plans and ironically might have saved Itzkowitz's life."

McTierney frowned at him.

"Taranovsky will kill people as soon as look at them, but I don't think Irina is cut from the same tree."

"Irina?"

"Yes. The texts you've been getting have been coming from Irina, that's why the English is a little questionable. It's not her first language, so she's prone to the odd mistake."

"But I don't understand. We called in on her last week, she let us search the house, and you're saying that she had Itzkowitz there all the time, but she remained calm, standing outside smoking with your mate Jackson."

"Yes, exactly. She was coolness personified."

"Was she ever!"

Bee's face was beaming as he shared his thinking. "You remember those fingernails of hers? Of course you do, you were fixated by the idea of them clawing your back!"

McTierney blushed momentarily, then shrugged his shoulders.

"She doesn't do the chores, how could she? When she popped back into the house, it wasn't because she was in the middle of her laundry. She did it to turn on the tumble dryer to create some noise; partly to keep us out of the utility room and partly to cover up any noise Itzkowitz might have been able to make from wherever she was being kept."

"So, Itzkowitz is being kept in the utility room of Taranovsky's big house?" asked McTierney.

Bee frowned at his colleague but continued, "Itzkowitz is in a hidden compartment, maybe a basement, but I guarantee it's connected to the utility room in some way."

McTierney's head tilted to one side as a smile stretched across his face, "She's a cool customer. No wonder she wanted that cigarette outside with Jackson, she kept one third of our team out of the way."

"I know and we helped her by offering to be only 15 minutes if she allowed us to have a quick look around without the hassle of getting a search warrant."

FORTY-SIX

BEE EXPLAINED HIS plan to Bishop and left her to look after Gandapur while he and McTierney pushed their way through the crowd milling around the entrance to the court. Once outside they were faced with a cordon of cameras, microphones and excitable journalists eager to fill their headlines. A further round of 'no comments' allowed them to escape, and they jogged back to the car park, Bee's car and ultimately back to Taranovsky's house in the Croydon suburbs. They parked opposite the house and waited for Irina to return.

"You can't come in; you don't have a warrant."

Bee pushed the door, "We don't need one. We're searching your house, we believe you're holding Fran Itzkowitz against her will and that her life might be at stake."

"You can't do this. I'll call the police!" She yelled.

"We are the police," said McTierney with a smile.

Irina took a swing at him, but McTierney caught her arm, twisted it around and pushed her back against a bench she had standing in the hallway. "Bastard! Dmitri will do for you when he's out. You're going to be sorry of this."

"Shut it, or I'll break one of your precious fingernails!"

Bee rolled his eyes and stood in front of Irina. "Calm down. Now let me help you. It's time to think about you and what's going to happen to you. Let's start with Dmitri; he's not coming home anytime soon. Lily Gandapur is in court, you've seen her. She's going to testify against Taranovsky, and he will be found guilty and be sent to jail for a very long time. But what happens to you is open to debate. If you help us find Itzkowitz and she's okay that will go in your favour. If you don't, we'll find her anyway."

"Even if we have to tear this place apart," added McTierney with unnecessary zeal.

Irina slumped on the bench and pouted.

"We know she's here. It's only a matter of time."

"Which is interesting," added McTierney, "because it's also a matter of time for you. Only for you it'll be years in jail, not hours in this house."

Bee turned and glared at him, "How about you make everyone a cup of tea, while Irina and I discuss her options?"

McTierney made the fastest tea in history, scampered back into the hallway and thrust a mug under Irina's nose. Bee reached for his mug, looked at the colour and put the mug back down on the floor. "Irina has agreed to help us; she acknowledges that Itzkowitz is here but says that she played no part in bringing her here."

McTierney shrugged his shoulders, "Where is she?"

"We haven't established that yet. One step at a time."

Irina took a sip of tea, screwed up her face, put her mug on the floor, folded her arms over her lap and retreated from the conversation.

"Fine, we'll do this the hard way. McTierney, you stay here with Irina and try not to antagonise her. I'll start taking the utility room apart. I've called Springfield, so she should be here shortly with some back up."

McTierney blew out his cheeks and took the opportunity to sit next to Irina on her hallway bench. "Look, you should do yourself a favour here. Help us and we can help you. If you end up in prison in a foreign country you're in for a terrible time. So come on, tell us where Itzkowitz is."

Irina turned to face McTierney and scowled at him, "You think you know me. But you don't know me at all. Don't pretend to be my friend. You're a pig."

McTierney smiled, "You're right, I don't know you." He paused, "But I do know fear. I see a lot of fear in my job, it's not pleasant, but I've seen it so often I can recognise it a mile away. But right now, it's here in front of me, not a million miles away, not even a mile away, but here etched all over you. It's in your eyes, on your face, your clothes smell of it. You're shit scared of what's going to happen, and you need a friend. Last chance."

Meanwhile Bee had disappeared into the utility room and called out Itzkowitz's name, but there was no reply. A shiver of self-doubt ran up his spine. He thought about smashing open each cupboard and cabinet, but a little voice inside him told him not to make too much damage just in case he was wrong. He looked around, he had to do something, McTierney would be expecting it. Internally he screamed at himself; stop over thinking this, you made a smart deduction, believe in yourself. He clapped his hands together, "Right." He walked to the external door, which was half-glass, half-panelled and opened out into a courtyard and turned around. In front of him was a row of 12 pure white cabinets. He could immediately dismiss the washing machine and tumble dryer, that left ten. He opened the first one, a full-length door moved and revealed a mixture of domestic bits and pieces mostly laundry related. He tried the second; that was cleaning chemicals, then came the two appliances. He continued along the row; tools, paintings, probably stolen he thought, a small safe, videos and DVDs, some video equipment and the last one just contained the fuse box for the house. He pushed the door back in frustration and leant against it. His thoughts were broken by the sound of an approaching police siren; *Bugger, Springfield would be here within the minute, and he'd look foolish again. He must have missed something.* Bee heard the front door bell chime and left McTierney to deal with it.

Moments later the entire entourage of McTierney, Springfield, Irina and two officers that Springfield had enlisted entered the utility room, but Bee was nowhere to be seen. He heard their entrance and called out to them from behind the false door that carried the fuse box. They looked into the darkness, and he flashed a torch up at the entrance.

"I'm down here. There's a secret compartment behind the fuse box. It took me a while to work out that it must be a secret door and that there couldn't be a lot of junk in front of it, if Irina needed easy access to this compartment."

The group in the utility room couldn't see Bee but they could hear him blundering around in the darkness, then he shouted out, "I've found her. She's still alive. Itzkowitz is here."

FORTY-SEVEN

THE DIM LIGHT of a single flickering bulb barely illuminated the damp basement where Itzkowitz had been held for ten days. The air was thick with the scent of mildew and fear. A faint muffled whimper came from the far corner of the room, as Itzkowitz struggled against her bonds. She was propped against a cold cement wall, bound at the wrists and ankles and with a gag across her mouth. Bee was fighting with the cords until McTierney passed him a kitchen knife. He swiftly cut through the restraints and gently lifted Itzkowitz up from the chair. She collapsed into his arms trembling; her face streaked with dirt and dried tears.

"It's okay. It's all over now. We've got you." He comforted her as Itzkowitz sobbed.

They stayed embraced for what seemed to Bee, like hours, McTierney spotted his friend's discomfort and cut in to take his place. "My turn. Come here Fran. It's so good to have you back."

Itzkowitz stumbled forward, her legs weak from the restraints and fell from Bee to McTierney. Together the two saviours helped her towards the steps that led out of the basement and back into the utility room. McTierney pushed the door open, but Itzkowitz recoiled from the bright light. A paramedic pushed through the small crowd and offered her a pair of sunglasses, before wrapping a blanket around her shoulders.

"We'll take her from here."

Itzkowitz took in a lungful of fresh air and allowed the paramedic to assist her towards the bench where five minutes before, her captor had sat. The captor who was now detained by Chief Superintendent Springfield and being read her rights as the handcuffs were applied. The paramedic made a few preliminary checks then led Itzkowitz to the waiting ambulance and whisked her away.

Bee turned to Springfield, "What happens now?"

"I expect the medical team will conduct a series of physical and psychological tests to assess her condition. There'll be the usual stuff; they'll do the regular vital signs, a physical examination to check for injuries, although I think the paramedic did a lot of that here. She seemed to be in reasonable shape, all things considered. I guess the other thing that they will check is if she's suffering from malnutrition. They'll probably try to get some food inside her this afternoon."

"She'll enjoy that," added McTierney who'd joined the conversation.

Two things come to mind; "We should get the forensic boys in here as soon as possible to go through the place with a fine-toothed comb – can you square it with Croydon, so we can use our own team?"

Springfield narrowed her eyes, as she pondered her answer. "Yes. They might put up a fight, but the kidnap of Itzkowitz is our investigation. I'll square it with ACC Raven first. What's your other point?"

Bee hesitated before speaking, "I'm hopeful that Itzkowitz can identify her kidnappers; not just Irina, but the people who abducted her from the industrial estate. Now, I strongly suspect that DCI Cooke is implicated somewhere, so I'd like to create a situation where Itzkowitz can identify him as soon as possible."

"That might not be easy to achieve," cautioned Springfield.

"No. But the risk we have is that he will learn of this rescue very soon, in fact he might even know already, and he does represent a flight risk. If he's convicted of kidnapping it's the end of his career and the start of a long spell in prison. He's going to do everything he can to avoid that. It wouldn't surprise me if he left the country and potentially Taranovsky is in a position to help him."

Springfield pursed her lips. "If Taranovsky feels inclined to help. He's already looking at a long sentence, plus his girlfriend is about to join him. He might not feel too keen to help a bent copper who he was expecting to keep him in the clear. But your point is well-made."

"Would it help if I get back to the court and keep an eye on Cooke?"

"Yes McTierney, that would be useful. Don't approach him but keep your eyes on him; see if he looks stressed and if he tries to make contact with Taranovsky. By rights Taranovsky shouldn't know what's happened here."

"No. But he'll be suspicious when Irina doesn't re-appear after lunch," said Bee.

"Not much we can do about that. So, to action; McTierney back to court, Bee you stay here and brief the forensic team and repel any Croydon boys. I'll take our kidnapper back to Reigate, get her charged and in the cells, then I'll speak to ACC Raven. Let's reconvene tonight."

FORTY-EIGHT

BEE WATCHED HIS colleagues drive away from Taranovsky's house in Kenley and felt like a little boy watching all his friends leave after a birthday party, except as far as he could remember he'd never had lots of friends come to his house for a birthday party. He turned back to the house, knowing that he'd have an hour or so before the forensic team arrived to assume control of the search. In the last three weeks there had been at least two searches of the property and neither had uncovered any compelling evidence, but that was before he had discovered the secret chamber in the bowels of the building. That was the place for him to start.

He retraced his steps into the basement; this time armed with a couple of torches. A brief search at the top of the stairs located two fluorescent strip lights. With these turned on, he surveyed the prison that Itzkowitz had endured. He squinted through the pallid light at the dingy set-up; considering the house was luxurious in the extreme, the basement looked like it belonged in another country; a musty earthy scent hung heavy in the air, mixed with the faint tang of mildew. The flickering tubes cast long jittery shadows across a rough concrete floor littered with dust and cobwebs and the occasional scuttling insect. Bee's stomach flipped at the thought of what it would have been like to be held captive in the room for ten days. Rusted shelves leant precariously against the walls cluttered with forgotten bottles, rotting cardboard boxes and discarded tools. Bee poked around the contents but couldn't find anything of interest and was happy to escape the oppressive gloom back up to ground level.

When he and McTierney had searched the property the previous week it had been in a hurry; not at all how it should be. Now was the time to do it properly. Bee had allowed McTierney to rummage around upstairs, so this time he began in the master bedroom. He pulled on a pair of thin gloves and yanked out all the dresser drawers, spilling the contents on the bed and sorting through what he found. Precisely nothing of interest. He switched his attention to the wardrobes and ran his hands over all the clothes, hoping to find a hidden package, but he didn't. He moved to the en-suite bathroom; in his experience this was a popular place for drugs. But not this time. He lifted the top of the cistern and peered inside, plenty of water but nothing useful. That left the bathroom cabinet which carried a hefty stock of medicines, but they all appeared to be legitimate.

Bee realised he was getting nowhere fast and considered that perhaps Taranovsky had expected a police search and had moved everything incriminating. Then he remembered something Taranovsky has said to him when they had spoken yesterday, 'when I look for inspiration I find it with Dostoevsky, you should try it inspector.' Bee smiled to himself, could it be that easy? He bolted down the stairs to Taranovsky's study, a room he had himself searched only a week ago. There was the Russian author standing proudly on the centre row of the tall floor to ceiling bookcase; not once but 16 times; it looked like Taranovsky had collected every book that Dostoevsky had ever written. Bee removed the first book and placed it on the huge desk, then thought how his colleagues might approach the task, man-handling all the books out in one thrust sending them sprawling to the floor. But Bee had a rare respect for books and gently transported each individual book over to the desk and his care was rewarded with the revelation of a small safe built into the wall behind the bookcase. That would be something for the forensic team to tackle.

Bee sat in Taranovsky's chair, adjusted his glasses and tried to imagine what the gang leader would be planning next. It was a tactic that Bee liked to employ in all his cases; try to stand in the footprints of the killer and see the world as they had done at the critical moment. He looked around the room; his books, his paintings, photographs of his key henchmen, his laptop; it was all here. But something was missing. Bee couldn't force his way into Taranovsky's head. Then the 1812 Overture burst into life again as Dr Kelly and the forensic team arrived and pressed the doorbell.

Bee gave them a quick overview of what had happened, and what he had discovered and left them to collect evidence. As he wondered what to do next, his mobile rang, it was McTierney.

McTierney had sat through an agonising courtroom session and was taking advantage of a mid-afternoon break to update Bee on what had occurred.

"The case against Taranovsky is falling apart in front of me."

"How can that be?"

"For a start, I don't rate the prosecution counsel; he

seems a long way off the mark, but the real problem is the judge."

"The judge?"

"Yes, he's dismissed the evidence given by Lily Gandapur."

"What? How? On what basis?" Bee slumped back into Taranovsky's leather chair. His face fell and his eyes, normally bright and attentive, lost their spark. This was a body blow for the inspector.

"Gandapur gave her evidence okay, but when the defence counsel was able to cross-examine her, he asked her about the time she'd spent under our protection."

McTierney paused and Bee fell silent on the other end of the phone; he had a bad feeling about what was to come.

"By the time he'd finished with her, he made it sound like she'd spent the weekend with a couple of friends; it was all Scott this and Ron that. She didn't use our titles once."

Bee exhaled deeply, but McTierney continued. "More than once the counsel had to stop her and confirm that when she used our names she was really talking about the two police detectives who were providing her with protection for the weekend."

Bee muttered something under his breath, but McTierney ploughed on, "Then he got to the bit where we'd staged the shooting. He ripped it apart. He made it sound like a game where we were making the Croydon police look like idiots."

"You need to get the prosecution counsel to call you to give evidence that we only did all that to protect her. Gandapur's life was in real danger. We had no choice!" Bee was standing and shouting down the phone now.

"I can try, but I think it's too late for that."

"Shit. What happened next?"

"The defence counsel suggested that we hadn't behaved in the manner expected of protection officers, and that we had groomed Gandapur to tell a story that would try to besmirch Taranovsky."

"What? Why would we do that?"

"It was suggested that we, you, were enraged by the death of your friend Jackson and were out to get someone for it. Regardless of the fact that Taranovsky was in custody at the time of the killing and had the perfect alibi."

"That's total bullshit!"

"You know that, and I know that, but the judge bought it. He told the jury that there was sufficient doubt around the protection of Lily Gandapur that her evidence couldn't be relied upon to be her own and that they should dismiss it from their deliberations."

McTierney waited for Bee to reply, but he said nothing.

"I hate to say it boss, but the way the defence counsel and the judge phrased it, I was starting to doubt it myself."

"Didn't the prosecution do anything?"

"No. I think he was rattled by the judge's ruling. You won't like this, but the way the case is turning, I think Taranovsky is going to get off. Our star witness has fallen flat; without her testimony, everything sounds a bit circumstantial."

Bee blew out his cheeks. "Okay, new plan, keep the case going as long as possible, I'll be there as soon as I can. I have an idea, it's crazy but it might just work."

McTierney returned to his seat and wondered if he should have told Bee about the moment when Taranovsky had stepped into the witness box. He had a scar on his face, a memento from his early days as an enforcer in Moscow, which twitched when he began to speak. He has eyes like a hawk, a short but solid stature, jet-black hair, and a vengeful look in his eyes. His vengeance was on display for all to see as he told the court that the police had stolen concert tickets from him while they were supposedly searching his property. His counsel had fed him some ridiculous questions to allow him to rant about this being outrageous and him wanting to see British justice conducted and an arrest. The episode had plunged to an awkward depth when Taranovsky had offered his help to the police saying, "I believe the offending officer, or should I say criminal, is DS McTierney and he's sitting in the public gallery – over there." Taranovsky had turned and pointed at McTierney, who felt himself blush as the courtroom turned, before the judge reminded everyone that the only person on trial today was Taranovsky himself.

However, the judge had taken a disgruntled attitude towards the suggestion that police officers had behaved badly and had instructed the jury to ignore the evidence gathered by the police when searching Taranovsky's house. This led to an outburst in the gallery and the judge had been required to slam his gavel demanding order in court. McTierney felt relieved that no one else from the Reigate team was present to hear the mini eruption but wondered if he could keep the secret.

As the case rolled on, McTierney sat fidgeting in the public gallery, sweat beads were beginning to gather on his forehead, he looked at his watch; it was a quarter-to-five; courts rarely ran beyond 5 p.m. He flicked his head up to the court clock 4:46 p.m. His mouth was dry; he needed a beer.

How was he supposed to delay the court case until Bee arrived? Then Judge Stephenson slammed his gavel down and announced that the court would break for the evening and resume the following morning at 10:00 a.m. The court rose and the key players got up to leave the courtroom. McTierney rose gingerly from his seat and stepped slowly towards the main gangway. He watched as Cooke spoke to prosecution counsel, waved to someone nearer the door and then turned to make his own way out. As he drew level with McTierney, McTierney dropped to the floor to pick up an imaginary pound coin; Cooke's attention was centred on his colleague at the back of the room, and he tumbled over the top of McTierney. Cooke picked himself up from the floor and turned to face McTierney, his face thunderous with rage, but McTierney took the sting out of the situation.

"Terribly sorry, I thought I saw a coin on the floor. Entirely my fault. Please allow me to make amends and buy you a drink."

Cooke was bristling for an argument, but McTierney's apology had taken the wind out of his sails.

"No, that's alright." Cooke looked around and realised there were too many witnesses for him to take offence.

Having broken the ice, McTierney pushed on, "Interesting case today. Do you think you'll win?"

Cooke eyed him suspiciously, "Do I know you?"

"I don't think so."

Cooke ignored the words and allowed his eyes to roll over McTierney's body as if searching for a weakness. He paused as if contemplating an insult, thought better of it and turned and walked away. As he strode out of the main court doors and down the steps leading away he was ambushed.

"That's him! That's the man who kidnapped me and held me captive!" Fran Itzkowitz pointed an accusatory finger at Cooke. His response was lost in a whirl of camera flashes and snaps as the media scrum turned to face him. Every reporter on the steps called Cooke's name, demanding a response. Cooke staggered backwards and looked ashen faced as the ITV news camera closed in on him. But before Cooke could offer them a headline for the 6 o'clock news, Bee stepped across the camera shot and said "DCI Cooke, I'm arresting you on suspicion of the kidnap of Fran Itzkowitz. You do not have to say anything, but anything you do say, may be taken down and given in evidence."

The rest of Bee's speech was lost in the furore. A furore that would be the lead item on every news programme for the rest of the evening.

FORTY-NINE

"Looks like we're going to nail Cooke, but Taranovsky will probably walk."

Springfield, Bee and McTierney were discussing the case while waiting in Reigate town centre for the rest of their party to assemble.

"That's outrageous," offered McTierney, "we researched some of his past misdemeanours and he's pure evil."

"I know. But it comes down to what we can prove and that's not a lot."

"I guess we should be grateful for having Itzkowitz back. That was always the priority for me," said Bee. "And here she comes with Bishop."

"Good. Let's refrain from talking about the case tonight and just enjoy the evening."

Itzkowitz had chosen the Hatay restaurant in Reigate to host her release party, although she didn't feel up to a real party, she was determined to mark her first day of freedom. The restaurant hummed with laughter and clinking glasses as the group collectively relaxed for the first time in ten days. Itzkowitz had been bullied into taking the centre seat, flanked by her two closest colleagues Bee and McTierney, with Kelly,

Bishop and Springfield facing them, Lily Gandapur and Nathan Rockford completed the line up.

To get the evening started Springfield proposed a toast to welcome Itzkowitz back into the fold. "Before I speak, I will preface my words by saying that I don't much care to hear about other people's dreams," her eyes fell on McTierney as she spoke. "Or their medical procedures, especially if I'm eating, so I know we are all delighted to have Fran back amongst us but let's leave the gory details to another time and just rejoice in her presence. Welcome back, Fran."

It was met with a huge cheer and yells of 'speech' from McTierney, who had already finished his first pint. Itzkowitz looked doubtful but gingerly stood up. Tears rolled down her cheeks as she thanked the team for their support. She saved her last line for Bee; telling him that she knew he'd never stop looking for her and it was that belief which kept her going through the dark nights. Bee looked embarrassed to hear the praise and flushed scarlet when Itzkowitz leant across and kissed him. Let's have a few words from the inspector, called McTierney as a waiter brought him a fresh pint. Bee resisted, but McTierney wouldn't take no for an answer. Eventually, Bee stood up. "I was just doing my job, but I will say that it's marvellous to have Fran back. I think we can all file this under 'a job well done'."

He moved to escape and sit down as quickly as he could but then remembered something and stood up again.

"You're supposed to wait to be called for an encore," jabbered McTierney.

Bee looked at him kindly, "You might want to pipe down for a moment, because this concerns you."

A sudden hush fell over the group and Bee realised that

he'd created an expectation. "I've remembered something that Itzkowitz should know. When McTierney and I were searching her house for clues, our beloved DS said to me that 'If we find her alive, I promise never to say, 'Action FBI ever again.'"

Everyone turned to face McTierney, who for once, was lost for words. "I er, perhaps maybe, I was stressed."

"Thinking that you might have to do some real work, if Fran disappeared," added Bishop.

McTierney started to glare but quickly broke into a laugh.

Itzkowitz placed her hand on McTierney's sleeve, "I don't care, honestly I'm so happy to hear it, you can say it all you want."

McTierney smiled, "Excellent. We need more beer on this table. Action FBI!"

The frivolity continued, McTierney looked across the table to check that Springfield was occupied, then asked "Was there a time when you thought you wouldn't get out?"

Bishop kicked him under the table, and he yelped, Itzkowitz laughed, "It's okay. I'm happy to talk about it; the medical team told me that it would help me assimilate the experience if I talked about it. So yes, there were times when I doubted I'd make it. When I was captured and bundled into the boot of the car, I thought I would be taken somewhere quiet and shot."

Slowly everyone around Itzkowitz stopped their conversations and listened intently as she spoke.

"I tried to think of what I'd been taught back in New York about building a relationship with the captors but all I kept thinking was *'why me?'*. It was only a short car journey, but I was terrified. We stopped somewhere, then carried on and stopped again. They left me in the trunk for a few hours, and I started to panic about the amount of air in there."

Itzkowitz looked around at her audience; the fun atmosphere had evaporated, and they were hanging on every word. She offered a half-smile, "But it got better. Although the cellar was ghastly, as the days went by, I started to believe that they wouldn't kill me."

"It probably helped that Taranovsky, the guy who owned the house, was himself, in jail by then, and he's the decision maker," added Bee.

"What kept you going?" asked Kelly.

"I tried to focus on some happy memories," Itzkowitz smiled as she recalled those happier times. "I convinced myself that I would revisit them. It was tough, but I had a lot of time on my own, so I could create my own environment. Does that sound crazy?"

"No, not at all," said Kelly gently.

Springfield seized the moment, "Talking of happier times; your mother came over to visit us when she heard of your disappearance."

Itzkowitz's face lit up.

"She's a tough lady, your mother. She gave me hell the day she arrived, demanding to know what we were doing to find you and threatening to take your case to the US embassy."

Tears began to well up in Itzkowitz's eyes. "That sounds like mama."

Springfield reached across the table and squeezed her hand, "She went to Edinburgh for a couple of days. I telephoned her earlier and she's on her way back tonight, you'll see her tomorrow morning."

Itzkowitz's lips began to tremble as she tried to say something, but the words wouldn't come. She inhaled sharply, but her chest tightened, and she gasped for breath. Then the dam broke and she began to sob.

After the dinner, the group split and went their separate ways; Bee and McTierney found themselves taking the last taxi back to Outwood. McTierney checked his phone and noticed a missed call. When they got home he dialled the number and was surprised to hear the voice of Jake Rivers.

"I saw it reported on the TV tonight that this Taranovsky bloke is likely to get off."

"It's possible, nobody really knows until the jury gives their verdict, but it's not looking good."

"That wouldn't be right. He's a bad 'un, a right bad 'un. Fran has suffered at his hands, and I know I haven't been good to her. You don't need to say anything. But she doesn't deserve what's happened to her, so maybe if I can testify that will help put this Taranovsky bloke away where he should be and also make Fran's life a little better."

"I don't think that quite makes amends for how you treated her, but it'll certainly help."

Rivers grunted.

"Good, so what do you know?"

FIFTY

It was Wednesday afternoon, Bee and McTierney had been summoned to Springfield's office and we sitting outside waiting to be called.

"I have a new theory on the Itzkowitz connection," said Bee.

"Go ahead."

"Taranovsky was running out of time to rid himself of the one witness who could get him convicted, – Lily Gandapur. He'd already made a couple of attempts, but each resulted in failure. So, he hatches a plan to blackmail a police officer into doing it. I imagine he thinks it should be easy for a serving officer to discover her location and he's comfortable working with the police."

McTierney nodded at the theory.

"So, he leaves the concert tickets where he knows they will be discovered and bingo, some greedy copper, in this case, you, picks them up."

McTierney jerked his head back in alarm at the suggestion but smiled and leaned back into the conversation.

"Once they were taken, all Taranovsky has to do is blackmail the officer into killing Gandapur or face exposure as a thief and the end of his career. I doubt he thought it would be a detective from Reigate, but once he'd worked that out, he abducted Itzkowitz as a back-up to apply a little more pressure."

McTierney grimaced, "Let's not share this detail with the boss."

As he spoke, Springfield opened the door, "Gentlemen, now would be good. Let's review the latest developments in the Itzkowitz case, and I have information."

The three officers took seats and Springfield opened the conversation.

"So, Jake Rivers has had a sudden change of heart and hopes to join the Good Guys' team."

"Something like that. He's not a pleasant individual but I don't think he's got what it takes to stand alongside Cooke or Taranovsky." McTierney continued, "There was a time when he was shaping up to be a murderer, we did find traces of Itzkowitz's blood in the back of his van."

Bee shook his head. "Yes we did. But remember she helped him shift his gear when he had the odd gig. She could very easily have taken the skin off her fingers loading an amplifier into the van."

Springfield nodded her approval. "My sources tell me that Rivers gave his testimony this morning; comprehensive and damning was the assessment. So Taranovsky is back on the ropes. His counsel will try to discredit Rivers as a credible witness, but DCS Harris feels we have sufficient to secure a conviction."

"That's a relief," said Bee.

"Yes, and with Itzkowitz's testimony we should have a solid case against Cooke."

"Good news all round."

"I understand that Cooke has been trying to cut a deal of some sort."

Bee nodded, "Yes. It was virtually the first thing he said when I questioned him this morning."

"Scumbag," muttered McTierney, shaking his head.

Springfield took control of the conversation, "I'm sure he can offer us some interesting evidence against Taranovsky, but I get the feeling that ACC Raven wants to set an example. He'd rather see Cooke rot in jail for a long sentence than offer him a deal. So, unless Taranovsky looks like he's going to wriggle away again, there's no deal for Cooke. Our new friend Rivers has stolen Cooke's thunder and has provided enough intelligence to put Taranovsky away for decades."

A small smile of approval crossed Bee's face.

"Incidentally, Harris is questioning Cooke over the murder of DI Jackson."

Bee perked up at the mention of his friend.

"I don't know the status of that inquiry, but with all the revelations that have come to light in the last 24 hours, Cooke must be considered a strong suspect. I've made Harris aware of the material Kelly collected from Cooke's car, before it disappeared."

"Jackson deserves justice at the very least," said Bee, his eyes suddenly ablaze as he leant towards the desk.

"Agreed. We all want to see the culprit brought to justice but leave Harris to pursue the perpetrator. He will also be following up on any potential misdemeanours at the scrap yard, so you may get a call from him. He's hoping to mop up as many of Taranovsky's gang as he can."

"Looks like it's all worked out for the best," said McTierney.

Springfield eyed him suspiciously, "Not entirely DS McTierney." She paused, "Harris filled me in on Taranovsky's claim yesterday that you had stolen a pair of concert tickets from his house a week or so ago and went on to suggest that probably that single incident had been the catalyst for the chaos that followed." She paused, took a deep breath and folded her arms across her chest. "I assume the two tickets were used by the pair of you. I think you'd better explain what on earth made you think it was a good idea."

Bee and McTierney exchanged nervous glances, before McTierney spoke.

"Ma'am. I must take responsibility for that incident. Taranovsky is correct, I picked up the tickets from the house when I was helping the Croydon team. I don't know why I did it, I know it was dumb, I just didn't think about it. I took my girlfriend to the concert; it had nothing to do with Inspector Bee. You should excuse him from any retribution. I will face it alone."

A flicker of surprise bounced across Springfield's face; she inhaled sharply and shifted in her seat. "Is that true inspector?" She asked with calculation in her eyes.

It was Bee's turn to feel uncomfortable, he paused, then nodded. "I believe so."

Springfield's brow furrowed and her eyes narrowed, but she nodded her acceptance. "It's good of you to take responsibility. I have to tell you that I'm inclined to suspend you from duty, although your work in the Taranovsky case, in particular your success in extracting a statement from Jake Rivers, does you credit, and DCS Harris is keen to record his appreciation of your work. So, consider this a final warning."

McTierney swallowed but didn't challenge Springfield's argument.

But Springfield hadn't finished, "I make this point to

both of you. Going forward, you come to me with any crazy idea before you take one step outside the station. Are we clear?"

Both detectives nodded and waited to be dismissed from the classroom.

"Good, then don't make me regret this decision."

As they walked back upstairs, Bee had his head down.

"You're welcome by the way."

Bee looked up, unsure of what he'd missed.

"I saved your arse in there."

Bee shook his head. "I know you think you did a good deed there, taking the rap over the concert tickets, but in reality you've screwed me over. You put me in a corner, and I've lied to Springfield again, but this time there's no redemption."

He stopped on the stairs. "I think I need to go back and explain."

He turned, but McTierney grabbed his sleeve. "No. You can't change it now. She'll axe both of us. This way you're in the clear, and I'm halfway. If we go back again, she'll do her nut. Leave it now."

They walked on to the coffee machine, McTierney pressed the usual buttons. As they stood Carol Bishop strode jauntily towards them, "Afternoon Gentlemen, I'm popping over to see Itzkowitz. Won't be long."

The men turned to watch her walk away.

"She seems happy," said McTierney.

Bee pursed his lips, "By the way, I've not forgotten your request for a motto. See what you think of this; 'veni, vidi, bibi'. It means I came, I saw, I drank."

"Cool. I like it. Veni, vidi, bibi. Thanks, I owe you one."

"Funny you should say that, as I know how you can repay me."

McTierney stopped in his tracks, "Are you seriously asking my advice on something?"

"I am."

"Go on then, let's have it."

"It's Bishop. She's asked me out on a date. I don't know what to say."

THE END

If you've enjoyed reading this story,
then sign up for more stories by Phil Hall.

Also in the series

PLUS

Inspector Scott Bee will return in …A Vote for Murder

www.philhallauthor.com

ACKNOWLEDGEMENTS

Thank you for reading this story, I enjoyed writing it and I hope you enjoyed it too.

If you did I can think of two things you should do.

1. Tell someone about the book. Word of mouth recommendations are pixie dust to an author.
2. Read another book in the series. 'Game, Set and Death' is a good place to start and available from Amazon.

I'd like to start at home and thank my wife Andrea and daughter Lauren for not complaining about my regular fights with our home printer.

No writer can succeed without a small army of beta readers willing to plough through early copies of their work. My battalion of unpaid warriors are Alex DuC, Andy G, Andy L, David H, Eleni C, Frank B, Jo C, Julia R, Karen H, Lesley S, Pat B, Robert B, Roger C, Stuart H, Stuart M and Tom G. All were generous beyond what I had any right to expect. Especially those blessed with reading the first draft, a tortuous process at any time.

I can't ignore the one professional involved in this process, especially as he kindly returned to fight again after the first book – and he really should've known better. Patrick Knowles – a first-rate cover designer and great sounding board.

My eternal thanks to you, one and all. It's been a slice.

As regular readers will know I like to weave my own stories around real-life events, and 'Ticket' was no different. The inspiration for this story was my failure to get a ticket for the Oasis concerts in London. Having set a book in the future, I hope the concert does go ahead!

Finally, all the crime related stats that I quote in the book are genuine, or at least they were when I copied them from the internet, most relate to 2023. I have nothing against Redhill or Croydon – they were simply stats to add colour to a story.

Printed in Dunstable, United Kingdom